THE AGONY OF HER

An Ohio Gothic

CASSANDRA L. THOMPSON

THE AGONY OF HER: AN OHIO GOTHIC
WRITTEN BY CASSANDRA L. THOMPSON
PUBLISHED BY QUILL & CROW PUBLISHING HOUSE

This book is a work of fiction. All incidents, dialogue, and characters, except for some well-known historical and public figures, are either products of the author's imagination or used in a fictitious manner. Any resemblance to actual persons, living or dead, or actual events is purely coincidental. Although real-life historical or public figures do appear throughout the story, these situations, incidents, and dialogues concerning them are fictional and are not intended to depict actual events nor change the fictional nature of the work.

Copyright © 2025 Cassandra L. Thompson

All rights reserved. Published in the United States by Quill & Crow Publishing House, Ohio. No portion of this book may be reproduced in any form without permission from the publisher, except as permitted by U.S. copyright law.

Edited by Lisa Morris, Tiffany Putenis

Cover Design by Fay Lane

Printed in the United States of America

ISBN (ebook): 978-1-958228-62-3

ISBN (paperback): 978-1-958228-63-0

Publisher's Website: quillandcrowpublishinghouse.com

For Women

PRAISE FOR CASSANDRA L. THOMPSON

"In *The Agony of Her: An Ohio Gothic*, Cassandra L. Thompson conjures a tale steeped in Midwestern folklore and charged with gothic unease, the land itself seething with haunted memory and buried dreams. Bound by the darkness of Haite Hill, Ada and Lori embody different eras of the same struggle. Together they find a way to rise against those who seek to erase them in a delightful twist of feminine rage and power."

— ANDREW K. CLARK, MANLY WADE WELLMAN PRIZE FINALIST AND AUTHOR OF *WHERE DARK THINGS RISE*

"When trauma is an inheritance, herstory is doomed to repeat in blood and tears. The Agony of Her is pure midwestern gothic, hitting all the right gloomy notes and landing with a hopeful, heartfelt finish."

— WENDY DALRYMPLE, AUTHOR OF *CREDENZA* AND *BED ROT BABY*

"*The Agony Of Her* is a nightmarish mix of slow Gothic horror and vicersal terror... Told through both Lori and Ada's point of view over different timelines, the tentative creepiness of Haite House sinks its clawed foundations in deep, and refuses to let go until the final pages...and lingers even after that. The strength of both female rage and motherly fury scream from this book, as both Lori and Ada battle a truly awful evil."

— L.V. RUSSELL, AUTHOR OF *THE BONE DRENCHED WOODS* AND *THE QUIET STILLNESS OF EMPTY HOUSES*

This book explores themes of violence and abuse, including harm done to women and children. Please be sure to consult the Trigger Index at the back of the book for more information.

PREFACE

Dearest Reader,

    I had to write a story about Helltown. How could I not?

    Growing up in Ohio was about as glamorous as you might imagine. With nothing much to do, I spent my teen years riding shotgun in someone's beat-up car, rolling up and down the hills of the Cuyahoga Valley, and exploring abandoned things. For legal reasons, I may or may not have frequented Jaite Paper Mill after it was condemned, and *maybe* an old psychiatric hospital in Sagamore. But at night, the best place to explore and scare yourself half to death was a place once called Boston Village. It was this little township that the locals dubbed "Helltown."

    If you drive down to the Boston Mills Historic District, as it is known today, you'll see a beautiful tourist destination for anyone who loves the great outdoors. Owned by the Cuyahoga Valley National Park, the original buildings that make an appearance in this book have been transformed into a visitor's center and a place to grab refreshments. You'll be able to see the old M.D. Garage, a Pure Oil gas station from the 1940s, and a few other historical barns and homes. But unfortunately, that's about all that's left of the place that once stirred the morbid imaginations of many an Ohioan.

    From Satanic rituals to mutants to dead schoolchildren, this spot

PREFACE

was positively brimming with legends. So much so that it captured the attention of ghost hunters and filmmakers; in fact, there is an actual "documentary" out there with so much fabricated information, it'll make your head spin. They even interviewed fake townspeople. The truth is, Helltown is simply just another Ohio town. The discovery of how much toxic industrial waste had been leaking out of the Krejci Dump site in the 80s led to stories of mutants and "melon heads." A school bus in the woods that served as a family's temporary home led to stories of a crazed bus driver and dead schoolchildren. An old Protestant church with interesting architecture became a place for Satanic rituals. And on and on it goes.

Fastforward to adulthood. My husband and I moved back to the area, and found ourselves regularly hiking up and down the CVNP. One of our favorite spots was the closed Stanford Road, where we discovered an abandoned barn and chicken coop up the hill to the left. I know they'll tear that down too, but for now, the dilapidated barn still sits, full of graffiti from the next generation looking for Helltown adventures.

It was on one of these hikes, in the middle of March, that I was startled by a weird sound and saw three vultures circling above me. The next day was too cold and rainy for hiking, so my husband and I grabbed coffee and parked at the Hines Hill campus near the trails. I'd driven by the strange buildings before, but never explored them. On an impulse, he and I grabbed our umbrellas and wandered through, learning that the house all the way in the back—the one you could see from Stanford Road—had once been the summer home of the Jaite family. And well, the story I came up with shortly thereafter, you will find in this book.

Whether it's ancient vampires or time-hopping hotels, my books are always inspired by history, but I love to twist the facts. I'm sure the Jaites and the early Boston Village settlers were lovely people; I'm happy to report that most of this tale comes straight from my own nightmarish brain. But that's why I love historical fiction so much. I can draw on my own experiences and the stories of others, blending them together into fresh lore.

Although some of the topics I explore are heavy, this story was a pleasure to write, and since my family and I will soon be moving, it feels

PREFACE

like my love letter to Ohio. It really is a beautiful place, if you ever find yourself up this way.

Just beware the Sisters Three.

Dreadfully Yours,
Cassandra L. Thompson

PROLOGUE
Unknown, 1881

A girl stood before her in a tattered yellow dress. Eyes hollowed and lips cracked, she said nothing, even as water pooled around her dirty feet. The skies were gray but rainless, creating confusion around the source of the spreading puddle. But when a metallic tang soured the air, the woman realized it was not water pouring from the girl's pregnant belly and out from between her trembling, bony legs. It was blood.

Before the woman could react, a man swooped in.

"Is she alright?" the woman cried.

"It's no concern of yours," was the retort as he whisked her away.

They disappeared behind the flimsy door of what the woman hoped was a doctor's office, their absence leaving behind cold silence. The woman supposed he was right; it was no concern of hers, no matter how strong her empathy for the young woman. She had just arrived and knew little about the seemingly desolate town and its happenings. She was also exhausted from traveling, and a sleepless mind often plays tricks on itself. Perhaps the girl was not bleeding after all.

She turned away, eager to find a place to rest. Crisp moisture bit the air, but it was too warm for snow, which left the lichen-coated limbs and peeling bark of barren trees exposed. For her entire journey, she'd seen nothing but the skeletons of haunted oaks and melancholy maples standing in faded copper grass. She'd named them the Guardians of Haite Towne, sentinels keeping watch of all who arrived.

Black shadows above interrupted her thoughts. She squinted against the sun to see three great birds quietly circling her. Vultures were not an uncommon sight in the country, but their ominous presence rattled her more than she liked. She looked down and immediately jumped.

The girl stood before her as if she'd never left.

The woman's heartbeat quickened as her confusion struggled to break through to reason. She wanted to ask the girl if she was all right, but the words were trapped in her throat. All she could do was stare, frozen by indecision, as blood continued to gush around the girl's feet. Her eyes fell to the girl's abdomen, and she gasped.

The soft, hopeful swell of belly was gone. It had been replaced by torn cloth and split flesh, a horrible grin spilling forth viscera as it laughed at her. The horror of it brought the woman to her knees, and she swallowed rising bile as the vultures above her let out a shriek.

Somewhere inside her rational mind, the woman knew vultures made no sound. Perhaps it was her own screaming she heard as she pressed her hands to her ears. Or perhaps it came from the girl, whose mouth began to slide open like her belly.

Her jaw drooped much too far and much too slack, eventually pulling her face apart. By the time it fully detached with a sickening crack, joining the collection of bloody pulp at her feet, the woman's eyes rolled back in her head. She collapsed onto the dirt, her vision darkening as she stared at the girl's fleshless, bloodied jawbone right before her.

The woman's last thought, as everything faded away, was whether the vultures would pick them both clean.

CHAPTER ONE
Lori, 1981

Lori stepped over the threshold, and immediately, her boot crunched glass. She looked up to see a broken window, the late afternoon sun catching in the remaining shards. This would have been the point where she listened to the home—observed it, smelled it, breathed it in—but the realtor hadn't stopped talking from the moment Lori stepped out of the car to greet her.

"Oh, don't you mind that." Jeanne Markle's nervous, high-pitched voice entered the room before she did, flooding the quiet, abandoned structure with the smell of overdone hairspray and powder. "I brought a broom!"

Her ill-fitting skirt forced out a grunt as she bent awkwardly to sweep the broken glass into the corner. "As you know, the house was painstakingly cared for while your relatives were alive, but it lay dormant for a few months before the estate was transferred to you. We took care of most of it, but you know, things happen."

"I anticipated repairs," Lori told her as pleasantly as she could. "Century home and all."

Jeanne navigated her pumps over the dusty wood floors. "The upper levels are the ones that need the most TLC, but the rooms are still livable. If you'd like to follow me, I can give you a quick tour—"

"Oh, that won't be necessary," Lori interrupted. "It looks exactly like the photos your agency sent over."

"It's no trouble at all, dear," Jeanne insisted, wobbling through the foyer to the back of the house.

Lori sighed. She'd hoped the handoff would be quick and painless. Her anxiety hadn't allowed her any sleep the night before, and after seven long hours in the car, all she wanted was to be alone to explore and plan her renovations. She sure picked a helluva time to quit smoking.

She gathered up what little patience she had left and followed Jeanne into the main parlor.

The realtor flitted about, attempting to show off the home's various selling points as if Lori hadn't already been bequeathed the damn thing. "The fireplaces have been boarded up, but they do work. You'll want to get them looked at, though, before you use them. Critters love to hole up when it's cold outside, and the last thing you need is rabies. The grand parlor features these glorious bay windows. Such a unique addition for an older home, don't you think? You could turn this into a fabulous great room, perfect for entertaining guests..."

While she babbled on, Lori surveyed the walls, happy to note they were structurally sound behind the faded, peeling wallpaper. Her eyes lingered on the intricate scrolled ornaments decorating the walls. Someone had maintained this place and had done it well. Beyond the inevitable country dust and occasional cobweb, the old manor looked like it must have ninety years prior.

"Like I said over the phone, you're lucky you were spared vandalism and squatters. No one wants to make the trek through the valley and up this hill. As you may have already guessed, the leftover townsfolk aren't too friendly either."

When Lori hit the last leg of her trip in from New York, she'd felt a sudden rush of energy to press on. She'd driven right through the empty town at the bottom of the hill, barely glancing at the old gas station and weathered storefronts. She hadn't seen a single soul that would enable her to agree with the woman, but she nodded just the same.

"So when will you and your husband begin renovations?"

"No husband," Lori informed her. "It's just me."

Jeanne's leathery features distorted in confusion. "The paperwork said Mr. and Mrs. Greene—"

"It's a formality. Our divorce hasn't been finalized."

"Oh, I see. Well, I must say, I'm pretty surprised anyone would agree to take on this place. Let alone a single woman."

"I'm actually a historian," Lori explained calmly. "I renovate old homes as part of my job. This house happens to be a very unusual type of Gothic Revival, an architecture rare for Northeast Ohio, let alone a summer home. I honestly can't even believe it was gifted to me. My mother died when I was a baby, and I never knew her side of the family."

"It is a strange situation, indeed," Jeanne said. "I'm not sure why anyone would spend so much money to keep this place maintained, but unlived in for years. Seems like a waste."

Lori shrugged. "In the words of the great Jim Morrison, people are strange. I'm just grateful for the serendipity."

Jeanne forced a grin that made her face turn red. "My, you really are a Miss Smarty Pants." She continued before Lori could explain what serendipity meant. "It is a pretty house, but there is nothing around. Ever since the paper mill shut down, there is no reason for anyone to stick around. The townies stayed because they have nowhere else to go, but they'll move on soon enough. Especially after..." She trailed off. "Soon, nothing will be left but woods and abandoned things."

Lori studied the frizzy-haired woman before her and considered her options. How could she possibly explain to anyone, let alone this woman, that the house had called out to her before she even received the phone call? That she saw it, and every house she'd ever worked on, in her dreams? They were spaces trapped in limbo, whispering their secrets to anyone who might be listening. Lori just happened to do so. Humans perplexed her, but reading a building's energy? Easy peasy.

"I plan to sell it," she said finally. "And if I can't sell it, I will live here."

"But—"

Children's laughter burst through the tension.

Lori grinned as her stepdaughters came barrelling into the room. "Careful, girls, there's broken glass."

"This place is spooky as heck!"

"Oh wow, look at the ceiling..."

"Girls, you can't just go flying through the house like that—oh hey, Lori."

Lori's smile faded as Sean entered, ducking to fit his tall frame under the low-hanging archway. Nikki, their oldest daughter, noticed the realtor and quickly tempered her excitement. She slid beside Lori, who lifted her arm up for a hug.

Jeanne looked perplexed. "Are you...? What...?"

Sean chose to be kind instead of hostile, turning on his special brand of Sean Greene charm. "Hiya doing there, Mrs. Markle. I'm Sean Greene. We spoke on the phone."

The realtor quickly composed herself, taking his extended hand. "Oh, forgive me, Mr. Greene. I didn't expect—you didn't—I'm glad you made it here safely. Your wife is quite lovely."

"Ex-wife," Lori corrected her. "So now that he's here, can we sign the rest of the papers?" She looked around. "Wait, where is Kellie?"

"Kellie!" Sean called, concerned.

"I'll get her," Lori said, realizing she knew where she went. She grabbed Nikki's hand, and the two quickly abandoned Sean and the flustered realtor.

"You inherited this place?" Nikki asked, her eyes wide as they walked back through the foyer to the main staircase.

"Crazy, isn't it?"

Lori couldn't help but feel pride as she watched Nikki drink in the details of the house with an appreciation similar to her own. Someday, she'd have to talk to her about reading the energy of old homes, too. Perhaps when her super-religious former stepmother wasn't still looming over her.

"Wish I had rich relatives that just appeared out of nowhere to give me a house," Nikki snorted.

Lori laughed. "I thought it was a scam at first."

"So this isn't like those other houses you fix and flip, right? You're actually gonna stay here?"

Lori felt a pang of guilt. "Well, most of the homes I worked on before were in New York, by our house. This one is out here, so I'm gonna stay here until it's done. Then I'll sell it." She intentionally left out how long the whole process would take.

Thankfully, Nikki didn't press the issue, distracted by the decorative finial that topped the end of the staircase handrail. "Aw, look at the baby angel."

She ran a red-fingernailed hand over the cherub, which was made of the same polished wood as the staircase, the beautiful dark wood stubbornly withstanding the test of time. "Ow." She winced.

Lori snatched her hand and quickly squeezed out the tiny sliver of wood. Nikki gave her a garbled *thank you* as she stuck the bloodied tip in her mouth.

"There are angels carved into the marble fireplaces, too," Lori told her. "I'll show you once we grab your sister."

The steps groaned as they climbed, but Lori knew the building was sound. The wallpaper wasn't as lucky as the staircase, its pattern lost between the missing patches. Lori couldn't wait to strip and restore it, drenching the entire home in a moody color palette that would bring out its true Victorian splendor. She also couldn't wait to polish the diamond-shaped glass that made up the lancet windows.

They reached the second floor, and Nikki stopped. Lori felt it too—the energy was different here, but she couldn't quite place it. She felt Nikki's hand find hers—an anxious tell of hers since she was little. A cool breeze whistled through the corridor, letting her know several windows needed replacing.

"So, how has your sister been?" Lori asked, attempting to distract Nikki. She located the second part of the split stairs and guided her up them.

"She's fine. She keeps asking Dad when you're coming home."

"Yeah, I thought that might happen. Did he fix up her room yet, like he promised?"

"It doesn't matter. We'd rather live with you. Even if this house is creepy as hell."

Another pang of guilt stabbed Lori in the stomach. "I know. I'll work it out with your dad...and Kellie's mom."

"Hi, I'm up here!" Kellie's joyful voice rang from above.

Lori couldn't help but smile. She knew her younger stepdaughter would fall in love with the tower. As soon as they reached the top, Kellie launched her little body at Lori, forcing her to catch her.

"Can this be my room? Please, please, please!" she begged as she kicked her feet, pummelling Lori's hips with the ridiculous mismatched rainboots she always insisted on wearing.

Lori laughed, happy to feel her in her arms. God, she missed them. "We gotta fix this whole house up first before we can even talk about that."

"How is this house not falling apart?" Nikki wondered out loud.

"The builders knew what they were doing," Lori explained. "This house is called a Carpenter Gothic, a type of Gothic Revival home. Traditional Gothic architecture used a lot of stone and iron, and though Carpenter Gothics used more wood, it kept the tradition. It's what kept them standing, even decades later. Plus, my crazy old relatives, who I have never met before, decided to keep it from falling apart even though no one lived here. Which is weird."

"Weird as heck," Kellie agreed.

Lori set her down to admire the big, circular room. The blurry photos she had been shown did not do the tower justice. It was tall enough that it felt nestled in the treetops, a window on each side creating a panoramic view that let sunlight pour in through the branches.

"It's crazy someone built this place in the middle of the woods," Nikki remarked. "In *Ohio*, too. It feels like a waste."

"Lori, why is there a lady standing out there?" Kellie interrupted, peering out the window.

"The realtor is probably showing your dad the conservatory," Lori said. "Get away from those windows. I don't know how safe they are yet."

"There's a conservatory?" Nikki whistled. "No shit."

"It's gonna need more love than the house. But maybe I'll finally be able to plant things that stay alive."

"No, the lady is just standing there, all alone. In a dress."

"Lori?"

Lori winced at the sound of Sean's voice coming up the stairs.

"I got her," she called back. "Come on, girls. I gotta sign this paperwork and get the keys so that lady can get the hell out of here."

Nikki snorted. "She seems like a real winner."

The girls followed Lori down the stairs to greet the realtor, who was standing awkwardly beside Sean, still holding a pen. Papers had been strewn out across the fireplace mantle, several inked with his name. From the look on Ms. Markle's face, Lori guessed Sean's charm had been a no-go. She took a moment to imagine what Ms. Markle saw. Eclectic Kellie with her rainbow barrettes, hot pink jacket, and army-print jeans; cool, calm Nikki with her freckles, glasses, and ironed cardigan sweater; anxious Lori with her ripped sweatshirt, undereye bags, and workboots.

Sean approached her, attempting to capture her eyes as she artfully avoided his gaze.

"Lori, look at me," he begged in a low voice. "Are you absolutely certain you want to do this? Move all the way out here?"

Wordlessly, she snatched the pen from his hand and began signing her name at every X. As she scribbled, the room quieted, and their presence slowly faded. It gave way to the sound of loose and swirling wind murmuring through the upper rooms. The house creaked and groaned with it, creating a somber requiem of a time long passed. She smiled inside. Finally, the house was speaking to her.

"Come on, girls," Sean said softly, scooping Kellie into his arms. "Let's explore the backyard."

Nikki seemed hesitant to leave but followed him out the door.

Lori signed the final page and handed the pen to Jeanne, who had been silently watching her. "Here you go," she said cheerfully.

"You have a beautiful family," Jeanne said as she gathered the papers. "It's very admirable what you're doing. Having a Black husband and kids."

Lori's face fell. "He's my ex-husband."

"Oh yes. Well, you still have mixed daughters. That's so *admirable*. Things have really changed since I was your age. Are they staying here with you once you fix this place up?"

Lori's mind drifted to a conversation she'd once had with her old college roommate.

"I know you love Sean, but are you prepared to raise Black kids?"

"Of course, why wouldn't I be?" she'd asked, offended.

"It's different, Lori," Lisa tried to explain, leaning her thin frame against the doorway. "You gotta protect them from more than just life stuff. You can't forget their Blackness. Just like we can't." She touched her skin for emphasis. "It's gotta stay in the back of your mind because one day, you're gonna meet someone who'll make sure you don't ever forget it."

"They're my stepdaughters," Lori's voice pushed the memory away, "so they'll be staying with their dad until we can work out a custody arrangement. Their mothers aren't quite in the picture."

"Mothers?" Jeanne clucked her tongue. "Plural? I bet they're on drugs, aren't they?"

Lori's cheeks burned with anger at the insinuation, but before she could retort, Kellie ran back into the room.

"Lori! Did you sign it? Is it ours now? I want to buy a boat for that lake. Daddy said we can go fishing when you clean it up."

"I said *maybe*." Sean came in behind her. Sweat beaded his forehead.

"There's a lake?" Lori asked in alarm.

"That old pond will be easy to fill," Jeanne cut in as she opened her briefcase. "It's half full of muck and dirt anyway."

"Say, I'm starving," Sean said. "Let's find somewhere to eat. Breakfast for dinner?"

"That's a great idea," Lori cut in before he could ask her to come. "I already ate, but you can take the girls while I survey the house."

Sean looked disappointed behind the rim of his glasses, but in typical Sean Greene fashion, he moved right on. "Any places you can recommend, Ms. Markle?"

"You certainly don't want to go any place around here," Jeanne said, shoving the stack of papers into her briefcase. "Folks out here aren't used to out-of-towners. There's a McDonald's in Akron, though. It's about a twenty-minute drive from here."

Nikki made a face.

"I sure could go for some fries," Sean said to the girls, refusing to give up his cheerful facade.

"Can I get a Happy Meal, Daddy?"

Nikki turned to Lori, all soft brown eyes and wistfulness. It reminded Lori of when she was little. "I want to stay here with you."

"It's all super boring stuff right now," Lori assured her. "Mainly writing out an estimate for Seth. But I'll see you all tomorrow before you head back home. Right, Dad?"

Sean nodded. "We'll be here, bright and early."

"Okay." Nikki wasn't pleased, but she still gave Lori a hug. Lori felt Kellie's little arms join hers, and she fought the rising lump in her throat. A part of her wished they could both stay, but she wasn't going to do that to Sean. Just because they couldn't make things work didn't mean she would turn the girls on him.

As easy as it would be to do.

Lori lingered near the doorway, watching as they climbed into the Dodge minivan. "Be careful, okay?" she called, her stomach twisting with nerves. A shadow crossed the yard, and she looked up to see three vultures circling above them.

"Right on time but in the wrong place," Ms. Markle said beside her.

"What do you mean?"

"The buzzards. Every spring, they migrate to the Buzzard Roost in Hinckley. They have a big celebration every year on March 15th at the Hinckley Reservation. They call it Buzzard's Day. You should go sometime. It's not too far from here."

Lori couldn't think of anything she'd rather do less.

"Well, thank you again."

Fortunately, the relator was done with the small talk and said goodbye before climbing into her sedan. Lori watched as both cars rolled down the steep "driveway" through the woods to the main street. She waited until she could no longer see them before taking a deep breath, anticipating the blissful quiet.

In the distance, she heard an animal's rebellious shriek.

CHAPTER TWO
Ada, 1910

Though autumn had come and gone, snow had yet to arrive, and all Ada could see out her window were the twisted remnants of empty trees. The faintest chirp of birds whistled in the distance, but their presence seemed like a faraway dream. She'd spent the entire journey staring out the window of Charles's Peerless Model 27 as it roared down the winding country roads, waiting for something more than the endless procession of trunks and limbs. But it was only interrupted by fields of cornstalks, bent and stooped by winter's chill.

"There is nothing out here," she finally remarked.

Charles squeezed her hand. "We've nearly arrived."

She forced the most pleasant smile she could muster.

The automobile lurched, breaking up a moment that, to any onlooker, would have seemed tender. But only Ada felt and saw the pressure marks he'd left behind.

The doctors told Charles that getting his delicate new wife out of the city smog would be better for her health, and the summer home had been his quick solution. He surmised it would be good for the children's health as well. Though advised to wait until the spring, he ordered the entire house packed up, and within a week, they found themselves headed to the country.

To all who listened, he insisted it was because he cared deeply for his ailing wife's temperament, but Ada knew the truth. A third wife falling ill would prove far too difficult for society to keep quiet about. She would surely make it into the papers, just as she had when Charles first brought her to Cleveland from New York, and Charles simply could not abide by any slanderous gossip. He needed to amend their predicament so he could continue his business affairs without interruption or scrutiny. The abandoned summer cottage he had built for his first wife seemed the perfect solution. Deep in the valley, it was close to the paper mill and company town he owned, but far enough from the city to keep any unpleasant talk at bay.

The sound of rushing water pulled Ada's attention away, and she found herself relieved to see something besides dead cornfields and woods. Standing right before them was a grand mill and smokestack, the words HAITE BAG COMPANY loudly displayed on its side. A newly constructed covered bridge took them over the nearby river, and soon, Haite Towne came into view. Though most labored in the mill, a few women and children strolled the dusty streets, stopping to stare at the procession of automobiles as they rolled by. Their piercing stares made Ada wonder if they gossiped about her here like they did in the city.

She had seen pictures of country towns but never witnessed them up close. Everything in the country smelled different. A lingering, sickly sweet aroma laced with the sharp bite of horse manure. Though the town was modern enough to include a modest train station, it seemed so small compared to what she knew. There was a general store, a hotel, and even a place for petrol, though she had her doubts that many cars made their way through. Down a road to the left, dozens of houses had been arranged in neat little rows, built to house the factory workers and their families. It all felt so strange, an entire town owned by the man beside her.

"It's just up a bit further," Charles said as the motor car continued to pull them upward.

Ada peeked out his window to see the shadowy outline of a residence through the trees perched high atop the hill. Though obscured by dead forest, she could tell it was much larger than she'd expected. She should have known better; it had been built by Charles Haite, after all.

If there was one thing she'd learned over the last years of marriage, it was that her husband spared no expense.

After a few more moments of being uncomfortably hauled upwards, the motor car sputtered and stopped at the entrance. At its mouth, a stone marker had been laid, etched with bold capital letters: HAITE HILL. After a pause, the automobile jerked them again as it began to move even higher upward, now winding them through the empty trees.

"It is a hill upon a hill," Charles said. "Which is why I brought Peerless and the Packard. No typical motor car can make it up these hills."

"Why make the house so difficult to reach?" Ada wondered aloud.

"For privacy, of course. The late Mrs. Haite wanted to ensure we'd be properly separated from the town."

Ada did not respond.

The moment the woods spat them out, they came up to an iron gate flanked by pillars made of oddly shaped stones. The same kind of mismatched stone had been used to construct a beautiful but abandoned carriage house covered in dead ivy. Three vultures were perched atop it, staring at Ada with cold, black eyes.

"I will have that converted into a modern garage, of course," Charles informed her. "You'll be permitted a car and driver for simple errands in town."

At last, the house came into view.

It took Ada a moment to comprehend what she was seeing, for what stood before her was no simple summer cottage. It was an outlandish manor, dreadfully out of place in the middle of the woods. Stretching two and a half stories high, it cut past the treetops and into the sky with severely pitched gables lined with lacy bargeboards. Lancet windows boasted diamond glass panes that stubbornly refused to reflect the light of the setting sun, while thick moss coated its roof. Dead plant growth crawled up the west elevation, reaching around to grip a protruding tower.

The back of the house boasted more of the veranda, as well as an abandoned conservatory and what appeared to be a murky, overgrown lake. Ada's eyes lingered on an old row boat that hung limply at the side of a dilapidated dock, and she wondered if it, or the boat house nearby, had ever been used. She couldn't help herself. "Is this place even suitable for living?"

Charles chuckled humorlessly. "The grounds do need proper maintenance. I will be sure to take care of that in the warmer months. I had the home cleaned and new furniture put in. More of it will arrive tomorrow. Soon, it will feel just as proper as the city house."

Ada forced a smile.

The Peerless finally rolled to a stop at the front of the house, next to the veranda. Though sprawling, Ada noticed the paint was peeling away from the wood like snail shells. The driver exited to open the door and, after Charles withdrew, left an arm up to assist her. Ada managed to exit the narrow automobile door without disturbing the wide rim of her motoring hat and was immediately startled by a loud swooshing sound. She looked up to see that the vultures had abandoned their perch for a dead tree beside the house. Wingspans fully spread, they looked like hideous gargoyles watching her. Waiting.

She frowned, composed herself, and hurried away from their gaze.

The second motor car door opened, and out popped young Josephine. With her usual disregard for ladylike behavior, she marched right up to Charles with a scowl, her dark hair and ribbons fluttering in the wind. "I still do not understand why I must live here with *her.*"

Charles scowled. "We have been over this many times, Josephine. Ms. Ada is your stepmother and will look after you until you are ready for finishing school. You have already suffered enough without the guidance of a proper mother. Besides, who else will help Mrs. Bessler care for Baby Margaret if you are not here?"

He gestured back toward the children's nanny, who clambered out of the automobile with Charles's four-year-old daughter. The sleepy toddler cried the instant her feet hit the ground. Josephine hurried over, snatching her hand out of the nanny's.

"Come now, Maggie," she soothed her baby sister. "Don't cry until you see the beautiful house Father built for my real mother. It's a pity we must live in it with his horrible new wife."

Ada felt nothing at her words. Though it had been several years since their wedding, Josephine's disdain toward her remained steady throughout. Ada had simply learned to accept it; there was no love to be found inside her husband, why would his children be any different? A part of her longed for the opportunity to be the mother she herself never had, but she would not force a warmth that did not exist.

"Mrs. Bessler," Charles scolded. "You must keep her under control."

"Better, sir," the old nanny said, furiously nodding. She spoke little English as it was, and by the looks she frequently threw at Ada, she despised her as much as the children did. The old woman took both girls' hands with a firm grip and marched them into the house.

The wind picked up around them, and Ada watched a few droplets of rain dampen the sleeve of her motoring coat.

"Come," Charles commanded.

At the front door stood a tall man with a thick, dark mustache. He looked too young to be a butler, his skin freckled by the sun and marred by a crooked scar running down the left side of his face. His butler's costume seemed too formal for the countryside, but a young, overdressed butler seemed to fit with the outlandishness of the household just fine.

"This is Mr. Garvey," Charles introduced. "He came highly recommended by the Ashtons. You recall the Ashtons from our wedding?"

Ada nodded, though she didn't remember anyone.

"Pleased to meet you, Mrs. Haite," the butler said with a nod. She heard the trace of an Irish accent. "Can I bring you tea in the parlor? Or would you like to tour your new home first?"

"She would love tea," Charles spoke for her. "I will leave her in your good hands. I must attend to other matters and head back to the city before nightfall."

A jolt of panic coursed through Ada. She hadn't expected to be abandoned so soon. Not before she understood the layout of the home, at least. "I thought you planned to stay with us for a spell before returning to your work."

His expression remained impassive. "I didn't want to alarm you before you had a chance to see how beautiful the home was."

It took everything in her to calmly meet his steely gaze. "Of course," she said. "After everything that has happened, it is quite reasonable that you wouldn't want to cause any alarm."

"Precisely." He smiled, but there was no warmth in the expression. "Business must always come first."

"I will make sure she gets acclimated, sir," Garvey gently broke in. "Mrs. Haite has a full list of maids to interview tomorrow. Once that is settled, I'm sure she will feel right at home here at Haite Hill."

I haven't felt at home since my mother died, she thought.

The front door revealed a hallway too small for the cherubic sculptures that jutted out from its walls. Ada immediately grew ill at ease; the house smelled stale, earthy, and unkempt. Foreign. Her heels tapped across dusty wood floors as they entered the foyer, and when she looked up, an involuntary gasp escaped her chest. The ceilings seemed cathedral high, painted over with a heavenly version of the Madonna and Child, surrounded by swirling clouds, each haloed in soft gold. The artist failed to capture any warmth in her eyes, however, and the hovering image provided anything but a comforting expression of maternal love. Ada shivered, for her eyes were not unlike those of the vultures who greeted her.

"My late wife is responsible for the decor," Charles explained. "I'm sure you'll come to love it as she did."

Ada shivered again as the drivers brought her luggage through the front door.

"Have all her things put in the master bedroom," Charles instructed them before turning to her. "There is a parlor to my left, beyond the stairwell. The room to the right was intended to be a study, which you would do well to avoid, as it is in complete disarray. You'll find all the bedrooms on the second floor and a nursery on the third. Avoid the tower; it is in need of repair." He swiftly kissed her on the cheek, then stepped back, his hateful eyes lingering on her face. "Be well, my dear."

Ada swallowed. "I shall."

Then, he was gone in a flash of wool, leaving her trembling in the foyer.

"Your tea is ready, Mrs. Haite," a deep voice rumbled beside her.

Ada turned to see Garvey gesturing her forward. She forced her body to be still, unwilling to let him witness any weakness.

"Let me show you to the parlor."

She gave a quiet, curt nod.

The grand parlor at the back of the house had apparently been fully furnished before their arrival, and Ada neatly settled onto the upholstered loveseat. The wallpaper displayed a green bold enough to rival the outside of the home, and if she stared long enough, the decorative flourishes became silhouettes of women posing amongst the flowers. She forced her gaze away to gently remove her hat and gloves, setting them both on the table before her.

Garvey brought in a tray holding a teapot and cup, which he poured before offering it with a mustachioed smile. Besides the curiosity of his age and attire, his presence should have been soothing for her—someone there to care for her and protect her and the home. But Ada knew better. Beyond all the pleasantries, his olive eyes were sharp and watchful. He'd been positioned there as a spy for Charles.

She watched him move about the room, stoking each fireplace to build their flames. Charles had no shortage of personal footmen working various jobs for him in the city; apparently, he had found one who didn't mind moving to the country and dressing the part. Ada took a sip from her teacup and winced at the bitterness. A butler, indeed.

"Mr. Haite tells me you're from New York City," Garvey said.

"Yes," Ada said carefully. "My family is originally from Norway."

"Ah, that explains the light eyes and hair."

Warmth crept into her cheeks. She did not care for his familiarity one bit. "Thank you for the tea. You are dismissed."

He seemed startled by her curtness but quickly composed himself. "I will take the rest of your luggage to your room. Please ring me at your leisure."

Ada nodded and watched him leave. Alone at last, she took a deep, calming breath. It was not Charles's departure that unsettled her; she enjoyed every moment spared of his authoritarian presence. It was what this place represented. Like her marriage to Charles, it was another prison, this time in an unfamiliar countryside, far from anyone Ada had ever known. She felt alone again, the sick, creeping reality that she must care for herself, just like she felt when consumption finished off the last of her family, taking her wealth and her choices along with them.

The fireplace popped, and Ada set her now cold tea back on the table. Though she'd just been shivering in the foyer, she felt a sudden rush of unpleasant warmth. It took her quickly—an awful, suffocating sensation that threatened to squeeze away her breath. She needed to flee. Now.

She scrambled to her feet, noticing the door that opened to the back of the house. She bolted for it—Garvey's suspicions be damned.

The smack of frigid air instantly soothed her as the house spat her out onto the veranda and down the steps. Above, the cobalt clouds had snuffed out any lingering bit of sun and now let loose a smattering of rain. She felt her hair grow damp, but she marched toward the lake unaffected, her boots sinking into the dampened earth with every step. Memories of what brought her there threatened to surface, but she pushed them down, focusing instead on the murky water that soon stretched out before her. She watched the placid surface devolve into an expanse of shivers, trembling with each tiny droplet like pinpricks on skin. The overwhelming urge to dive in gripped her, and she imagined being pulled to the bottom by unseen fingers, releasing her from this life and all that went with it.

This behavior will get you put away. You must not let them see you.

The rippling water shifted to reveal what looked like tiny faces under the surface. They stared at her with the same longing she felt for death, all soft eyes and sad, open mouths. They were children trapped in the lake, like the cherubs trapped in the walls, calling her to join them. Ada took a deep breath and forced herself to look away.

They will lock you up, Ada. None of this is real.

She gathered her skirts up and away from the developing mud and headed back toward the house. Her life had never been easy—from her mother's death, to the journey over the ocean to a new country, to the moment she watched her sister and father waste away before her—this was just another trial for her to endure. And endure it she would.

A new determination settled over her, but not before a flash of movement caught her eye. She looked up to see a girl staring down at her from the tower. Alarmed that Josephine was so close to the window, Ada quickened her steps, hurrying back into the house.

Garvey stood waiting at the bottom of the veranda, visibly bewildered.

She ignored him, flying up the steps and through the open door, ready to call for Mrs. Bessler, but was immediately greeted by both children and the nanny. They were waiting for her in the parlor she'd just fled moments prior.

Confused, Ada opened her mouth to speak, but Josephine interrupted her attempt. "Father has locked the door to the tower, and we cannot get in. I'll need you to find me the skeleton key."

CHAPTER THREE
Lori, 1981

From the moment she'd pulled into the driveway, Lori felt like the heroine of a Gothic novel. A strange, abandoned manor surrounded by forest at the top of a hill, waiting just for her. The whole thing was pretty unbelievable, but she'd long learned not to look a gift horse in the mouth. She was also tired of sleeping on her friend Janet's couch, scouring the newspaper, looking for apartments that didn't cost double their house payment. The news couldn't have come at a better time.

Lori headed outside to grab her tent and supplies. She was no stranger to staying overnight in dilapidated houses—it was just like camping, something she'd joyfully done since she was a child. As soon as her foot hit the grass, she was immediately startled by the three vultures she'd seen circling earlier, now perched on the roof of her Ford pickup. Unmoving, like a trio of grotesques, their great wings were spread to their full extent. Lori had seen vultures sunning themselves before, but only in the early morning and never so close.

"H-hello, there," she said awkwardly.

Their beady black eyes glared at her from within shriveled, blood-red heads before all three took off in an uproarious rustle of feathers. Lori wasn't sure why the sight of them bothered her, but she quickly shook the feeling off and re-focused. She had planning to do.

The late afternoon breeze picked up around her, and she shivered through her old KSU sweatshirt. Although Ohio had been blessed with an unnaturally warm spring, the evenings were still cold, and Lori had the foresight to pack a big stack of blankets along with her flashlights and lamps. She'd been assured the house was wired for electricity, not long after it was built, but she didn't want to take any chances.

She managed to haul in all her supplies, plus her suitcases, in only three trips, deciding to set up shop in the study immediately to her right. It was the smallest room on the first floor, so in her mind, it was the coziest. Its high windows and lack of fireplace would also keep any nipping spring wind at bay.

This room had no fancy scrolled ornaments or sculptures of angels, presenting a more masculine representation of the entire home. The plain, symmetrical wainscotting of smoky wood was mirrored on the ceiling, which gave the room an almost claustrophobic feel. Lori imagined it filled with stately, dark wood furnishings with even darker wallpaper. It opened to a similarly designed parlor, which was complete with a chipped black marble fireplace, but she closed the connecting door to keep out the draft.

She pitched her tent and threw in the blankets, then she took an old beach towel and laid it down across the floor to sit on. She spread out her stack of floor plans right above it. Then she opened up her Igloo cooler to retrieve her thermos, happy to learn the coffee she grabbed at the last rest stop was still warm. She poured some into the thermos's metal cup and settled down to examine the home's skeleton.

So far, the house seemed content to have her there, and she enjoyed its murmurations as she made faint notes with her pencil. Thankfully, whoever had sketched out the plans had a steady hand and legible handwriting, the name HAITE HILL etched neatly at the bottom. Lori usually appreciated the symmetry Victorians were so fond of in their house building, and it was interesting to see a home dedicated to doing the opposite. The window placements had no rhyme or reason, the doorways were sporadic, the stairwells were disjointed, and the tower ruined it all. But its quirks gave the home character, and she intended to do her best to honor that in its renovation.

She gently removed each sheet of the plans until she reached the last page. It took a moment for her to understand what she was seeing, and then her stomach sank. The house had a basement. Basements in older homes only meant one thing: a huge, expensive pain in the ass. She hoisted herself to her feet and grabbed her flashlight.

Having just memorized the home's layout, she headed toward the back, into the grand parlor. It seemed more majestic without the spinning realtor, its bay windows revealing an overgrown but generous backyard, complete with a private lake and boathouse. She pushed all thoughts of a rotting basement aside and stood before them for a breath, appreciating the view. The sun had finally disappeared, leaving the sky the color of a bruise. Its eerie, leftover glow settled along the surface of the lake's murky water, making it seem almost tolerable. But she still had no desire to observe it close up—stagnant water made her skin crawl. Seth could figure out how to drain and fill it, or the right guy to call. He'd been working for her since she flipped her first house, and he knew a guy for everything. That is, if he didn't kill her over a nightmare basement.

She sighed and walked through the dining room. Her spirits were lifted when she saw three chandeliers, each hanging from its own plaster medallion, kept intact. She was going to love polishing them to their original shine. She pictured what kind of table would be long enough to fit the room, complete with gracefully sculpted chairs. But her uplift in mood was brief. She still had a monster issue to deal with. She pushed open the baize door to the kitchen and paused in surprise.

It hadn't been modernized. At all.

Why would a house be kept in good condition but the kitchen left inoperable, she wondered, as her eyes swept over the wood-burning stove and ice box. Maybe the owners wanted to keep it that way for authenticity—but then how would anyone have lived here comfortably? *Unless the house had been empty for the full seventy years...*

It was one thing to think of the house lying dormant for a few decades. But for one to remain empty and maintained since the moment it was built for nearly a century was, quite frankly, insane.

Lori shivered, suddenly wishing it were daytime. She shook off her growing unease, attempting instead to appreciate the simplicity of another era. Of course, she'd have to replace the stove and add a

Frigidaire to sell the home, but for a moment, she stopped to imagine what the kitchen would have been like. Servants in aprons bustling about to prepare each course for dinner. At a time when families dined together at the table. A pang of longing for the girls struck, and Lori broke into a stride to dismiss it, walking toward the end of the kitchen where the door to the basement had been bolted closed.

In most Victorian homes, the basement was the place where the servants slept and congregated. Some houses even had secret halls and stairwells to prevent upper-class families from having to share their living space. It was so strange to see it all laid out before her in what she had been told was just a casual summer home in Ohio, but she'd visited enough Newport mansions in Rhode Island to know how much Gilded Age aristocrats loved to spend their money. Apparently, the original homeowners were no different.

Lori fished out the skeleton key the realtor had left for her and tried it in the door. Surprisingly, it worked, but age had firmly stuck the door into the jamb. She pulled the handle as hard as she could, but it only creaked, mocking her frustrations. This would be the point where she'd call for Sean to help, the mere sound of her feminine distress causing the suffragettes before her to roll in their graves. But Sean was no longer here, and he wouldn't be. She had to get used to doing things on her own. She was ready for it.

Re-determined, she mustered every ounce of strength she had and pulled. At last, the door gave way with a resounding crack. She folded, taking a moment to catch her breath. That's when the smell hit her.

Horrified, she pulled out the handkerchief that she kept in her back jeans pocket to mute the stench, trying not to gag at what she'd just released. She debated closing it back up again—there could be a myriad of awful, gross things down there, from dead animals to sewage. But she needed to know what to tell Seth. And she needed to find out if the house was even salvageable.

She stepped back and wrapped the handkerchief around her head like a mask. It restricted her airflow but saved her nostrils from the torment. She flicked on the flashlight and pointed it into the black void. Its steady fluorescent beam revealed nothing but the top of a narrow, twisted stairwell. She took a tentative step forward and observed an eerie silence devoid of scurrying mice or even dripping water. She took another step, testing the stairs. They seemed as steady as the ones in the main stairwell, and the craftsmanship of the entire home led her to believe she could trust them. Still, her heart rate picked up, remembering every single scary movie she'd ever seen where they warn you not to go into the creepy basement.

This isn't the movies, Lori.

She took another step and then another. Servants once regularly made this same dark climb—if they could do it, so could she. A brief thought about the lack of cobwebs floated by, but she ignored it. The smell grew stronger, forcing its way past the fabric of her handkerchief. Bile hit the back of her throat in response, and she took a moment to collect herself. She was immediately glad she did, for as soon as the light from her Eveready settled, she realized what she was seeing. Not more than two steps ahead of her was completely still and stagnant water.

Panic seized her as she recalled every warning she'd ever received from her fellow abandoned house hunters, including her ex-boyfriend, Robbie. *"Keep your ass away from stagnant water. All kinds of shit gets in there—mosquito larvae, brain-eating bacteria, microbes that will rot your skin..."*

Shaking despite herself, Lori took a careful step backward. She didn't even want to move, her eyes fixated on the slimy, flat, spotted expanse only a few feet before her. It swallowed the rest of the stairs, and if she had walked a few more steps down, she would have stepped right into it. Every part of her wanted to run back up screaming, but she forced herself to take another steady step backward, taking the flashlight's beam along with her.

It moved across a strange lump she hadn't noticed before—that she didn't want to notice now—but she couldn't help but squint to see it better.

It was a skull.

In the murky, bacteria-saturated slop before her floated a human skull.

Lori whimpered, not wanting to know anything more, but the realization forced its way inside her brain regardless—it was an entire skeleton. *Mosquito larvae, brain-eating bacteria, microbes that will rot your skin—and human fucking remains.*

She had no idea how long it had been there, and she didn't want to know. Fuck this place. Fuck this house. Fuck it all. She'd drive into town and call the cops from a payphone. They could deal with it. She turned to race back up the stairs, to flee to fresh air and hope. But as soon as her foot hit the next step up, it crumbled under her weight.

The broken stairs fell first into the putrid water, and then the flashlight.

Then, her body followed.

She squeezed her eyes shut, but she knew there was no hope—no stairs left, no one there to reach down to grab her. Just millions of organisms sinking into her skin, her mouth, her eyelids, ensuring that even if a miracle happened, she'd die within days. She wanted so badly to scream at the absolute horror of it all, but she refused to open her mouth to the sludge.

All she could think about was joining the other body trapped in the stagnation and wondering if anyone would ever find them.

"Lori? Lori."

Lori bolted upright.

It took a minute for her eyes to adjust and her brain to realize where she was and who was standing before her. The answer to the first part was the floor of her new Victorian fixer-upper; the answer to the second part was Seth, her construction guy. As the sleep fog slipped away and her sense of reality returned, she learned she was soaked, but not from water. Sweat dampened her undershirt, and drool clung to her face, which had smeared the ink on the blueprints crumpled beneath her.

"Shit." She hurried to blot the moist papers with her sweatshirt. How could she have passed out like that? And all night?

"Blueprints *are* pretty boring."

"Oh my God, Seth, I'm so sorry," Lori groaned, remembering he was there. "I haven't been sleeping well, and it must have caught up with me."

"Eh, no worries." The broad man, wearing a flannel and faded blue jeans, shrugged. "The crew's not coming for another hour, so you have time to get your shit together. Hey, you got a lil' smudge..." He smiled as he made a rubbing gesture on his cheek.

Lori groaned again, taking her sweatshirt sleeve to the side of her face. "I don't even know if this place has running water yet."

Water.

The memory of her nightmare resurfaced, causing her skin to prickle with disgust. It had all been so vivid that she found it difficult to push the sensation away.

"You do, but it's not drinkable. I scoped out the house while you were catching up on your beauty sleep. I still gotta locate the boilers. Just make sure to run the faucets until you see the water clear. My electric guy can't make it until Friday, but you should be okay there, too."

Lori nodded, though she was distracted. She continued rubbing at her face as if she were scrubbing away the revulsion that had sunken through her pores. God, she wished she had a cigarette.

"I gotta say, I'm pretty shocked. Someone took really good care of this place."

"The basement," Lori finally managed. "The house has a goddamn basement."

It was Seth's turn to groan. "And here I thought shit was gonna be easy. Alright, I'll check it out. You go do whatever you gotta do to—" he gestured around at her unkempt appearance, "—fix all this up."

"Yes, go."

As soon as he left, Lori hurried to the bathroom behind the stairs, her hands shaking as she closed the door behind her. She placed them on the sink, taking a few deep, steadying breaths as she centered on the sensation of porcelain beneath her skin.

Then she turned the faucet, watching the water run from cloudy to clear before she splashed it across her face. The cold was just the shock she needed. She'd known Seth for years—they'd even hooked up once in high school—but she still felt embarrassed to be caught snoring in a puddle of drool. There was no mirror in the small, authentic water closet, but she made do, combing through her long, reddish-brown waves with her fingers and pulling them into a scrunchie before wiping her face with her back pocket handkerchief. She emerged semi-renewed but still worried about what Seth would discover when a familiar voice burst through the house.

"Hey, Lori!"

She looked up to see Nikki and Kellie coming toward her. She'd completely forgotten they were coming back to say goodbye. "Hey, girls. How was the hotel?"

"Gross," Kellie said honestly. "Can I sleep in the tower tonight?"

Lori gave her a quick kiss on the head. "Dad's taking you girls back tonight, but maybe after I get everything all fixed up—"

"Actually, I wanted to talk to you about that." Sean marched in from behind them, Kellie's backpack in hand. "There's an emergency at the office, and Shawna can't take them because of her church thing. Can they stay here with you for a day or two?"

Lori's stomach sank. She shouldn't have been surprised, but she was a fool not to have seen this coming. Typical Sean.

"Sean. I'm working."

"Come on, Kellie," Nikki said, recognizing the tension. "Let's go explore the carriage house."

"I know, I know," Sean said with a sheepish grin in the same flippant way he always did. "I'm sorry to ask. You know Jen isn't an option. I don't even know which trailer park she's even living in now—"

"Oh please. Nikki would kill you if you called her birth mom. What about school?"

"They don't come back from spring break until next week. And they brought their bookbags with them to study."

Lori couldn't believe what was happening. It wasn't the girls—she loved having them around. But she'd genuinely believed once she left, maybe Sean would finally understand that treating her as nothing more than a live-in babysitter was part of why she left. Or using her quiet longing for a motherhood that she herself never had—and would never be able to biologically experience—to his advantage. Wishful thinking.

She could still hear herself screaming: "*You treat me like I'm just part of the house—a piece of furniture waiting here when you're tired and need comfort! I'm not your fucking sofa, Sean!*"

"There's no place for them to sleep," she pressed. "It's an abandoned house."

"So, I packed their suitcases for a couple of days just in case something happened, and their sleeping bags are still in the car from last weekend. Kellie even brought her beanbag chair."

Anger sparked in her chest. "So you planned this."

"Lori, look—"

"No, no. It's fine," she said coldly. "This just helps prove that the divorce was the right choice. You go ahead and be a workaholic, fuck your new girlfriend, and I'll take care of the girls like I always do. And deal with Shawna's anger when she realizes you left Kellie here with me. Like I always do."

"Please don't do this. You know I have it hard—"

"*You're* doing this, not me. It's been almost a year since we separated, and I've asked several times that we make a plan for visitation. Not just you dumping the girls on me whenever you and your girlfriend decide you need spring break to yourselves. I want to stay in their lives, but not like this."

"This has nothing to do with my girlfriend."

"Way to miss the point," Lori snapped, wishing he would leave. "I need to get back to work. Is that all? Can you please go now?"

"I appreciate it." He dug into his pocket to grab his wallet.

"I don't need your damn mon—"

He pushed a few bills into her hand, regardless. "Just take it, please. Just in case."

"You know I don't have a phone here, right? If you need to get ahold of me, you'll have to call the hotel in town. If they're even cool—I didn't get a chance to introduce myself yet."

"I'll find their number in the phone book," he said. "But I promise I won't be gone more than a couple days."

"Hey, I'm not interrupting anything, am I?" Seth tentatively entered the hallway from the kitchen, his hands up like he was entering a war zone.

"Oh hey, what's up, Seth?" Sean greeted him with a nod. "I'm just heading out. Lori, I'll put the girls' stuff on the front porch."

"That's fine," she said, eager for him to leave so she could address the pressing issue at hand. Her anger had dissipated, allowing her paused anxiety to resume its climb.

"Did you get a look at the basement?" she asked Seth.

Seth shook his head. "I can't get over how lucky you are, kid," he said with a chuckle. "We're talking minimal repairs, if any. Being up on this hill probably helped mitigate water damage. Gotta imagine the valley wasn't so lucky."

Relief flooded over her. "Oh, thank God."

"I found and turned on the boilers. I was worried they still ran on coal, but at least that part's been modernized. I'm telling you—someone made sure this place never felt a minute of abandonment. Oh, and they left the old servant bell system installed on the wall. You should come check it out."

She felt a twinge of excitement before her face fell, remembering she needed to be Mom before she could play explorer. "Actually, I have to make a run into town. The girls are going to be staying here with me, and I need to make sure there's a way for their dad to contact me."

Seth nodded. "Ah. So that's what all that was about."

Lori shrugged. "You know how he is. Nothing's changed. I planned on introducing myself to the locals anyway, but got sidetracked...as you might have noticed."

"Well, listen, I got Steve on the way with the crew, but this is gonna be a breeze. Where's your list?"

Lori winced. "Can you give me like ten minutes to write it?"

Seth shook his head again at her, thankfully still wearing a smile. "Man, you're all over the place today."

"I don't know what's gotten into me," she admitted. She wasn't lying—this was so unlike her; normally, she'd have everything mapped out and strategically planned before Seth even arrived.

"Hey, it'll all work out. I've worked with you long enough to know your style. I have all the Victorian-inspired wallpaper, paint, and wood furnishings you could think of. Remember those ridiculous floorboards we put in the Watkins Glen house? I have the remnants in the truck."

Lori nodded, grateful for his calming words.

The girls slowly crept back into the house as if testing the waters.

"Did Dad leave yet?" Nikki asked innocently.

"Yes," Lori replied. "You both are staying with me for a couple of nights."

Kellie let out a squeal of delight, and Lori accepted her hug. Now that she'd gotten over Sean's bullshit, she should have been thrilled to have them with her. But she couldn't shake the uneasiness her dream had left behind. It all felt so real... She'd been hoping the house would welcome her warmly like the others, but it sent her nightmares instead. Something wasn't right.

She didn't want the girls to feel it, too.

CHAPTER FOUR
Ada, 1910

Drip. Drip. Drip.

Ada's eyes fluttered open. It took them a moment to adjust to the darkness, and when they did, she witnessed another droplet falling from her bedroom ceiling right onto her forehead. The cold, rude splat filled her with rage, and she threw off her quilt and blankets as frustration burned away her grogginess. The rain had yet to relent, creating a steady pattering on the window glass that on all other occasions would have been pleasant to slumber to.

Ada felt around to find and pull at the lamp strings, and they flickered on with a lazy sputter, bringing dim yellow light into her room. She squinted up at the ceiling, wondering how rainwater managed to come through to her second-story bedroom, right at the spot where the bed had been laid. But she had not imagined it: a jagged crack collected a line of shimmering water that bloated into a fat droplet before falling right on her pillow.

Ada considered her options.

She hadn't left the master bedroom since she entered it, wanting nothing more than to be alone with her thoughts. It hadn't mattered to the rest of the household; Josephine refused to be away from Maggie and abandoned her beautiful second-story room for the third-floor nursery, which forced Mrs. Bessler out. The old nanny moved to a smaller, closet-sized room nearby, even when Ada suggested she take Josephine's room.

"Care *aus* Maggie," she had argued.

As soon as that was settled and they bounded up the stairs, Ada informed Garvey that she was exhausted from traveling and would retire early. He'd accepted it without comment and agreeably took to the servant's quarters below the kitchen, but asked her to call upon him if needed. A part of her wondered if he was grateful to be dismissed early, lest he be forced to prepare supper until the actual cook arrived. She wasn't even certain if he was a real butler, let alone someone who could properly prepare a meal.

Ada had fallen asleep the moment her head hit the pillow, though she couldn't help but wonder, as she drifted off, if Charles's other wives had slept in her bed too.

She eyed the house bell, but the last thing she wanted was to rouse the slumbering pretend-butler. She'd done enough damage with her rain-drenched outburst and did not want to give him anything more to report back to Charles. But she couldn't sleep in her bed either. She thought of Josephine's abandoned room and sighed. It would have to do.

She found her robe and wrapped it around her body, fighting the chill seeping through her nightgown. She then located a portable gas lamp and the ring of keys Garvey had left her. Then it hit her—the tower. The tower was located directly above her, right above where the bed was positioned. Perhaps one of the windows had been left open, letting the rain pour through.

Her eyes again found the house bell. She could let Garvey know, but it would be nothing for her to just close the open window on her way to Josephine's room. Her stepdaughter had claimed the tower door was locked, but Ada knew better. Josephine had a relentless curiosity, and she'd try anything to get her hands on the skeleton key. Ada put the keys in her robe pocket and lit her lamp.

The dark, empty hallway that greeted her was soundless enough that the pitter-patter of rain followed as she exited the room. Its shadowy, contorted shapes might have given her a fright if the corridor hadn't felt so somber. Its rooms should have been filled with children, and it seemed to lament the loss. Ada positioned the beam of the lamp to locate the stairwell that led up to the tower, leaving the corridor to its melancholy. The temperature dropped immediately as her foot hit the first step, and she clutched her robe a bit tighter as she ascended.

She reached the top, and no sooner did she see the door than she heard the captured tempest whistling behind it. It shuddered like a giant attempting to break it free of its hinges. Ada tried the handle, and as she suspected, it was unlocked. It flew aside to reveal that, indeed, all three windows had been left open. Wind blasted her skirts and face as she entered, whipping her hair clean of its fastenings and stealing the flame of her lamp. But not before she saw the huge puddle collected in the corner where, logistically, her room would have been.

She fought against the howling squalls to reach each window and struggled to pull down the frames. Rain spat at her as she heaved, taunting her attempts to stop its onslaught. She grunted as she finally succeeded in slamming the first one down. Then came the second, and when the final window clattered shut, the tower went still at last.

Panting from the exertion, she brushed the wet, tangled hair out of her face and retrieved the felled lamp. Fortunately, it relit easily, giving her a chance to examine the room. A bookcase full of wet, and most likely destroyed, books had been set against the only windowless wall. Beside it was an old bedframe and a small desk that one might gift a child. In fact, the bed was small, too, as if it were also intended for a child. Ada imagined the view from the tower was quite beautiful in the daylight, a cherished spot for a child to hide away and play. But now, standing in the damp, dark space, Ada realized it brought her nothing but dread.

A crack of thunder added to her unease. A winter thunderstorm. The rarity of such an occurrence was enough to unsettle her completely, and she decided exploring the tower would be tomorrow's adventure. For now, it was best to simply sleep. She would let Garvey know of the leak in the morning. She started to turn back just as lightning flashed, revealing a white shape below.

Her jaw fell open.

It was a child standing near the edge of the lake.

Ada nearly dropped the lamp as she plummeted down the stairs. She tore through the house as fast as her skirt would allow, hurrying past the grand parlor and out into the backyard. "Somebody help me!" she managed to screech as she flew out the door to the veranda. The rain had turned into a hammering pour as she ran barefoot in the mud, fighting to see the little white nightgown through sheets of unrelenting water.

"Maggie!" she screamed.

Her soaked nightgown weighed her down, making it harder to fight the slippery mud. She finally lost her footing, hitting the wet earth with a painful thud. She abandoned her lamp, scrambling to get back to her feet as the small white shape wavered before her.

Finally, she reached her.

Maggie looked at her blankly, a little expressionless doll. Ada instantly recognized the look. It was the same her sister once had...the same she knew she had when Charles's men found her wandering around the grounds after dark. *Somnambulism*, the doctors called it. Walking while asleep.

Ada slowed her pace, careful in her approach.

Never wake a sleepwalker, her aunt once warned them, *lest they be trapped in the space between worlds...*

"Maggie, baby, wake up," Ada called as firmly as she could. "Wake up, Margaret."

The child didn't reply, just continued to stare at her blankly. Her bouncy curls had become streams hanging down her expressionless face, her soft blue eyes now dark and haunting.

"Maggie, it's Ada," she said. "You are sleeping, baby. You need to wake up."

Maggie simply turned, and before Ada had a chance to reach forward, she took a step into the lake.

"Maggie!" Ada screamed, launching herself into the rainy black.

Pain bit through her skin as she fell into the water, a blinding, brutal cold. She had no time to think, flailing as her body sank, desperate to connect to something. As soon as her finger grazed what felt like a limb, she clamped down and pulled Maggie to her chest. She kicked her legs to push them up just as a pair of strong arms lifted her shoulders from behind. She landed with a smack on the bank, sputtering for air through the downpour, Maggie's weight pressed to her chest.

Garvey stood above them, yelling over the storm. "Get her inside!"

Ada scrambled to her feet and hurried back to the house, cradling an unconscious Maggie. They all burst into the parlor, bringing buckets of rain with them, and Garvey slammed the door shut against the accompanying wind. Mrs. Bessler stood frightened in the doorway, holding back a sobbing Josephine.

"What happened?" Josephine cried as Ada rushed to the fireplace.

"She was walking while asleep," Ada explained calmly as she knelt as close to the flames as she could. She brushed Maggie's dark, wet curls from her face as the little girl coughed and spat.

"Mama..." she moaned.

"Mrs. Bessler, let Jospehine go."

The old woman obeyed, remaining helpless in the doorway, horror slackening her wrinkled features. Josephine ran forward and fell to her knees beside them.

"I need clean clothing and blankets immediately," Ada told Mrs. Bessler.

"I can do it," Josephine offered, furiously wiping away her tears.

"Yes, good, please help Mrs. Bessler."

Josephine's bare feet slapped the wood floor as she hurried away. Garvey stood, dripping in the middle of the room, seemingly at a loss for what to do. "Ma'am—"

"Fetch Maggie some warm tea, but not so hot that she can't drink it," Ada told him. "I will also need the flattest, dullest knife you can find in the kitchen." She met his stare, which was blank with confusion. Annoyed, she lifted the hem of Maggie's dress to show him the fat black leeches stuck to and suckling her pale little legs.

Garvey bolted into action.

In her arms, Maggie burst into tears, finally awake and conscious. "Mama, Mama..."

"Shhh, baby, it's Ms. Ada," Ada soothed as she began to rock her. "I have you now. You're safe."

Josephine darted back into the room on furious legs, carrying a stack of blankets taller than she was. Mrs. Bessler shuffled after her.

"Fetch the antiseptic and bandages," Ada told the nanny as soon as she reached them.

"*Es tut mir leid*, I sorry—"

"Mrs. Bessler, please do as you are asked."

Ada turned to Josephine. "I need you to sit as close to the fire as you can. I'm going to take off Maggie's wet nightgown and wrap her in the blankets. Then, you will hold her close and use the warmth of your body to heat her skin. Can you do that for me?"

Josephine nodded, grateful to be given a helping role.

Ada moved quickly, concerned that Maggie had stopped moaning, her teeth chattering behind blue lips. She tore away the girl's sopping nightdress and wrapped her shivering body in the heavy quilts. Josephine then cradled her sister, trying to be brave through tears that stubbornly threatened to break through.

"What's on her legs?"

"Leeches."

Garvey entered with the tea, which he set on the table to hand Ada the knife.

"Is it tepid?"

"Yes, ma'am."

"Josephine, help her drink this," Ada instructed, taking the cup from Garvey and passing it to her. "Then I'll need you to hold Maggie still, okay?"

Josephine nodded.

Ada took a steadying breath, pushing her wet hair from her face to see clearly. The room grew still as she focused on the slimy, plumping bulges attached to the toddler's legs. She began the gruesome work, holding each leech by the tail as she carefully broke the suction of its mouth with the knife, then tossed the wiggling creature into the fire. Maggie erupted once more in cries as tiny rivers of blood ran down her skin and onto the rug.

Mrs. Bessler returned with the bandages, her eyes widening at the sight before her.

"Thank you, Mrs. Bessler," Ada said. "You may take your leave."

"But Maggie—"

"Maggie is under *my* care," Ada said, with more bite than she intended. The elderly woman was far beyond the age of child-rearing, and Charles was a fool to have kept her on. "You insisted upon sleeping near the children, yet you were unable to notice a four-year-old leave her bed, head to the stairs, descend them, and then find her way outside. I have no hatred towards you, but you have not fulfilled your obligation to this family. Therefore, her care is now mine."

Josephine remained silent, an unspoken agreement.

The old nanny withdrew, and Ada set back to work. Once she'd finished removing the leeches and treated Maggie's legs with ointment, she wrapped them in clean bandages. She was grateful to see Maggie's color return, and her shivering subsided. She had taken to sucking her thumb, watching Ada work from against her sister's chest with wide, soft eyes.

"How do you know how to remove leeches?" Garvey asked.

Ada frowned, not wanting to give him any more information than necessary. "When I was a young girl, we vacationed in the country."

"And here I thought you were just a city girl."

Ada didn't appreciate how he looked at her. "Mr. Garvey, wire Charles immediately in the morning and let him know we've let Mrs. Bessler go. I am afraid she cannot properly care for the children anymore. We will hire a nanny as well as the servants tomorrow."

Garvey fumbled in surprise. "Well, I can ask—"

"No, you will do as I say," she snapped. "My husband has hired you to look after his wife and his children; what do you think he will do if he believes you are not up to the task?"

"Well, I, uh—"

"An elderly nanny is no fault of ours, and we can quickly fix the problem without Charles needing to be bothered."

A look crossed over Garvey's eyes as if realizing Ada wasn't quite what he'd expected as the lady of the house. "Yes, ma'am."

"Thank you." Ada softened when she turned to an unusually quiet Josephine. Her dark brown eyes had been wide and watching.

"Are you feeling okay taking Maggie to bed?"

"What if she does it again?" Josephine asked worriedly.

"She won't," Ada assured her. "But even if she does, I will not be sleeping tonight. I will ensure nothing happens to either of you. In the morning, we will rearrange the rooms so that you are closer to me."

Josephine nodded. "Come, Maggie," she said in her sister's ear. "You can sleep in my bed."

"Mr. Garvey, please carry Margaret to her room with Josephine."

"Yes, ma'am."

The butler removed his housecoat, exposing a plain cotton shirt beneath. Ada was surprised to see faded lines of tattoos peeking out from under his sleeves. "I'm gonna lift you up now, Miss Maggie," he said gently. "Is that alright?"

Margaret nodded, appearing comfortable with his touch as he lifted her with ease. Josephine stood and swept her hands down her night-dress. She looked at Ada with a serious expression, her eyes wiser than her years. "My deepest gratitude for saving my sister."

Ada gave a faint smile. "You're welcome, Josephine. Sleep well."

The young girl trailed after Garvey, and Ada listened as their footsteps faded, then disappeared up the stairs. She looked back at the fire and down at her lap, remembering she was still soaking wet and covered in mud. Brown muck covered the rug where she sat, ruining its pattern. In the quiet, her mind settled, allowing her to process what had just occurred. It was sleepwalking that had convinced Charles to send her away; she wasn't sure how he'd react to finding out his daughter now did the same. She closed her eyes, focusing on the sensation of warmth on her skin.

Garvey's voice forced her eyes back open. "The girls are safely in their room, ma'am."

"Thank you, Mr. Garvey. For all your help."

"Would you want me to do the honors?"

Ada looked up at him, confused. Then she realized what he meant. She lifted her soiled nightdress to see her own little friends dotted along her skin. Her legs were so cold and numb that she hadn't felt them. Pulling leeches off Maggie had been instinctual, done breathlessly and without much consideration. But she had since calmed, and the thought of pulling their angry mouths from her own skin made her feel ill. "Yes, please. Thank you."

Garvey knelt down beside her, and she caught the scent of fresh tobacco and pine. Though his arms were muscular, his hands were gentle, and as he set to work, she found herself hoping the dim light wouldn't reveal the bruises Charles had left behind. If Garvey noticed, he didn't speak of it. Instead, he let the silence be, interrupted only by the occasional sizzle and pop as he sacrificed each engorged leech to the pyre.

"How did you know she was out there?" he finally asked.

"I saw her from the tower windows."

"The tower?" He paused to look up at her. "The tower is locked, ma'am."

A chill spread across Ada's flesh, and she quickly decided that insincerity was her only option. She thought she'd entered the tower, but what if she was wrong? Since the event, there had been many times when she couldn't tell her dream state from her waking one, and she certainly didn't want to provoke unnecessary suspicion if she was. "Right, I meant the third floor. It's all so high to me that it feels like a tower. I went to check on the girls in the storm and noticed Maggie was missing from her bed. I ran down here immediately without thinking of calling for you."

She held her breath, hoping her words would be accepted.

Garvey seemed to accept her answer. "Why did the little lass wander out there anyway? With all the rain and cold?"

Ada took a moment to consider how to answer. This time, sincerity seemed to fit. "The doctors call it *somnambulism*. It means—"

"To walk in one's sleep."

Ada was taken aback. "Yes, exactly. Since...since the autumn, I've been suffering from a similar affliction. It's the reason why Charles thought it best for me to be out of the city. He believes what ails me is in the unclean air."

Garvey threw another leech into the fire. "Yet, here his youngest daughter is suffering from the same affliction. Perhaps it is a sickness common in your bloodline."

"Maggie is not mine," she said gently. "Nor Josephine. They each belonged to Charles's wives before me."

Garvey paused to meet her eyes. "Ah, but they are yours. You protect them like a mother, and they look to you as one. That is all that matters."

She quieted, his words soothing a restless sorrow that had long been nestled in her chest. "I suppose you're right." His words were too nice, his touch was too calm, and the fire roared a bit too pleasantly. It was artfully deceptive, and for the briefest of moments, she forgot her awful predicament.

Then she winced as he pulled at another leech, bringing her back to reality.

"That's the last of them that I can tell."

"Thank you, Mr. Garvey," she said, throwing her damp skirt back over her legs. She was grateful to be startled out of her lull. It would do her no good to be comfortable around any man in her husband's employ, no matter how kindly he appeared to be. "You may take your leave. Try to get some rest before sunrise."

"Ah, I don't think I'll be able to settle down again, Mrs. Haite. If it's all the same to you, I'll take care of this rug while you go up to change your clothes. Would you like some coffee? It's an awful vice of mine, but it does wonders for the long nights." He stood, shaking out his pants before offering a hand so she could stand.

She hesitated before she took it, allowing him to hoist her to her feet. Strong coffee did sound wonderful. "I would like that, thank you."

"Very well, then."

"Also, I'll need you to look at the ceiling in the bedroom. I believe there is a leak in it, which has ruined my bedding and pillows."

"Yes, ma'am. I can take a look as soon as I bring the coffee."

"Thank you." Ada wiggled her hand free of his grasp and turned to head back toward her bedroom. She paused. "Also, Mr. Garvey?"

"Yes, ma'am?"

"I want that lake filled."

CHAPTER FIVE
Lori, 1981

Lori's Ford rumbled down the hill, the exhaust kicking up the dried leaves that scattered the forest floor. It had been a mild winter, but Ohio was notorious for its last-gasp spring snowstorms, and she couldn't imagine trying to get down the poorly cleared path through the woods in the snow. She made a mental note to talk to Seth about having it paved as soon as possible.

The truck bounced as it exited the woods and hit the actual road, which was just another steep hill to maneuver down. Beyond the worn pavement stretched swampy marsh and, in the distance, rusting silos and tumbledown barns.

"Wait 'til you see the creepy church," Kellie piped up from where she sat next to the window. "It's Satanic!"

Nikki clicked her tongue. "It is not. It's just an old building."

"Yeah, huh! It's got a cross that goes upside down on the front of it. Mommy says that's what Devil worshippers use."

"Actually, an upside-down cross isn't Satanic," Lori told her as she wound the truck down the hill. "It's called Saint Peter's Cross because he was crucified upside down," she continued, then winced as soon as the words left her mouth. The last thing she needed was Shawna getting wind that the religious bullshit she routinely fed her daughter and her former stepdaughter was being debunked.

They reached the bottom of the hill where the road forked.

"You have to go left," Kellie told her.

Lori looked in the direction she had pointed to and saw faded old buildings in the distance. Concrete barriers had been set up in front of them, one wearing a sign that read "ROAD CLOSED."

"Please!"

Lori turned the truck left to humor her, and sure enough, they saw an old church with a cracked bell tower and painted white brick. She smiled as it came into view. "That upside-down cross shape you see at the top is just part of the architecture," she explained. "Those are called bargeboards; our new house has them, too. That hanging part right there is called a pendant."

"Still creepy," Kellie remarked.

Lori had to admit she was right, but the fading church was the least ominous part of the town. Right across from it was another building with peeling white paint that looked like it might have once been a school. Its windows and doors were boarded up and covered with spray-painted signs that said "KEEP OUT." Beyond that, an abandoned house sat with a yard full of rusted car parts. This one had a fancy government sign with printed letters that warned "No Trespassing by Federal Law."

How had I not noticed this on the way in? Lori wondered.

She turned the truck around and headed back down the main road. They drove past their street and met another faded sign that boasted the Boston Hotel. The old boarding house behind it was the largest building in town at two stories high, with dark shutters and a wrap-around porch. Lori noted the Federal-style architecture in the fan-shaped lunette above the front door, meshed with Greek Revival-style Ionic pilasters. The hotel sat beside a gas station that hadn't been updated since the fifties, with a bait and tobacco shop perched next to that.

Lori pulled the truck into the unpaved parking lot, and a man in dirty overalls immediately came out of the hotel to investigate. She offered him a tentative wave through the window, which he did not reciprocate. It suddenly dawned on her that this place looked very similar to the sundowning towns she'd seen during her travels. The ones Sean warned her about. Fear prickled in her chest as she looked at the girls, feeling very much the ignorant white stepmom. Jesus Christ, how could she have been so stupid?

"*...are you ready to raise Black kids?*"

Before Lori could put the truck in reverse and stage a quick retreat, Kellie pushed open the passenger door and hopped out.

"Kellie!" Nikki hissed, jumping out after her.

"Oh hey, there, young lady," the man called, his voice friendly. "How ya'll doing today?"

Lori exhaled with relief. She turned off the ignition and followed them out, slamming the door behind her. "Hi, there," she called up to the man. "I'm the new owner of the house up on the hill."

The screen door opened again, revealing a heavy-set woman wearing old blue jeans and a flannel come to join them on the porch. "You're Lori Greene, right? Your man, Seth Baker, is staying with us. Said he works for you."

"Yes, Lori Greene. These are my daughters, Kellie and Nikki."

"Welcome. This here is Ed, and I'm Carlene. Carlene Duncan. Ed owns the bait and tobacco, but he mostly hangs out here and drinks all my beer."

Ed whistled. "Aw, save it, Carl."

"Why don't you folks come on in? It's getting chilly with the sun going down."

Nikki caught her eyes, and Lori nodded, letting her know that it was safe. So far, so good. But now, Lori understood what the relator meant—there was nothing here. Just a fading town and a handful of folks fading along with it.

They walked up the porch steps and into the hotel, their footsteps creaking on worn floorboards. The inside was pretty much what Lori pictured; everything was outdated, with faded rugs and tobacco-smoke-stained paint. But however stale the air, the atmosphere was light. A shabby front desk with a telephone had been pushed into the small foyer next to the main staircase, and there was a little shop with candy and newspapers in the back. Through the opposite doorway, Lori observed an attached restaurant and bar with little plastic flowers set in vases on the tables.

At one of them sat a wizened man smoking a cigarette, tufts of smoke swirling around his face as he watched them with glassy eyes. Lori was ashamed to admit that the smell of it made her mouth water. He didn't break eye contact with her as he took a long sip of his beer. Kellie had gone from curious to shy, walking so close to Lori that her bright purple boot heel smashed into her toe. Lori bent down and lifted her into her arms.

"Ya'll hungry?" Carl asked, leading them into the dining room. "Dinner isn't for another hour or so, but I can whip you up something small."

"Oh no, I'd hate to intrude—"

"Nonsense," the woman said as she disappeared into the kitchen. The mirror behind the bar had the words *Jim Browne Tavern* painted across it in peeling gold letters. "Have a seat at that table near the bar. And don't mind ol' Tom. He's older than this town and can't hear a goddamn thing to save his life."

Lori exchanged another glance with Nikki as they settled around one of the tables. Behind them, Tom's cigarette hissed as it went out inside his beer bottle. His chair creaked as he pushed it away from the table, and he shuffled out of the room without a word.

Lori cleared her throat. "I was hoping to use your phone number until I can get a line installed," she called to Carl. "Just in case the girls' dad needs to get a hold of us."

"Your husband ain't helping you fix up the ol' Haite House?" Ed asked as he rounded the bar to help himself to another beer.

"Don't think I can't hear you," Carl warned him from the kitchen.

"Put it on my tab." He popped the top off with a bottle opener attached to the side of the bar and took a long swing before continuing to address Lori. "Seems to me that he ought to be helping you with such a big task."

Lori decided it would be too much to explain. "He needed to get back to work. We're from upstate New York."

"Got it. That one yours?" He nodded toward Nikki.

Lori shot a look at her oldest stepdaughter. Because of her light complexion, people always assumed that Lori was her mother, which stressed out Nikki, who wanted to pretend her birth mother didn't exist, and Kellie, who didn't quite understand why no one ever asked her that question.

"They're both mine," Lori said firmly.

"Well, you feel free to give him our number," Carl interrupted as she came back in, armed with a tray. "There are little cards on the front desk with our phone number if you need it." She'd brought with her three egg-salad sandwiches, each with a handful of chips, and two cans of Pepsi for the girls. She set a can of Pabst Blue Ribbon in front of Lori. "I know it's early for some folks, but you really look like you could use a cold one."

"Thank you so much." Lori cracked open her can. It was a little flat, but she was grateful for it all the same. The entire afternoon had rattled her more than she wanted to admit.

Nikki made a face at the mashed-up egg and mayonnaise concoction pressed between slices of white bread, but Kellie happily munched away on her sandwich and potato chips. Lori's stomach growled, but she silenced it with another sip of beer, not quite ready to eat yet.

"If you or the girls need anything, you just give me a holler," Carl said as she went behind the bar. "Now that you're official residents of Boston Village and all."

Ed snorted. "We ain't even a real town, Carl. Not anymore. Damn government snatched up half our houses."

"Is that why there are so many 'No Trespassing' signs?" Kellie asked, her bravery restored with each bite of sandwich.

"Well, look at you," Carl whistled, impressed. "That's exactly why. Ford's new bill let the National Park folks come in here and try to grab everything up. They marched into town a few years back, making threats and flashing around their money, and people fell for it. At least ten families sold their properties to 'em and moved on. But after all that talk, not a damn thing happened. It's like they all found something better to do. The houses are just sitting there, boarded up and attracting teenage mischief."

"They tried to set fire to the Holmes's barn last week," Ed told her. "Bobby ran 'em off with his shotgun."

Carl shook her head. "Goddamn shame."

Lori's stomach sank as they continued to talk. How could she possibly flip and sell Haite Hill without a nearby town? She took another sip of her flat beer. *I might just end up stuck here.*

"How are you still in operation, if you don't mind my asking?"

"Fair question," Carl said as she lit a cigarette. "Folks still pass through here for various things. There's a big ol' arena in Richfield called the Coliseum, about thirty minutes down the road, that plays all sorts of concerts. It's cheaper to stay down here than in a hotel in the city. I inherited this place, so I'm staying, come hell or high water."

"Lori inherited her house, too," Kellie said, ignoring Nikki's poke in the ribs to be quiet. She crunched her potato chips loudly as she spoke. "Some rich white people gave it to her."

Both Ed and Carl turned to look at Lori.

"How'd that work out?" Ed asked her. "I thought the Haites were long gone."

"I'm just as confused by the whole thing," Lori admitted. "My birth mom died when I was young, but apparently *her* mother has been alive up until last month. In her will, she named me her sole heir. I never even met the woman in my life."

"Josephine."

Lori looked up to see a Black man in the doorway. He looked to be about Ed's age, with thick, salt-and-pepper whiskers under his baseball cap.

"Hey, Comfort," Ed greeted him. "These are the Greenes from Haite House."

"How did you know my grandmother's name was Josephine?" Lori asked.

"Boston Village is a small town," Carl explained. She set a beer down in front of the man called Comfort as he settled himself onto a bar stool. "I shouldn't be letting you drink on the job, but it's not every day new folks move in."

"You know I appreciate you, Carl," Comfort said with a smile.

Carl turned back to Lori. "Josephine was the daughter of Charles and Julianna Haite. You see, Boston Village started small, but it was a booming town back in the canal days. The railroad ruined everything.

Everything was falling apart when Haite came in to build his paper mill. He bought up everything for miles and turned it into a company town for his workers. Called it Haite Towne, even. He built Haite Hill as a summer home for Julianna and their boys."

"Spoiled that woman rotten, he did," Ed chimed in. "You see that ceiling? Had an artist sail in all the way from France for it."

"Oh, stop spreadin' rumors, Ed," Comfort chimed in. "No one knows who painted that damn ceiling."

"Regardless," Ed continued, undeterred, "Charles Haite spared no expense building it. Filthy rich, that one."

"Things were all fine and good until the papermill burned down the first time," Carl continued. "At least four families were left with no parents. Unlike her husband, Mrs. Haite was a real godly woman. She took in the kids and apparently liked the work so much that she took in city orphans as well. Haite Orphanage ran for almost ten years before she died."

"I *knew* that place had kids," Kellie remarked as she ate another chip. "The boathouse has all these little boats too small for adults."

Lori shot a look at her oldest, who was supposed to be keeping her sister far away from the lake.

"I was watching her!" Nikki said defensively.

Lori sighed, suddenly feeling exhausted again.

"You know, if ya'll need some help with the little one, my niece is an amazing sitter. She just turned nineteen."

"Oh no—"

"Becky!" Carl yelled up the stairs.

"I do *not* need a babysitter," Nikki hissed in Lori's ear.

"I know, but you're gonna be helping me fix the house, remember?" Lori took her last sip of beer. "It would be nice to have a little help with everyone running in and out of the house."

They heard footsteps coming down the stairs, and a shy-looking blonde poked her head around the corner. "What's up, Auntie Carl?"

"Becky, this is Lori, Nikki, and Kellie Greene. They bought the old Haite House up the hill."

"Oh, wow." Becky walked into the room, her eyes widening behind her wide lens glasses. She seemed younger than nineteen, with little contrast between her skin and the hair she wore in a long French braid down her back. Her yellow cardigan was in a style similar to Nikki's, giving her a charming, studious look. "That place is so beautiful. I've always wanted to see inside it."

"There's a spooky church painting on the ceiling," Kellie informed her. "And a tower."

"That's amazing," Becky said genuinely. "Do you like candy? I have a ton in the shop."

Kellie raised an eyebrow. "But do you have PopRocks?"

Becky reached into her back pocket to reveal the obnoxious red, pink, and yellow packet of fizzling sugar.

Kellie squealed in delight as Lori looked the teenager up and down, trying to get a feel for her. She wasn't the type to ask for help, especially when it came to the girls, but it seemed more reckless *not* to. There was no way she was going to be able to focus on the house and make sure Kellie didn't find her way into something dangerous. She also hated burdening Nikki with her care when she knew Nikki'd rather be helping her with the house.

"Becky is here on break from Akron U," Carl said proudly. "She's going to school to be a teacher. I told her mom she could work here with me until the fall when she goes back. Earn a little to help pay her tuition."

"Awesome," Lori said. She gestured to her sweatshirt. "I went to Kent State myself. What's your concentration?"

"History."

"You're hired," Lori said, half-kidding. She felt Nikki nudge her under the table, which she ignored. Kellie stuck her tongue out at the grimacing Nikki, wiggling her hissing, red, Pop-Rock-coated tongue.

"Are you sure she wouldn't be needed here?" Lori asked Carl.

She chuckled. "If we suddenly get a rush of customers, I'll send Ed up to fetch her."

"Rush of customers," Comfort repeated with a wheezing laugh.

Lori looked down at her empty beer can, frozen by indecision.

Carl must have noticed. "There's no need to stress about it today," she said as she came around to clear the table. "If you decide ya'll need the extra hand, just let me know. The offer stands."

"Great, thank you so much. For everything." Lori began to fish out the money Sean had given her.

"You put that back in your pocket," Carl said. "Your first meal at the Boston Hotel is free."

Lori hated even a glimmer of charity, but she also understood that it was how relationships were built. She needed allies in this strange town, at least until she figured out what to do with Haite Hill. "Thanks again," she said. "It was nice meeting you all."

They all said their goodbyes, and she and the girls walked out onto the wrap-around porch. Lori was startled by a low creak and turned to see Tom, the old man from earlier, sitting in one of the rocking chairs as if waiting for them. He pointed a long, gnarled finger her way.

"You better do right by that house, young lady," he wheezed.

"Don't mind ol' Gramps," another man called as he jogged toward them from across the street. "He's cranky, but he's harmless, I promise."

"No problem," Lori said pleasantly, though she guided the girls away from the porch. They met the younger man at the bottom of the steps.

He pulled off his baseball cap to reveal a crop of dark hair, which he ran a hand through before sticking out his hand. "The name's Finn. Finn Garvey."

"Nice to meet you," Lori said, finding herself uncharacteristically nervous under the sparkle of his green eyes. He was tall but broad, with a working man's hands and a five o'clock shadow freckled with auburn. Though he seemed a few years older than her, his wide, playful grin made him seem younger than his years.

"I'm Lori Greene—actually, it'll be Lori Byrne now—um, and these are my daughters, Nikki and Kellie."

"Nice to meet you, girls," Finn said with a nod. "So you getting married? The name change," he added after he saw her blank expression.

"Oh! Um, no. The opposite. Byrne is my maiden name."

"Can we go now?" Kellie said impatiently.

"I'll take her to the car," Nikki said, pulling her sister's arm.

"Shotgun!" Kellie said.

"Well, wait—I'm coming too—"

"I won't keep you," Finn said. "You must be the new owner of Haite Hill?"

"If you couldn't tell by how awkwardly we stick out," Lori said with a nervous laugh. She was suddenly very aware of her unkempt appearance and wondered in quiet horror if she still had caked spit in her hair.

"Nah, if the house called you, you're meant to be here."

That took Lori aback.

"My granddad was Haite Hill's groundskeeper for years before I took on the heavy lifting," he explained. "We used to stay in the old carriage house. Since Ms. Josephine died and gave you the house, we've been staying at Carl's."

Lori frowned. "Oh, I'm sorry. I had no idea."

Finn shrugged it off, genuinely unbothered. "Nah, don't be. But if you do need any help with the grounds, just gimme a holler. It's been a few weeks since we've been over there, so I'm sure she's in bad shape. The lake definitely needs work before summer."

"Sounds great. Once I make the inside look decent, I can think about the grounds."

Finn brightened. "Oh, I can help with that, too. Interiors, exteriors. Feel free to ask around: I'm a jack-of-all-trades..." He trailed off as if realizing how overly eager he sounded. "To be honest, I just want an excuse to hang out with you. It's not every day a beautiful woman moves into town."

The trunk horn honked, causing them both to jump.

Lori felt her cheeks burning. "Oh, yeah. Sure. I'll see you around," she stammered awkwardly as she backed up toward the car.

Finn gave her another big smile with a bob of his head and headed back across the street where he had been working.

Lori climbed in the truck to greet a snickering Nikki and an agitated Kellie.

"What's up with you and Irish guys?"

"Daddy's not Irish! He's *Black.*"

"He's both, so we're both, dummy."

"I'm not a dummy, stupid—"

"*Girls, please,*" Lori said shortly, trying to let her swirling thoughts settle. They both went quiet as she threw the truck into gear. They exited the parking lot, and she tried not to look back at old Tom in the rocking chair. She could feel his eyes on her as she drove away. Besides the surface-friendly townsfolk and the angry old man, meeting a handsome, charming stranger had not been expected.

"Why is it so dark outside?" Kellie asked.

Lori looked out the car window to see rain clouds moving in to snuff out the last gasps of sunset. She cursed under her breath, hoping Seth would notice and bring all the supplies into the house before they burst over them. She wished her old pickup would move faster, the Ford sputtering as it pulled them up the paved hill and into the woods.

As soon as they hit the bend, another truck came barreling toward them.

"Lori, look out!"

She swerved out of the way just in time. The tire twisted in and out of the shallow ditch as she struggled to correct it. She looked back to see an old, red pickup truck with a rusted tailgate and billowing exhaust speeding away.

"What the heck was that?" Kellie cried.

Lori brought the car to a gentle stop to catch her breath. "Are you girls alright?"

A strange look had crossed Nikki's face.

"Nikki?"

"I saw two white guys driving," Nikki told her. "They looked—I don't know. Their faces looked weird. Distorted, I guess. Through the window."

"Guess we're meeting all the townies today," Lori muttered. "Why they've come up here is the question."

"Maybe they live in that old barn," Kellie said.

"We saw an abandoned barn when Dad drove us up here," Nikki explained.

"Who knows," Lori sighed. She put the car back into drive and proceeded back up the hill to the wooded elevation. "I'm happy your dad let you girls stay with me, but I wish he had given me a chance to get a feel for it first. Some of these country towns can be…"

"Racist?" Nikki said.

Lori frowned. "Maybe we should find a nearby hotel."

"That hotel is gross!" Kellie whined.

As if in response, the Ford promptly stalled out.

"Shit." Lori tried the key. Again. And again. "Ugh, not now..."

A scream pierced the air.

"What was that?" Kellie asked in alarm.

"It's just a fox, baby," Lori replied, distracted. She wasn't exactly sure what a fox's scream sounded like, but she didn't have time to consider it. To add to the building calamity, a clap of thunder resounded above, and the skies promptly opened and poured.

Lori fell back in her seat, defeated. The beer on her empty stomach had temporarily dulled her stress, but no part of her wanted to mess around under the hood of the truck in the rain. In the middle of the woods. After nearly being hit by a car.

"What are we gonna do?" Nikki asked.

"Well, we can wait it out or walk." She turned to give Kellie a weak smile. "At least you have your rainboots."

"Yeah, but I don't," Nikki protested. "And I'm *not* getting my hair wet."

Lori sighed. "Fixing the car in the rain, it is." Her fingers went to hit the latch at the same time that another piercing shriek rang out from the distance. This time, Lori paused.

"That doesn't sound like a fox," Nikki murmured, reading her thoughts. "It sounds like a woman screaming. What if it's from that barn?"

"Lori, I'm scared."

"There is always a logical explanation for things," Lori assured Kellie, though she was starting to get spooked herself. In the wind, the empty branches began to sway and twist, scraping against the roof like fingernails. It reminded Lori of the old urban legend where the killer left his victim hanging above the car.

"I don't like this place anymore."

"Come here." Lori scooted over so Kellie could crawl over Nikki's lap to the middle. The trio grew quiet as they watched sheets of rain pour down the pitch-black windows surrounding them and listened to the scraping sound above.

Lori waited for a pause before trying the ignition again. It was most likely the damn battery; she should have known better than to haul the old Ford across so many miles. It seemed she was failing at everything.

"Do you think our basement is going to be flooded again?" Kellie asked.

Lori paused. "What do you mean?"

"Like before. When that lady got trapped in there and drowned."

"Shut up, Kellie," Nikki snapped. "No one wants to hear your scary stories right now."

"I'm not telling scary stories!"

"Girls, please st—"

The shriek rang out again, this time, so loud it rattled the car. They jumped, and Kellie let out her own scream. Heart racing and hands shaking, Lori slammed the key forward again, hard, praying to any god that would listen that the car would *just fucking start!*

And then, a miracle.

The Ford roared to life, and she threw it into gear. The truck hurtled up the rest of the hill, churning up the mud as the girls cheered in the background. It pushed for a bit longer, then sputtered out again when she reached the old carriage house, but it was good enough. She saw Seth jogging toward her, an umbrella in hand. Relief washed over her as she opened the door to greet him.

"Where the hell have ya'll been?" he called over the rain. "I almost went after ya."

CHAPTER SIX

Ada, 1910

Evening seeped into the sky like ink, ruining the sunset. Ada gazed out the front parlor window into it, wondering what sort of adventures tonight would bring. Would she see children's faces in the lake? Would she wander into a tower that had been locked, mysteriously unlocked, then locked again? Would she wake to find Maggie drowned?

"Ma'am?"

Ada looked back at the prim woman seated before her. She blinked before she remembered she was in the middle of an interview. "Oh, forgive me, Mrs. um, Mrs..."

"Thornbury."

"Mrs. Thornbury," Ada said with a nervous chuckle. "Yes, of course. Thank you for your time, Mrs. Thornbury. I find myself growing tired as the hour grows late, as I have been interviewing potential caregivers since early this morning. You may go. We will be in contact with you once the decision has been made."

The older woman stood and bobbed her head. "Thank you, ma'am."

Ada let out her held breath as she retreated, exhaustion settling into the corners of her eyes. She rubbed at her temples, longing for a good cup of tea. The past few days had flown by in a flurry of furniture and bodies. Although her suspicions of Garvey remained, he proved to have quite the knack for household management, and soon all was taken care of, as he had promised. A new housekeeper was quickly and efficiently hired, as well as four additional maids. The leak in the ceiling had been addressed immediately, and a brand new bed was brought in, which was positioned on the other side of the room, near the two beds belonging to Josephine and Maggie.

Mrs. Bessler had been officially dismissed, which both children seemed remarkably content with. Life was settling into a semblance of routine, but Ada still had yet to shake the impression the house had given her—a general sense of foreboding and discontent. Nor had she yet to find a suitable replacement for Mrs. Bessler. She hadn't minded the absence of a nanny so far; since the harrowing first night, the girls had warmed right up to her. It was something Ada hadn't realized she needed in her life—the love and companionship of children. But still, Josephine needed her lessons, and Ada needed the freedom to manage the affairs of the home. And so, Garvey arranged for potential nannies to be interviewed.

Ada reached for the bell to ring for tea when Garvey surfaced.

"I was just about to call Elena for tea."

"There is another girl here to see you, ma'am."

"Another hire? I thought that was the last of them."

Garvey looked apologetic. "I told her to come back tomorrow, but she begged me for the opportunity to speak to you. I think she's a local from town, which means she walked quite a ways and up the hill to see you..."

Ada sighed as she stood. "I will take care of it."

"Yes, ma'am."

Ada headed to the foyer to greet the potential hire in question. In the doorway stood a young girl dressed in yellow cotton under a shabby coat. She wore a waist-length, straw-colored braid beneath her hat. When she looked up, she revealed a round face ruined by thin, cracked lips and shadows under her eyes.

"May I help you?"

"Yes, ma'am. Good evening, ma'am. My name is Rebecca, ma'am. Rebecca Crane."

"Good evening, Rebecca. I interviewed all the maids a week prior."

The girl's eyes widened. "Oh, forgive me, ma'am. I-I didn't know—"

"No need to apologize," Ada said. "Mr. Garvey can escort you back home—"

"Oh, madame, please," she said frantically. "I live right in Haite Towne with my grandma and grandpa, and since the mill shut down, we haven't had any money comin' in. They're too old to move, and I need to provide for them."

Ada blinked. "The mill has closed?"

"Yes, ma'am. All the families got told last week. He doesn't know if it will reopen soon or next year. He's lettin' us stay in our houses, but we have no money without the mill work."

"How old are you?"

"Fourteen, ma'am."

"You're but a child. Josephine is ten years old, nearly your age."

"It's true, but I've been watchin' little ones for years. When the mill was open, I kept watch over all the children in town so their parents could work. I love kids, and they love me, too."

Ada studied the young girl before her. "The children were attached to their nanny, and I have assumed her role as of late. I must say, I am hesitant to hire someone so young when the girls need to be closely watched and cared for. What else can you do?"

"I can cook good, and I can clean."

"I have a cook and several maids..." Ada frowned, waiting for a pause before the solution came to her. "I am in need of a lady's maid, however. Do you think you could manage that? Preparing my daily attire, running my baths, and anything else I may need throughout the day?"

Rebecca brightened. "Absolutely, ma'am. It would be my honor, ma'am."

"Then you can assist me with the girls where needed."

"That sounds wonderful, ma'am."

"Alright, then. You can start tomorrow."

"I-I'd like to begin today if I can," the girl said, resuming her pleading eyes. "The woods can be hard to navigate in the dark."

Ada searched her face and found nothing but innocent enthusiasm. She stepped aside, inviting the girl in.

Rebecca grabbed her faded bag and entered, her eyes widening immediately at the sight of the ceiling. "This place is beautiful!"

"Garvey?" Ada called, sensing he was near. "Please tell Elena to get Ms. Crane settled and acclimated to the ways of the house."

Sure enough, Garvey surfaced from the front parlor. He gently pulled her to the side. "The servants' rooms are full—"

"She will be my lady's maid, so we shall put her on the second floor, near me and the girls."

"A lady's maid, eh?"

"Yes," Ada said defensively. "My mother had one when I was a young girl in New York, and I see no reason why I cannot have the same. Surely, we are not that far removed from the generation before us."

Garvey continued to look concerned.

"She can also assist me with the girls."

"Ah." She watched him fight a maddeningly charming smile. "Now I understand. Of course, Mrs. Haite."

Rebecca remained mystified by the mural on the ceiling, clutching her bag to her chest as she stood waiting. She looked down as Ada approached. "Thank you for hirin' me, Mrs. Haite. You won't be disappointed, I promise."

After a few moments, Elena came from the kitchen. She was a plain, smileless woman, though her demeanor remained perpetually pleasant. Her thick black hair had been wound tightly into a bun at the nape of her neck. "How can I help, ma'am?"

"Elena, this is Rebecca Crane. She will be coming on as my personal lady's maid to assist me in caring for Miss Josephine and Miss Margaret. Please show her around the manor and have her settled in the room directly next to ours."

Elena nodded. "Good to meet you, Ms. Rebecca," she said plainly to the girl beside her. "You may call me Ms. Brennan. Right this way."

Rebecca beamed, happiness turning pink in the apples of her cheeks. "Thank you again, ma'am."

Ada nodded and waited as they disappeared down the hall.

Once she was confident they were a distance away, she walked into the dining room, where she found Garvey in the midst of teaching one of the new maids how to arrange the table.

"Mr. Garvey? May I speak with you?"

"Yes, ma'am."

Ada headed to the former study and waited for him to enter before she shut the door. A draft whistled in, swirling around the empty, dust-coated room. Without a fireplace, the room was bitterly cold, even with the back door opened to receive the warmth of its accompanying parlor. Although Charles had instructed her not to use either room, she'd had them opened and cleaned. For what exactly, she was unsure.

Ada faced Garvey, hands at her hips. "I need complete honesty from you, Mr. Garvey. In fact, I insist upon it."

Garvey met her eyes. "Of course. What seems to be the problem, ma'am?"

"You are no butler. Or maybe you have been trained as such, but I have it on good authority that your main position here is to watch over me. You were a valet to Charles, and you now watch me and report to him regarding my well-being."

He studied her face before he spoke. "You are nearly correct in your assumptions. I have been hired as both a butler and your keeper. I served in a household as a child, shadowing the butler as an apprentice until I became one myself. I had every intention to follow through, but as I grew older, I found myself better suited for work as a valet with special...talents."

Ada wasn't sure if she felt better or worse that her suspicions were confirmed. "And your findings?"

Garvey caught her meaning. "You have given me nothing to report. You've been a wonderful mother to the girls, and I've seen no concerning behavior. I honestly didn't expect to, either."

"Oh?"

"Wealthy, powerful men have been sending their wives away for years. It doesn't necessarily mean the reason behind it is well-intentioned."

His sincerity took her aback, softening the wall she'd been struggling to keep up between them. Just a bit.

"Why wasn't I made aware of the mill closing?" she asked him.

Garvey crossed his arms. "Have you ever known Mr. Haite to be forthcoming about his business? I wasn't even made aware until I received the post yesterday."

Ada frowned. He had a point. "And how does Mr. Haite plan on me operating this household properly without a nearby town? We are in the midst of winter; what if there is a snowstorm?"

"Fortunately, it's been a mild season. We have plenty of stores in the pantry for several months, and I plan to visit town before it's fully closed. I can tell you, Mr. Haite assured me it is a temporary shutdown based on equipment failure, and everything should be back to normal by the spring."

Ada grew quiet, considering the information. She hadn't even considered life there beyond the winter. She couldn't shake the feeling that Charles was leaving everything that no longer suited him behind to waste away in the valleys and cornfields. While he and his two older sons continued to live in luxury at the Cleveland manor, she would be trapped here with the girls.

"Everything will be alright, Mrs. Haite," Garvey promised. "I will make sure you and the young misses are cared for." He added, attempting to sound professional, "It is my job, after all."

Ada decided to believe him. "Continue to run the household, but let Elena take over the menial tasks. There is no reason to keep up with the façade when we are the only ones here."

Garvey cracked a sideways smile, his pale green eyes sparkling. "I rather like bringing you tea."

Ada felt her cheeks grow warm, and she turned away. She suddenly felt too close to him, and she took a step away. "I would also like to fix the inoperable rooms, such as this study." She paused before she blurted out, "And the tower. It would make a lovely space for the girls to take their lessons."

Garvey nodded. "Yes, ma'am. I can focus on that for the time being."

"Thank you, Mr. Garvey."

She withdrew without another word, her steps quickening as she hit the hallway. The Madonna and Child stared down at her, but she refused to meet their dark, hollow eyes, marching forward instead. She was relieved by the soft sound of children giggling in the back parlor. The warmth from dual fireplaces blasted her as she entered to see Rebecca in the midst of a story.

Ada smiled. "I see you have met the girls."

"Is Ms. Rebecca to be our new nanny?" Josephine asked immediately.

"She is here to assist me in all things, including your care," Ada explained. "So we must be polite and mindful, just as you would any nanny."

Josephine bobbed her head in compliance. "Ms. Rebecca says she knows of my mother, the one I never met."

Ada blinked, though she shouldn't have been surprised. Charles's two dead wives were high society's worst-kept secrets, following Ada around in whispers wherever she went; why wouldn't those whispers follow her to his town? Although Charles never spoke of the girls' mothers, there was no lack of conversation regarding the force that was Julianna Haite. She was a formidable powerhouse of a woman who managed the entire family estate while running an orphanage once located in the very home they now resided in.

"How wonderful," Ada murmured.

"She took care of my brother here at Haite Orphanage after my folks died in the mill fire," Rebecca explained. "I was just a babe then, so Grandma took me in, but Jeb lived here with Ms. Julianna until he died of the wastin' disease. She was a great lady. You kinda look like her with your brown eyes and hair." She smiled as Josephine.

Ada frowned, struck by a sudden wave of uneasiness.

"I knew Ms. Eleanor, too," Rebecca continued, oblivious.

"You knew Mama?" Josephine's words poured out in a whisper.

The pit in Ada's stomach grew. Besides the knowledge of her fate, Eleanor Haite remained a mystery to Ada. She only knew of two things for certain: that Eleanor was originally the Haite children's nanny, and that she was very young when Charles married her. And, according to the portrait Charles kept in his desk drawer and reaffirmed by Maggie's dimples, blue eyes, and curly auburn hair, Eleanor was also quite beautiful.

"Only a little," Rebecca told her. "She hid in the house while she was pregnant with Miss Maggie here. The only one she spoke to was Grandma Amity."

Ada decided it was time to move on from the conversation, but before she could speak, Josephine turned to address her.

"I lived here with Maggie's mother before you, Ms. Ada," she said. "It's hazy, but I remember being in this house before she sent me back to the city. Sometimes, it feels like she's still here... I called her Mama. I can call you Mama too, if you want."

Emotion pooled in Ada's chest. "Ada is fine," she said quickly and moved to scoop up Maggie. She turned to Rebecca. "I need the girls bathed and dressed for dinner."

Rebecca jumped to her feet. "Yes, ma'am."

"I hope Elena will make another pie!" Josephine said, thankfully distracted. It was not that Ada wanted them to forget their mothers. She just wasn't sure their mothers needed remembering.

"As my lady's maid, I'll need you to prepare my outfits as well," Ada continued to address Rebecca. "Tonight is your first night with us, however, so you may retire to your room and prepare yourself for tomorrow. You will have a full day, so be sure to get your rest. Report here first thing in the morning when Elena brings my tea. We will discuss your duties then."

"Yes, ma'am," Rebecca bobbed her head. "Thank you, ma'am."

The three girls disappeared down the hall in a whirl of fabric and hair.

The parlor suddenly seemed too quiet without them, and Ada wandered back down the hall. Dim, unsteady electricity cast its golden glow across the decorative woodwork and angelic sculptures around the house. No matter how safe they promised electricity was, it never ceased to fill her with unease. Shadows moved across the cherubic finial at the end of the staircase, the eyes watching her as she moved. She suppressed a shudder, unwilling to observe what the lighting did to the judgmental eyes painted above.

She ducked into the study, its chill pulling her back from her building trepidation. Soon, the help would emerge from the kitchen with dinner preparations, the girls would appear with scrubbed cheeks and proper dresses, and she would eat with them as if all was well. She would pretend that Garvey was simply a butler and she was simply the lady of a fine household. All would be well. Until she was alone again.

She thought of Maggie's sweet, cherubic face, and her eyes wandered to Charles's desk. She wondered if he kept pictures of his previous wives in this desk, too. Though he'd never verbalized his sentiments about either wife, the fact that he kept both their portraits spoke loudly enough. She walked over to the mahogany monstrosity, eyeing the keyholes. Of course, he locked his drawers when he was not present; she was foolish to think otherwise. But still, she reached her hand underneath just to see if he'd hidden the key.

Her fingers hit metal.

Surprised at her luck, she felt around to discover that a single brass key had been secured by leather to the underside of the desk. She removed it easily, realizing she'd found the key that Josephine had originally asked her about—the skeleton key. Smiling, she slipped it into her pocket. Josephine would be so pleased. Charles's desk would have to wait.

She hurried up the stairs to dress herself for dinner. After they moved both girls into her bedroom, she had the other two rooms turned into a dressing room and a playroom. The third had been left empty—a spare bedroom now occupied by Rebecca. Before entering her bedroom, she peeked in on them in the dressing room. Josephine was in the midst of showing Rebecca her extensive wardrobe, and Maggie smiled up at her from her spot on the floor. "Hi, Mama."

Ada's anxiety from earlier began to surface, but Josephine quickly soothed it.

"She wants us to call her Ada, Maggie," she scolded her gently. "We have to respect our stepmother's wishes."

"Thank you, Josephine," Ada said, crouching down to smile at Maggie. "But know I care deeply for you both, as any mother would. Look what I found."

At the sight of the key in Ada's palm, she ran over to her with an excited squeal. "Can we go into the tower?"

"After dinner," Ada promised.

She helped Rebecca finish getting the girls ready for dinner, then retreated to her bedroom while they played. Her room had an attached toiletry for dressing, filled with all her finest dresses per Charles's orders. It seemed ridiculous to have brought them here; most were the latest fashions from Paris, suitable for formal events in the city. All the fine silks and beaded trimmings wasted in the country for no one to see. Not that it mattered. She made a lousy debutante. She hoped whoever Charles found to fill her place would enjoy what was left of her wardrobe in Cleveland. With a sigh, she selected one of her most casual dresses. Then she hurried against the cold to wash up and comb any loose blonde hairs back into her low pompadour. She met the girls in the hall, and the moment their feet hit the bottom step, she heard them bringing up dinner.

The scent of roast chicken confirmed it, which provoked Josephine to break into a run.

"Josephine, mind your manners," Ada gently reminded her.

They settled around the table as Elena and the kitchen maids brought baked sweet potatoes, green corn, cauliflower, plum sauce, and bread to the table. Ada contemplated requesting wine with her meal, but thought better of it. It didn't seem like the time to be caught unaware.

"Mr. Garvey, we're going into the tower," Josephine said as soon as the pretend butler came in to pour their drinks.

One of Garvey's dark eyebrows raised as he filled her glass with milk. "Is that right, Ms. Josephine? I couldn't get that lock to work to fix the leak for Mrs. Haite. Will you be breaking the door down then?" he asked playfully.

"Ada has found the skeleton key."

Garvey looked at Ada. "Well, that's wonderful news. I'd love to accompany you to see about that leak."

Ada nodded. Fortunately, the rain had relented enough that the dripping water that had awakened her ceased, but Garvey had her bed moved, regardless. She hadn't pressed the issue any further; most of the fortifications she'd put up between them had been dismantled, and she didn't want to ruin it by raising suspicion.

Garvey withdrew, leaving the three to their meals. Ada began cutting Maggie's food into small portions. "What do you girls think of Ms. Rebecca?" she asked.

Josephine shrugged. "She seems sufficient. Don't you think she's too young to be a proper nanny?"

"I do agree, which is why she is simply a helper, not a formal nanny."

Josephine bobbed her head. "She said her grandmother is the oldest woman alive. She's been here since the town was founded, from before Father even bought it for the mill."

Ada raised an eyebrow. "Is that right?"

"She's so old that she outlived Rebecca's grandfather, too."

"Well, that's strange. She told me both her grandparents were alive."

"I'm simply relaying the information," Josephine said, taking a generous gulp of milk from her glass. "She said her grandmother Amity was one of the first people who lived here, when she was but a child. There were only a few houses that made up the village then, and they all belonged to a church that followed the teachings of the first man who settled here."

"Well, Rebecca certainly has a lot to say."

Josephine impaled a piece of meat with her fork. "She also said her Grandmother Amity worked with my real mother here at Haite Orphanage and taught all the children their ways."

Garvey surfaced from the kitchen with coffee. "Are you ladies ready for dessert?"

"Is it pie?" Josephine asked immediately.

"No, just pudding, little miss," Garvey told her.

"Then we shall skip it," Josephine decided for everyone. "We simply must go on our adventure to the tower as soon as possible. Right, Ada?"

Ada nodded. Her anxiety regarding the tower, now blended with her growing suspicion of Rebecca, ruined any hope of appetite. She dabbed her lips with a napkin and pushed herself from the table. "I'll take my coffee in the parlor after our excursion," she told Elena, who had arrived to clear the dishes.

Josephine wiggled in her seat until Ada properly dismissed her from the table. She grabbed Garvey's hand to pull him forward as Ada scooped up Maggie from her pressed-back high chair. The little girl found Ada's loose tendrils of hair, wrapping them around her chubby little fingers as they ascended the stairs.

"Mama," she said.

Ada gave her a tired smile before gently correcting her: "Ada."

When they reached the tower door, Ada fished out the skeleton key. "Would you like to do the honors, Josephine?"

She snatched it excitedly from her palm and jammed it into the lock. Sure enough, it worked, and the door fell open with a loud creak.

Ada's mouth went dry. She remembered her experience in the tower clearly—the sopping wet books, the child's bedframe, the small, old desk. But now there were no furnishings, simply a bookcase filled with dry books and a nice, clean wood floor with a rug. She looked at Garvey with immediate suspicion, but he also looked surprised.

"I thought for sure this place would be soaked to the bone," he remarked. "Or at least smell of wet wood."

"You saw the leak, as I did," Ada said carefully, a statement more than a question.

"Yes, ma'am. Pooled and pouring right on your pillow. I don't understand it."

"Ada, look at all these books!" Josephine interrupted excitedly. "I remember now—this used to be where Mama used to spend her time. These are all hers."

Ada set down Maggie, who toddled over to her sister.

"A lady who likes books?" Garvey whistled. "No wonder you and your sister are so smart."

"So does Ada," Josephine informed him as she pulled a faded leather-bound tome from the shelf. "She read to us all the books she fell in love with when she was learning to speak English. Before Father forced her into marriage, she acted as our governess."

Ada was stunned into silence.

"A house full of lady geniuses," Garvey remarked, genuinely impressed. "I am honored to care for such a house."

Josephine thrust the book into Ada's hands. It was an older version of the Bible, the Geneva version preferred by those who colonized America. "You should read us a passage."

"Alright then." Ada opened the book, deciding that she would ponder the curious state of the room later. But she paused, alarmed to see that the original pages of the book had been torn out and reglued so that in between the Old Testament and the New, a written-out section was included. Curiosity got the best of her, and she turned to it, her eyes sweeping over the words:

"The Book of Ruth. Towne of Hope, 1703. Take heed the Sisters Three."

"What is it?" Garvey asked.

"I-I don't know." She closed the book, deeply unsettled. "Let's read a different book, Josephine." She thrust it back on the shelf and grabbed another, which she was relieved to learn was a volume of poetry.

"Let's retire to our room for the evening," she said. "We can curl up in bed, and I'll read to you like I used to when you were little. It's much too chilly in this old tower, and I'm eager for the fire's warmth."

Josephine seemed content with her suggestion and hurried to grab a few more books. Ada picked up Maggie and as she stood, caught Garvey's eyes.

"I'm simply tired, is all," she said quietly.

"I understand, ma'am."

CHAPTER SEVEN
Lori 1981

The rain slowed by the time they reached the front door, leaving a gentle pitter-patter on the veranda's roof. Droplets slipped through the cracks in the old wood, and Lori found a dry place to stand and squeeze her sopping wet hair while the girls ran screaming into the house. "Fucking battery stalled halfway up," she told Seth as he shook out and closed the umbrella.

Inside, at least a dozen men were in the midst of packing up for the day, a few who she recognized from previous projects. "Hey, Stacks," she called with a wave.

"Hey, Greene. Nice hair."

"I'll have to give you a jump tomorrow," Seth told her. "We're headed out."

"So soon?" she said, half-kidding.

"Don't tell me you've never heard of an Ohio spring—also known as mud season. We only have so much time before that hill right there turns into a Slip n' Slide."

Lori frowned. "I gotta do something about that."

"I already planned on calling Bob in the morning for an estimate on the lake. Maybe he can give us a two-for-one special if we tell him we also need a driveway laid. In the meantime, Steve measured the windows—he's gotta order them special for the tower, so it's gonna be a little more than you estimated. Everything else on your list, I can order. I brought in some stuff already—the dining room table and some chairs—and the rest of the furniture should be delivered by the end of this week. Oh, and Bill managed to get the beds set up for the girls. Put their suitcases in there for 'em, too."

"He's such a sweetheart. How are things with his boyfriend?"

"Guess they're living together now." Seth shrugged. "Listen, I would still consider getting the basement waterproofed. Like I said earlier, I'm shocked at how well this place was kept up, but you never know. I'd hate for you to put a ton of money into this thing just to have the basement flood."

Lori winced. He was right. "Things just keep getting more and more expensive."

Seth chuckled and gave her a clap on the back. "Still nothing like that Pennsylvania house. If you and I could get through that, we can get through this shit, no problem."

"True."

"Oh, and did you know that tower is full of old books? I figured you'd want to handle them, so I had the guys leave it be."

Lori blinked. She hadn't even noticed a bookcase when she was up there before. That was very unlike her—she had a soft spot for old volumes.

"Lori! They set up our rooms!" Kellie burst back into the foyer, her rainboots squeaking. "I wanna put my dolls up."

Lori didn't have the heart to tell her it was only temporary. Instead, she gave her a big grin. "How awesome! You can hang out up there—just no tower without me or your sister with you, got it? It's still kinda dangerous. Did Dad pack your books?"

"Yup!"

"Hey, does the hot water work?" Nikki interrupted. "I want to take a shower or a bath, or whatever people did in the old days."

"Yes, but you have to use the bathroom by the kitchen," Lori explained. "The upstairs ones need new windows and flooring before we can use them." She turned to Kellie. "Stay in your room and read until Nikki is done—no exploring. Can I trust you?" After she received an emphatic nod of rainbow-colored clips, she turned back to Nikki. "And can you please hang with her when you're done?"

Nikki sighed. "Yes. Now let me get clean."

Lori nodded, and both girls retreated to their rooms.

"I don't know how you manage it," Seth said with a chuckle. "I got one, and he drives me and the old lady up a wall. Oh, look what I found hanging in the basement," he added as he handed her a chunky set of keys.

Their weight surprised her; some of them looked at least fifty years old. "Good. Having only one skeleton key was making me nervous."

"There's a key for *everything* on that ring. Even the kitchen cabinets."

"They used to keep them locked so the staff wouldn't steal the silver," Lori told him with a grin.

"Rich people." Seth snorted. "Anyway, everything is good to go, but if you need to check the boilers, they're in the basement. We'll be back in the morning."

"Sounds good. Thanks again."

"Hey, can I...talk to you for a second?"

She looked up to see that Seth's face had shifted into an uncharacteristically serious expression, which, in turn, led to him looking uncomfortable. Man, she didn't need more bullshit. "Sure, what's up?"

Seth ducked into one of the parlors, empty of work guys. He dug into his pockets as he spoke. "I was examining the upstairs bathroom flooring and found these." He pressed something small and hard into her palm.

She looked down to see that it was a polished tooth. "I-I don't understand."

"Most of the tiling is your standard marble in grout. But if you look closely at the patterns...they also used human teeth."

"What the hell?"

"That's what I said. They look kinda small, like baby teeth, so maybe it was just the owners' way of memorializing them? Who knows. It's creepy as hell, and I have no issue pulling it all out and re-tiling the whole thing. I just figured you should know how weird your house is."

Lori frowned, turning the tooth back and forth in her hand. "Yeah, let's pull it out. I'll figure out what to do with the, um. Teeth."

"Yes, ma'am." Seth stepped back into the hall and let out a whistle. "Come on, guys! Let's go get some hot food and beers. On me."

Lori joined him as the crew began shuffling out, offering their respective hellos and goodbyes. Then she stood in the doorway, watching a chorus of car engines upset the vultures perched nearby before rumbling down the hill. The rain had stopped, but a distant crack of thunder resounded in the distance. She hoped they would make it to the hotel before any rain returned. She wondered what the townies would make of them.

She reached for her pack of smokes, then remembered she had quit, which prompted a frustrated sigh. Even though she and Sean were no longer trying for a baby, it had been a whole year, and she didn't want to throw it all away. Deep down, she knew she needed to kick the habit for good. Knowing didn't make it any easier.

There was a flutter above her, and she looked up to see that the vultures had returned. They were the same ones Lori had met when she arrived at the house, three monstrously big creatures that seemed even bigger up close. The tree branches groaned and bobbed with their landing.

"Ah, so this is your home, too."

She did not receive a response.

Uneasiness settled in as she stood in the gaze of their dark eyes, and she stepped back inside. The house was eerily silent, amplifying her tension as she searched her pocket to find and examine the tooth in her hand. How could she possibly live in a place like this? But after her conversation with Carl, she knew she wasn't going to be able to sell it quickly, either. Her absolute best-case scenario was that someone would buy it to turn it into a bed and breakfast, but even then, what would the draw be? A dilapidated town? Cornfield scenery?

She wandered into the ladies' parlor and sank into the loveseat. Sculpted cherubs with missing cheeks and chipped wings smiled at her from the fireplace. Maybe the government would want to buy this land from her, too. It would be a loss, financially and historically. She closed her eyes to listen to the house again, but it had decided to withdraw from her. She couldn't even be upset; between the nightmare, the townies, the screaming foxes, the rain, and now the teeth, she was frazzled to her core. Far from calm enough to receive any kind of communication.

"Where's my suitcase?" Nikki asked from the doorway. She'd already dressed in pajama pants, her hair neatly piled under a silk bonnet.

"Do you remember Bill from PA? He set up your bedrooms. It should be on the bed."

"Okay. I'm starving. That egg salad was gross."

"All I have is the snacks I brought and whatever Dad packed," Lori told her. "It's gonna have to do until tomorrow. I'll go shopping after Seth gets back."

Nikki fell into the seat beside her. "This is nice. Did you thrift it?"

"Actually, Seth and I found a woman who creates authentic Victorian-era replicas," Lori said, her vision stuck toward the fireplace screen. For a moment, she thought she saw faces in the pattern. "Figured the ladies' parlor could do with some fanciness."

"Men and women had different parlors?"

Lori nodded. "Ladies received company during the day when they would sip tea and gossip. Men received guests in the study during work hours and retired to their own parlors for drinks and cigar-smoking after dinner."

"Sounds like it would be more fun to be a man."

Lori laughed. "No corsets or teacakes for you?"

Nikki made a face.

"Come on, let's go find Kellie. I bet she's getting restless up there." Lori stood and realized she was lightheaded. "Can you grab the lunchbox?"

Nikki slid off the sofa and retrieved the Igloo cooler from the study while Lori grabbed her bag. Wind battered the house as they headed to Kellie's new room, and Lori found herself grateful that the guys boarded up the open windows. There were four rooms on the second floor: an old master bedroom with an attached bathroom, and three bedrooms intended for children. She knew from the blueprints that there was an additional nursery and an attached nanny's room on the third floor, but she hadn't had a chance to investigate anything beyond the tower. She assumed those windows had been boarded up, too, since there was no extra racket above.

Lori found the button for the lights, and the wall sconces that lined the hallway flickered on, filling the hall with a dim and ugly white. It illuminated the wallpaper samples Seth had tacked up for her to choose from, deep forest greens and rusty maroons making patterns along the wall.

"I like all the gold in the red one," Nikki remarked. "Pick that one. Then, you can make the light fixtures gold to match. The *accents*."

Lori smiled. "I like the way you think." She located the only doorway with a glowing strip beneath it, logically deducing that it was the room Kellie chose.

Nikki walked into the room right beside it. "Oh look, a real light switch," she remarked as she flicked them on. A flood of proper, modern light revealed a plain room of wood embellishments and fresh, pale paint. She located the suitcase on the unmade bed set up for her. "This will do."

Lori bobbed her head, then walked to Kellie's door to gently knock on it.

"Who is it?"

"Lori."

"You may enter."

Lori smiled as she opened the door, pleasantly surprised to see the bedroom Kellie picked was almost fully finished. She'd already unpacked her little pink suitcase, setting her Barbie dolls along the white marble fireplace. Sean had only let her bring a few books, but she had already put them on the pre-installed bookshelves. Lori tried to ignore the little red travel Bible eyesore that her mom forced her to take everywhere she went. Instead, she focused on how her princess sleeping bag and beanbag chair matched nicely with the faded pink roses on the old wallpaper.

"It's a princess room," Kellie said proudly.

"It looks absolutely perfect."

"Can we go get some more books from the tower to fill up my shelves?"

Lori frowned. Even Kellie had noticed there were books up there—why hadn't she? "I dunno, Kells. It's getting dark, and there are no lights up there..."

She wrapped her little arms around her legs. "Pretty please? I stayed in my room, just like you said."

"I don't have my handling gloves. Old books get damaged by the oils in our fingertips."

"I promise I won't touch any old ones!"

"Okay. But after that, we all need to get to bed." Lori poked her head out the doorway to see Nikki curled up in bed with a fashion magazine. "You want to come to the tower with us?"

"Sure," she said, throwing off the blanket.

"Grab your flashlights," Lori called as she hurried downstairs to find some kind of gloves. "I don't think there's working electricity up there."

She located a pair of thin work gloves and returned to guide them to the tower staircase. Threatening thunder rumbled in the distance, interrupting the steady squeak of Kellie's boots as they walked down the corridor.

"I hope all this rain doesn't flood us," Lori murmured, trying not to think of the basement.

"Then we can sleep in the tower!"

"Great plan," Nikki snorted. "Then we'll get struck by lightning."

"Lori, Nikki's being mean."

"Girls."

They climbed up the narrow spiral until they reached the door at the top. Lori pointed her flashlight at the doorknob, and Kellie excitedly flew past her to push it open. Seeing the tower at night was a completely different experience from in the daytime, with black gaping holes where sunlight once poured in. In the weak beam of Lori's flashlight, the empty tree branches seemed to reach like protracted fingers. She frowned, reminded of being stuck in the car. What *was* that scream in the woods?

She turned her gaze away from the windows, and sure enough, there was an old bookcase leaning against the only windowless wall. She must have missed it in all the chaos. "Watch those windows, Kellie," Lori reminded her as she darted for the books.

"It's creepier up here than downstairs," Nikki remarked as she looked around with her flashlight. She pointed the beam at Lori's feet. "Look at that rug."

Lori followed it with her eyes. Covering the floor was an anachronistic rug made of a strange, straw-like material. She knelt to examine it, learning it wasn't straw at all but some kind of thin, blonde string. She thought of the tooth in her pocket and bolted upright, her stomach twisting with nausea.

"What is it?"

"Let's head back, girls—"

"Look at this one! It's got pictures," Kellie said excitedly, showing Lori an old version of Mother Goose. The beam of her flashlight wiggled around the room.

"Careful that the pages don't fall out," Lori said, coming closer. "Wow, that one looks like it might be from the '20s."

"For someone so worried about things being Satanic, you sure don't worry about books being haunted," Nikki said from her perch near the doorway. "I am *not* stepping any closer to those."

Lori couldn't help but scan a row herself, immediately drawn to a faded leather tome at the farthest end. Any foiling on the spine that would have given her a clue to its contents had long faded away. She sensed something then, a palpable energy that burrowed its way into her stomach like a parasite. Finally, the house spoke to her, but not how she had hoped. She wanted to honor her body's response to the very clear warning to move on, but her curiosity was forever the victor. She put the flashlight under her arm and wiggled on a glove to begin the slow and careful process of removing it from the shelf. As she did, a slip of paper beat it to its journey, fluttering to the floor near the awful rug.

Lori abandoned the book and bent to retrieve it. Worried the delicate parchment would fall apart in her fingers, she unfolded it as gently as she possibly could. Discovering the ink was still legible replaced the sick, sinking feeling in her gut with excitement—she was potentially holding a clue to the house's history. She pointed her flashlight and began to read.

August, 1906

If you are reading this, may God bless your soul, for you might be my daughter. Or worse yet, you might be another wife of Charles's, and I am long since dead. He believes me mad, but is that not what all men think when a woman has clear thoughts that are her own? I could be mad, but believe me when I tell you, I am not nearly as mad as the woman who lived in this house before me.

You must understand that I am not a covetous woman. I have loved Julianna Haite's daughter as if she were my own. But Julianna was a wicked creature, possessed by the Devil himself. She was a witch, a cruel murderess, who offered the blood of the innocent to the pagan fiends that lurk in these lands. You might ask how this could be. The entire town and city know her to be the Saint of Orphans. But I know the truth. The orphaned children she took into this very home to raise as hers, the children she slowly, painfully murdered, have shown me the truth. In dreams, they guide me to the places she bled them, offering them to her gods—her fiends! The house that demands I either sacrifice my own children or my body will also be given to this home, my blood used to paint the walls.

And so you see how I sound mad. I am mad—mad because they want my Jo—Julianna's own daughter! An old hag lurks these woods, beckoning she follow her into the dark woods. My sweet girl refuses to heed her call, but no sooner does the girl fall asleep at night, *does she walk to the very lake where her mother once dumped the children's bodies! It took much convincing to send my Jo away, and it is truly God's miracle that Charles granted my request. But what of my own child? The one who grows in my womb?*

This house, this place... the fields around me demand my own blood and birth, or my flesh this house will take. Flee this place, my dear, sweet friend or daughter!

Flee this place and take the children, too.

There is no God in these lands. Only three... the scalpless, blood-thirsty, demonic three. Heed my warnings! My time here is brief. Either the men in their coats or the Sisters Three will take me.

Please take care of my baby.

Yours,
Eleanor Haite

A loud pounding from below caused Lori to drop the letter and her flashlight. She cursed, scrambling to collect it all and stick it back on the shelf. Her hands were shaking, making the task that much more difficult.

The knock sounded again.

"Who is that?" Kellie asked fearfully.

"It's probably Seth," she murmured.

"What if it's those men from the truck?" Nikki hissed, her eyes wide.

Fear hammered Lori's heartbeat into her throat. She didn't want to think of the unthinkable, but here, alone with the girls, she had to. The last thing she read was imprinted in her mind like an old marquee: *Please take care of my baby…*

"Stay here with your sister and lock the door."

"I don't want to stay here!" Nikki hissed.

"Then follow me and go to Kellie's room. Don't come out until I get you."

The girls nodded and tiptoed behind her down the stairs. Once they parted on the second floor, Lori went to the stairwell and paused to listen. From where she stood, she couldn't see the visitor clearly and wanted them to have the same predicament. They knocked again but said nothing. Lori slipped off her shoes so her socks would ensure no noise as she hurried to the kitchen. In the dim light streaming in from the other rooms, she saw nothing but shapes. Refusing to look in the direction of the basement—that was all she needed—she crouched down to better examine the tools left on the floor.

At last, she located the bag Seth had left behind. She found and stuck a screwdriver in her back pocket and withdrew a hammer to keep at hand. Then she walked steadily to the door, ready to do whatever it took to defend her girls. When she reached the front of the house, she took a deep breath and raised the hammer. Then she threw open the door.

"Jesus, Mary, and Joseph!" a man cursed as he dropped his flashlight, sending its light bouncing along the veranda.

Lori squinted into the darkness. "Finn?"

"And me, Becky," came a girl's voice behind him. "From town."

Lori exhaled. "Oh shit, I'm sorry. Is everything alright?"

"I know I came on a little strong before, but really? A hammer to the skull?" Finn grabbed his flashlight and stood, collecting himself. "We've come bearing supplies and bad news about the weather."

"Oh yeah, come in." Lori stepped aside to let them in. As they entered, Lori noticed they both carried baskets full of food, matches, and batteries. Cheeks flushed with embarrassment, she pushed the hammer into the belt loop of her jeans.

"Sorry for my reaction. A red truck nearly hit us on the way up from town, and we're still a bit rattled."

Finn let out a grunt of disapproval. "Those damn fatheads. Bob and Bill Wheatley."

"You know them?"

"Their dad used to own the abandoned barn on this road. They've taken it upon themselves to patrol the area—and the whole town, really, since the park bought everything up and left it to rot. All these abandoned buildings gave the rumor mill plenty to talk about."

"They call it Hell Town," Becky piped up. "Well, out-of-towners do. They say all kinds of spooky things happen here at night. We let it go because it's good for the hotel, but it also causes problems."

Lori gestured for them to set their baskets down on the table.

"Teenagers like to sneak down here at night and cause us all kinds of problems," Finn explained. "The Wheatley Brothers like to scare 'em off, but they need to be more careful. I'll have a talk with them in the morning."

"Gosh, this place is something else." Becky's face was stuck in an expression of awe, her head swiveling around like a rapt tourist as she took in the dining room.

"I'm hoping it will be," Lori said lightly. "I have a great frame to work with. So this storm is going to be a nasty one?"

"Yep." Finn set down his basket on the table and began fishing through it. "At least three days of heavy rain. Carl packed you some eggs and veggies from Szaylen's farm. Want me to make you and your girls a quick omelette? I can't cook a lot of things, but it's hard to mess up an omelette."

"Oh, no, you don't—oh shit, the girls." She jogged back to the stairwell. "Girls! It's okay, you can come down!"

Kellie came bolting down the stairs, but Nikki lingered at the landing. Obviously, she did want to be seen in her pajamas and bonnet.

"Who's here?" she demanded.

"Becky and...Finn."

Lori winced, prepared for the teasing.

Nikki simply snorted. "I'm going to bed."

"Okay, I'll be up in a bit." Lori followed Kellie as she bounded into the dining room to greet Becky.

"You got more PopRocks?" she demanded.

"Hey there," Becky said, unaffected. "I do have PopRocks, but I also brought a bunch more."

"What kind?" Kellie asked suspiciously.

"Jolly Ranchers and Laffy Taffy."

"Gross."

"What about gumdrops?"

"Depends on the color."

"Kellie, be nice," Lori told her. "Where did Fin—uh, Mr. Garvey, go?"

Becky pointed to the kitchen.

Lori left Becky and Kellie to their candy negotiations and walked into the kitchen, where the smell of burning wood met her nose. He'd already lit the stove and was in the process of chopping vegetables. She looked to see he'd brought a pan, oil, and even a large spoon to stir with. Also in the basket were napkins, plastic forks, and plastic plates.

"How do you know how to work the stove?"

"Caretaker, remember?"

"Oh yes, yes, of course. You lived here."

Finn cracked an egg into the pan. "Yeah, the carriage house. It's fixed up all modern."

"Wait—so—" Lori suddenly felt woozy.

"Whoa there, girlie." Finn dropped his knife with a clatter and went to catch her arm. He guided her around the various tools and leftover materials to a small nearby table. "Good thing I didn't take no for an answer on feeding you. You might want to take that screwdriver out of your pocket before you sit."

Lori pulled it out and set it on the table. "It's—it's been a long day."

"Yeah, I had a feeling. I chatted with your guy a little bit at the hotel. Coming all the way from New York has to wear on a person."

Thunder rumbled above them, rudely announcing it was back for more.

"Ah, there she is," Finn said. "Next storm, right on time." He pulled a bottle of Coke from the basket and twisted it open for her. "Here, drink this. For the sugar."

Lori took a sip. She would have to scold herself for letting a charming man into her house and cook her dinner later. Right now, his presence was a relief—he knew the strange town and the strange house, and it brought her a modicum of ease. "Why did Josephine make you move?"

"Oh, it wasn't her," Finn said. "It was the will. We were only caretakers until she died. Then it's up to the new owner—the next Haite in line—to keep us around or hire someone new. We're obviously hoping you take us on, but we didn't want to push you when you first got here."

"Oh," Lori said quietly, taking another sip. She wished her head would stop spinning. "I suppose we can talk about it tomorrow."

"Of course," Finn said. "No pressure. That's not what the cooking is about, either. I'm doing *that* because I want to hang out with you. We can talk shop another time. Nothing to be done with this storm, carrying on anyway. Ol' Grandpa isn't exactly a hiker."

"You walked up here?"

"Sure." Finn shrugged. "Can't bring a car up in the mud."

"But won't you need to hurry back before it—"

Thunder cracked again, followed by rain.

Finn slid the vegetables onto the frying pan, which sizzled as they hit. "We'll wait for a break in the storm. Becky's a tough kid. Don't you worry."

The warmth of a lit stove felt good in the drafty kitchen, and the aroma of sizzling vegetables and burning wood added to the pleasant vibes. Lori fought a yawn, her thawing body finally made aware of how exhausted she was.

"I smelled food." Nikki appeared, fully dressed and sans bonnet, her braids pulled back into a low ponytail.

"Grab a plate," Finn said with a smile as he flipped the contents of the pan.

In a whirlwind, all of them settled around the dining room table with their plates, and Lori had the first hot meal in what felt like centuries. Finn cracked jokes, and Becky shared stories about college life. Lori couldn't believe it, but she actually felt content. Good, even. She clanked her plastic fork against her Coke bottle to grab their attention. When they all quieted, she lifted it up for a toast. "I'd like to thank our new friends, Becky and Mr. Garv—"

"Have 'em call me Finn. Mr. Garvey is my granddad's name."

"Becky and *Finn.*" Lori smiled. "On behalf of the Greene girls, we'd like to thank you for the food…and for bringing us a little bit of warmth on this cold, dark night."

"Hear, hear!" Finn said.

The girls joined in and clinked their cups and bottles together.

And then, as if to remind everyone that good moments seldom last long, thunder boomed, and the lights promptly went out.

CHAPTER EIGHT
Ada, 1910

Morning brought with it a gentle frost, but the chill that settled around the house was far from gentle. Though Ada was dressed in her warmest attire, she fought an inescapable shiver, even as she sat as close to the fire as she was able. The girls kept to the playroom with their toys and new books, tended to by Rebecca. It offered Ada a few moments of peace, and she'd intended to enjoy it as fully as possible. The ladies' parlor, situated directly between the first and main parlor, proved to be the warmest room, and that is where she planted herself with her tea.

Though she'd been able to distract them all from her discovery last night, she could not shake the feeling that had settled in her bones. Something wasn't right at Haite Hill, and she found herself needing to know what it was, like an itch that desperately needed scratching. And whether it was the isolation or Charles's absence, she felt emboldened like never before.

Garvey appeared in the doorway, cap in hand.

Perhaps he helped a little, too.

"Good morning, ma'am. I'm sorry to disturb you, but I've received word of a storm coming our way. Should be here by midnight tonight. Whether it be rain or snow is left to the good Lord above, but I do know it'll be a real doozy."

"This dreadful cold leads me to believe we should prepare for snow," Ada murmured as she stole a glance out the window. "I wish to make a trip into town beforehand to ensure we have all the supplies we need."

Garvey looked surprised. "Is there something specific you'll be needing? I can fetch whatever it is—"

"It has been a week since we've arrived, and I find it ill-mannered that I have yet to make an appearance in the very town my husband owns. Now that Charles has closed the mill, perhaps my presence will give them a bit of hope."

"Or they could take their frustrations out on you," Garvey pointed out.

Ada rose to her feet, trying to hide her annoyance. "I also wish to bring a basket to Rebecca's grandparents as a token of my gratitude for allowing her to work here."

Garvey's mouth twitched under his mustache, still skeptical of her proposal. "Are you certain you feel up to subjecting yourself to the cold?"

Her cheeks burned. "After you retrieve the shopping list from Elena, have the motor car brought around front, Mr. Garvey," she said firmly, reminding him of his place. Then she turned and went to the call bell to ring Elena, who was supervising the breakfast clean-up in the scullery.

"Yes, ma'am." Garvey withdrew without another word.

Ada sighed. So far, he'd been nothing but kind to her, and certainly didn't deserve any venom from her. But she needed to know more about Rebecca's grandmother and she didn't want to be questioned.

Elena arrived at the door, dressed in extra layers including a wool skirt. Apparently, Ada wasn't the only one sensitive to the encroaching chill. "You rang for me, ma'am?"

"Have Mary gather my warmest motoring coat, my fur-lined gloves, and a hat. I am accompanying Mr. Garvey today on his errands in town. Rebecca is with the children."

"Yes, ma'am."

"I also need you to check the pantry for any goods we can spare. I wish to deliver supplies to Rebecca's grandparents so they might comfortably weather the storm."

"Yes, ma'am."

Ada hurriedly dressed, following Elena's lead with extra petticoats and stockings, hoping the layers plus her winter attire would be sufficient for an outdoor excursion. With the addition of her fur-lined coat and gloves, she felt added confidence in her choices. She still gasped, however, when she took a step out onto the veranda; the addition of wind was an unexpected source of discomfort.

Garvey stood near an old, sputtering Model T, waiting for her with the door open. Of course, a motor car that was so plain and unloved was the type Charles thought was suitable for his discarded wife and daughters. Ada sighed as she walked toward it, tucking her head down to use the fur collar against the wind.

Garvey was dressed in his own warm motoring attire, the stitching of his coat bringing out the green in his eyes. As she gazed at him, Ada found her anger from earlier slowly fade away.

"Your chariot awaits, Mrs. Haite," he said playfully, his nose ruddy from the cold.

She climbed into the automobile, which was not much warmer than outside, and tried not to regret her decision to venture into the elements.

"If you must know," she began as soon as Garvey slid into the seat beside her. "I want to meet Rebecca's grandparents. Rebecca told Josephine that only her grandmother is left, but she told me she needed to work to support *both* grandparents. A simple mistake or a white lie, perhaps, but it isn't sitting well with me. She also knows more about Charles's wives than I do, and quite frankly, the whole thing makes me unsettled." She added after a pause, "I also want to learn more about the mill's closing."

"So now you are the one watching," Garvey said with a grin, throwing the motor car into gear. "Are you sure it's good to pry?"

"Are you going to stop me?"

"I don't think anyone can stop the likes of you, ma'am."

The automobile began its descent down the wooded hill, and then the paved one, billowing out thick black exhaust that seemed trapped around them. The bitter air was already heavy with moisture, another confirmation of impending snow, and Ada crouched down so that her collar better covered her ears. Though the weather was less than desirable, it felt good to be away from Haite Hill and all the worries it brought, although descending into an unfamiliar town didn't make her feel much better. She knew the weather would keep most of its inhabitants indoors, however, which would prevent dozens of judgmental eyes from following her like they did when she arrived.

They reached the bottom of the hill where the road forked, and Ada noticed an old Protestant church down the road in need of repair. She wondered why she hadn't noticed it before, but considering what a state she had been in that day, it was no surprise. Garvey guided the automobile to the right, and Ada made out a beautiful but empty hotel with an attached tavern, several small shops, and the petrol station she remembered when she first arrived. The town seemed completely abandoned, save for gaslamps burning in a few shop windows, but the Model T's motor made sure to boisterously announce its presence to anyone who might have been around. It echoed even louder as they went through the covered bridge, though the roaring river below gave it quite a run for its money.

As soon as they popped out the other side, the bold white letters HAITE BAG COMPANY taunted Ada from the mill. This time, there was no billowing smokestack or clusters of mill workers. It was just as lonely and quiet as the rest of the town. Abandoned, just like her. Garvey pulled the car to the opposite side and parked in front of a building called Haite Company General Store. It was the closest building to the train tracks, and from the lonely state of the train station and the layer of ice built up on the metal, Ada ascertained that the train had not come through for weeks.

As if reading her mind, Garvey said, "When I last came into town, I was told it had been a few weeks since their last delivery. I did wire Charles, but have yet to hear a reply. Hopefully, Mr. Zanski still has enough to offer us."

Ada frowned. "Well, we shall see what he can spare. I want to give Rebecca's grandparents a proper basket and stock our own pantry without taking from the townspeople who need it."

Garvey smiled at her. "Very good, ma'am."

He held the door open for her as she hurried in, finding herself grateful to see a small coal-burning stove heating the store. But that was where her relief stopped. Bins she assumed were once full had only a few rotting potatoes and turnips left in their baskets. They sat before shelves holding a few slumping sacks of flour. She could barely read the Haite Bag Company logo on the front.

"Good morning, ma'am."

Behind the counter, a man with hair that should have been white but looked yellow climbed to his feet. Stale cigar smoke and coal dust clung to his loose overalls and stained his fingertips. "And to you, Mr. Garvey."

"Good morning, Mr. Zanski. This is Mrs. Ada Haite, the wife of our industrious benefactor."

"Charmed," the man said, though he did not look charmed in the slightest. "What brings you both down here? Getting ready for the storm blowing in? They say it's a proper nor'easter."

"Yes, sir. Mrs. Haite wanted to accompany me as I gathered supplies."

"Picked a hell of a day for it," Mr. Zanski remarked as he glanced outside. "I hate to be the one to tell you, but we still haven't had another train come through since you last came by. They're probably done for the winter."

"How will you make it through?" Ada blurted out in alarm. "There's nothing here."

Zanski chuckled. "Must be a city thing. This ain't the first time we've had a hard winter down here, Mrs. Haite. Most folks have root cellars. Every fall, ol' Szaylen brings down the harvest from his farm a few miles up. Folks buy up what they can afford to can and pickle for later. The Swarksi brothers like to hunt, so I buy up their venison. We all get by. With or without the mill being closed."

Ads saw her chance. "Did Mr. Haite tell you the reason for the closure?" she asked, as casually as she could.

Zanski exchanged glances with Garvey.

"Our Mrs. Haite has a real heart for charity," Garvey told him. "Ever since she heard of the mill closing, she's been worried about the townspeople."

Zanski turned back to her. "Repairs," he said flatly. "But we have our suspicions. It's hard to keep up operations down here in the winter.

Gotta pay more for the snow plowin' and for the extra coal. Guess he don't tell you any of that. Come to think of it, I'm not sure why he stuck you here with us. Seems to me he should be keeping an eye on such a pretty young wife like you."

Ada decided to ignore his words and their implications, and held up the basket she'd brought instead. "I have a care package I'd like to give to the grandparents of my new hire, Rebecca Crane. To show my gratitude for allowing her to be in my employ at Haite Hill."

A strange look crossed over the old man's face.

Ada continued, "Can you show me where Amity Crane lives?"

"I know where an Amity *Goodeman* lives," the old man told her, studying her face. "She stays in the oldest house on Main Street. She turned it into an apothecary when the town doc left for winter."

"Very well." Ada snatched the grocery list from Garvey's hand and slapped it on the counter. "Please give us what you can, including some extra coal, if you can spare it."

The strange look remained planted on his face. "You really don't need to be bringing ol' Amity anything like that. She gets on fine all by herself."

"It's a kind, neighborly gesture," Ada informed him. "Is that *a city thing* you're unfamiliar with, as well?"

Zanski chuckled, gracefully owned. "Whatever you say, Mrs. Haite. I'd hurry, though. The first dusting has already begun, and you gotta get that contraption of yours back up the hill."

He moved to load her basket with a sack of flour, potatoes, and a few slabs of salted venison. Then he grabbed a pack of coffee from one of the shelves. "Amity likes her coffee," he explained. He took longer to prepare the order for their household, and after a few minutes, emerged from the room behind his counter with a bin of coal.

"Thank you, kindly," Garvey said as he gathered up all the supplies.

They exchanged farewells, and Ada and Garvey braced themselves for the cold. Just as Zanski had warned them, a gentle flurry of snowflakes had begun its descent, melting as they hit the dead grass. It would be some time before the flakes became piles. Ada found the soft dusting beautiful, peaceful even, if only for a moment. No matter how rude, the shopkeeper was right—snow in the city was much different than snow out here. She wasn't sure exactly what to expect, but so far, it didn't seem so terrible.

"So much for the snowless winter the Almanac predicted," Garvey remarked as they slid into the car. "Say, are you sure you want to disturb this Amity woman? It sounds like she isn't the type to be bothered."

Ada slid him a look, a reminder of their previous conversation.

Garvey remembered and gave a quick nod before he cranked the old auto back to life. It let out a sputtering grunt of discontent as it lurched forward. Ada scooted a bit closer to him for warmth, peeking out from her fur collar as they retraced their path back over the covered bridge.

Garvey took a left down Main Street, where all the company houses were neatly arranged on both sides of the road. Though all the hastily-built homes could have used a fresh coat of paint and some general repair, the apothecary stood out amongst them. The last house on the street was an old, single-pen house with a faded sign nailed to the front. Though it was only a floor high, it seemed to groan and sway in the wind.

"This must be it," Garvey murmured.

The uneasiness Ada felt at Haite Hill returned in a wave, and she held the now-filled basket close to her chest, a physical reminder of her purpose there. Garvey helped her out of the car once more, the sparkling white from the sky sticking to his hat and mustache. He led her to the door and knocked once, waiting for any sign of life.

The door opened with the rude creak of rusted hinges, accompanied by the sounds of critters fleeing. An old woman peeked out from behind it, dark eyes hooded with skin appraising them both with hostility. "I'm closed. Be gone with you."

"Good morning, ma'am," Garvey began. "We've come—"

"Are you deaf, boy? I said I'm closed. You and your trollop can get your pennyroyal another t—"

Ada stepped out from behind him. "My name is Mrs. Haite, ma'am. Might we have a moment of your time?"

The old woman opened the door wider, exposing herself in the gray sunlight. Ada was surprised by her vitality; by all appearances, the woman was older than any living person she had ever seen. Her skin hung from her bones like thin sheets of yellow parchment, riddled with liver spots that crawled up her neck. Wisps of straggly white hair poked out from her bonnet. Despite the bitter cold, she was barefoot and stockingless, wearing nothing but a stained cotton day dress. "Haite, you say?" she croaked. "You're his new wife?"

"Yes, ma'am. I just moved into Haite Hill."

The woman let out an uproarious burst of laughter, which Ada worried would shake her very flesh loose from her bones. "Come in, then, come in." She widened the door to allow them entry, exposing them to the formerly trapped stench of pipe tobacco and sour cat urine.

"We can't stay too long," Ada said as she took a hesitant step forward. "I've brought you some extra supplies for the approaching storm. I wanted to thank you for letting Rebecca come work up at the house."

"Who?"

"Rebecca."

The old woman's glare remained blank.

"Is Rebecca Crane not your granddaughter?" Ada asked.

Again, the old woman laughed, spittle flying through her loose teeth and gums. "If she says she is, she is. My, my, if Rebecca has already gotten to you, then I have nothing left to do but stay here, rotting away."

Confusion silenced Ada's bravery, and she moved to set her basket on the front counter. Behind it were shelves of apothecary bottles, some filled and some empty, all coated with dust.

"I moved in here when the doctor moved out," the old woman said. "Right before the cold weather hit. Good riddance to him, I say. I keep the tinctures and the herbs safe for the folks in town. Say, did you bring smoke and coffee?"

"Coffee, yes—"

"I have tobacco," Garvey interrupted, pulling a pouch from his coat.

"Give it here, then."

Amity took it, then gestured for them to join her near her dwindling fire. She hobbled over the coal bin to add a scoop into the hearth, which released sparks into the air. No part of Ada wanted to sit on the ratty old armchairs she'd arranged near it, but she forced herself to. She hadn't come here for pleasure; she needed answers.

"Put on the coffee, will ya?" Amity barked at Garvey. "Make yourself useful while you're standing there." She looked back at Ada. "I can always pick out a service man."

If Garvey was offended, he didn't let on. He located her tarnished pot and filled it from her water bucket, then placed it on the rack over the freshly stoked fire. Then he set to finding cups.

Amity slumped down into the chair opposite Ada, her legs spread like a man's under her skirt—the ultimate defiance of formalities. She snatched the smoking pipe left on the table near her chair and began pushing tobacco into its mouth with her gnarled fingers. Her long, yellow nails matched the length of her fungal toenails. "Do you got children up in Haite House?"

Ada cleared her throat. "Yes, as a matter of fact. Both Charles's daughters, Josephine and Margaret, are living with me. That's why we hired Rebecca to assist."

Amity stared, her jaw drooping to reveal cancerous gums. "Josephine, you say? And Maggie?"

Ada felt an unexpected flush of protectiveness. "Yes, those are their names. Do you know of them?"

"Do I know them? I delivered Maggie right out of her raving lunatic mother's womb." Amity snorted. "Before they sent her away, of course."

Ada tried not to reveal her surprise.

"Mrs. Eleanor Haite died in childbirth, ma'am," Garvey gently broke in.

The woman let loose another cackle. "You and I both know that ain't true. They locked her up in a looney bin and threw away the key. Is that coffee ready?"

"Uh, yes, almost, ma'am."

"Rebecca mentioned you knew her, Maggie's mother," Ada broke in. "Josephine's mother, Julianna, as well. You assisted her at the orphanage...?"

"The finest woman you'd ever meet," Amity said, lighting her pipe with a match. Soon, the scent of pipe tobacco and brewing coffee filled the air, struggling to overpower the stench. "Reminded me of myself in my younger days. I was the matron of this town, you see, before your husband snatched it up. Even the Stanfords respected my husband and me."

"Speaking of your husband, where is he?"

Amity snorted. "The good Reverend Wolcott has been dead longer than you been alive, my dear."

"I'm sorry to hear that," Ada offered. She was right. Rebecca had lied.

"Eh, no need for it. I work best in solitude, going where the Lord tells me. I ran Haite Orphanage right alongside Mrs. Haite for ten years before her untimely passing."

"What happened to her?" Ada pressed, curious to have her input.

"The Great Flood of 1901, that's what. The entire town had to be rebuilt. Not even Haite Hill was spared. Two maids drowned in the basement, and Julianna was found the next day, face down in the lake. All the children were moved to the Light of Hope Orphanage on Gore Road in Vermillion."

"Glad the children survived, at least," Ada said softly. "What a terrible tragedy."

Amity didn't echo the sentiment.

"So Julianna and Eleanor's daughters are back at Haite Hill." She shook her head in wonderment. "Seems too good to be true. This explains why the Lord sent you here. It's all a part of his Divine Plan, you know. You got a child of your own?"

Ada was taken aback. "No-no. I have not."

Amity stared at her, nodding. For as old as she seemed on the outside, her cold eyes betrayed a sharp mind. "Bled out, did ya?"

Instantly, the room began to spin, and Ada fought to compose herself. The old woman's words had caught her brilliantly off guard. Powerless, Ada squeezed her eyes shut, fighting away the memories of what brought her to this place, forcing her mind to think of anything else—refusing to think of the blood—*oh God, all the blood*—

Garvey's warm hand touched hers. "Here is your coffee, ma'am."

She looked up at him, an oasis in the harrowing desert that was her mind. She focused on his face instead of her racing thoughts, and the snow trickling down outside the grimy window, even the cracked, dirty cup steaming with hot black liquid...and soon her senses returned.

Amity just stared at her, taking a careful puff of her pipe.

"'He maketh the barren woman to dwell with a family, and a joyful mother of children,'" she finally quoted. "Your purpose is greater than birthing, like mine. A mother is nothing but a vessel for her children. An empty house to be filled, then emptied in pain and suffering. It is the punishment for Eve's sins: 'And unto the woman He said, I will greatly multiply thy sorrow and thy conception; in sorrow thou shalt bring forth children.'"

"We should be heading back," Garvey interrupted, keeping his voice even. He pointed out the window. "The snow is starting to stick."

"Yes," Ada murmured, feeling as though she were trapped in a horrible dream. She accepted Garvey's outstretched hand and rose shakily to her feet.

"Bring the girls to visit me," Amity said, remaining planted in her chair, circled by smoke. "When the weather breaks. I'd love to see them again."

"Yes, indeed..."

"Take care, ma'am," Garvey told the old woman as he hustled Ada out the door.

Three fat vultures were waiting for them, perched on the roof of the motor car. White snowflakes coated their inky black heads and feathers, but they seemed unaffected, watching them with beady eyes.

Garvey attempted to shoo them off. "Go on now."

Ada heard a slight tremor to his voice despite his best attempts to sound firm. The birds did not seem apt to leave their perch, so Ada, finally finding her bearings, marched toward the car. They hissed as she grew closer, a garbled, grating sound that arrested her movements, before they took to the sky.

"Never seen buzzards in the winter before," Garvey muttered as he hastily wiped away the melted snow from the front seat.

"I never heard such horrid sounds." Ada watched as the swirls of white swallowed their dark, flapping bodies.

Once the seat was dry, she slid in. The automobile cranked to a start, and they rode in sputtering silence, as if both were in the midst of processing all that had happened and what had been said. Garvey finally broke the quiet.

"That woman was full of lies. Ms. Eleanor was not sent to an asylum. I would have been informed of such things."

"It's true," Ada argued gently. "I found the paperwork in Charles's drawer not long after we married."

"But I *knew* her. When she was just a lass, she worked as a housemaid's helper at the same home where I apprenticed as a butler. We parted ways, but I heard she became Josephine's nanny, years before Charles married her. I worked with the girl and broke bread with her at the servants' table. She was a bright, lively young woman. Certainly not mad."

Ada's mind flashed to her and Charles's wedding night when she first realized he was the type of man who refused to make love—his preference was causing pain. Enjoying fear. She took a moment before she spoke, careful with her words. "Charles is as formidable with his family as he is in business."

Realization settled on Garvey's face, twisting his features as he stared ahead at the road. "My God. That is why you fear me reporting back to him. You're afraid he will send you away as well. For your sleepwalking."

Ada was quiet.

"Oh, Mrs. Haite. Forgive me."

"You've done nothing but be kind to me, Mr. Garvey."

"Dammit, just call me Tom."

Ada turned to hide her budding smile. "Alright then, Tom. But when we are not around others, you must call me Ada in return."

There was a pause, and the two shifted closer together in unison, an unspoken agreement shared between them. Outside, the snow had shifted to an icy rain that caused the old Ford to struggle its way up the road.

"Poor Maggie," Garvey said quietly. "All this time, she's been kept away from her mum."

"Someday I will find Eleanor for her," Ada said with determination. "I just have to figure out how. I cannot delude myself into thinking I'm free, even all the way out here. I still belong to Charles."

His name hung in the wind, widening the gap between them they'd just tried to close. And then there was a scream, radiating from far out in the distance. Ada jumped.

"An animal, most likely," Garvey assured her. "We're nearly to the house."

Ada heard it again, a screech unlike any creature she'd heard before. It was a sound worse than the hiss of the vultures, eerily similar to a woman's screaming. Its unfamiliarity made her hair stand on end. She was grateful to see Haite House appear around the crooked bend, the roof now coated in snow.

Garvey managed to get the Ford up the wooded hill and Ada smiled when she saw Josephine and Maggie's little faces in the front parlor windows.

"Come," he said. "Let us prepare for the storm."

CHAPTER NINE
Lori, 1981

Lori's cheap plastic umbrella was no match for the angry squalls of a relentless storm, and no sooner had she stepped from the veranda did it fly right out of her hands. The wind took her scrunchie too, rain splattering her face as she struggled to capture her thrashing hair in the hood of her raincoat. She heard Finn's playful laughter as he darted for the carriage house, fighting his own battle against the storm.

"Hurry!" he called. "Before we get stuck in Oz!"

Lori rushed after him, trying to keep her old Keds steady lest they send her ass-first into the mud. The power outage had spooked the girls, but Becky suggested they grab their blankets and sleeping bags and have a sleepover in the parlor while Finn and Lori retrieved extra flashlights and candles from the carriage house. Kellie was skeptical until Finn told them the parlor fireplace had been recently cleaned and he could make them a fire. And so, the two hurried in the rain while the girls patiently awaited their return.

As they drew closer, Lori realized she hadn't had time to appreciate the carriage house properly. Constructed with mismatched stone that must have come from a nearby quarry, its pitched gable roof and slanted windows offered the same Gothic beauty as the home it belonged to.

Finn unlocked and pulled open its double doors, and they entered, leaving the storm to carry on without them. He flipped the switch, and the lights came on with a buzz and a flicker, revealing a modern living space with an open floor plan. Though furnished with couches and even a TV, the apartment worked with the old construction rather than against it, its fixtures built into the varied stone, including a fireplace still loaded with wood.

"Oh wow, this place looks nice," Lori said as she attempted to smooth her hair back in line. "You didn't move your things out?"

"Well, Granddad and I didn't know if you'd want us around, so we just packed a suitcase each. We figured there's no use moving everything until we have to." Finn headed into the kitchen and began rummaging through the cupboards and drawers.

"Grandad fixed this place up to live in decades ago," he continued. "Then I modernized it a few years back when I moved in. He didn't even have electricity. I installed it myself, and hooked it up to a generator..." He paused and made a face. "...which I *probably* should have also done with the house before you moved in."

"Well, I'm not sure we're actually going to move in," Lori admitted. "I didn't realize the entire town got bought up by the park."

"Damn government always messing with things," Finn said with a sigh. He went over to the fireplace with a garbage bag and started piling up a few logs of wood. "Haite Hill is a special place, though. No one—not even the National Park Service—can take it away from you. I know it hasn't been smooth sailing with the storm and all, but I promise you'll grow to love her. I know I do."

Lori thought back to the tower, the letter, the weird books. The teeth. "So, how did you and your grandfather start working for my grandmother anyway?"

Finn wrapped the wood in the makeshift tarp and stood. "That is a very long, complicated story that I'd love to share with you once we get that fire going for the girls."

Lori nodded. "Can I help you carry anything?"

"The bag over there. I stuck in a few flashlights and taper candles."

Lori retrieved it, and the two braced themselves to step back into the uproarious night. It seemed to have gotten worse. All around them, trees thrashed and creaked, their branches whipping in the furious wind. It didn't take long before they broke into a run for the house.

"Christ, what if one of them falls?" Lori cried, hurrying to keep up with Finn. His lack of response was enough response for her, and she picked up speed until they reached the veranda. Once protected from rain under the roof, Lori paused to catch her breath. "There's no way I can send you and Becky home in this," she shouted over the wind.

"Only one date, and you're already inviting me to spend the night?" Finn called back, equally breathless. "Damn, I must still have my boyish charm."

"This is *not* a date!" Lori sputtered.

He laughed. "Relax, I'm only messing with you. I want to take you on a proper date anyway. One where we have someone *else* cook and I have to give the waiter and all the other men in the restaurant dirty looks for gawking at you."

She froze, at a loss for words, and he leaned in to push the front door open. She caught his scent, an earthy mix of rainwater and aftershave. Flustered, she followed him in, and soon water streamed from their jackets onto the foyer floor. Lori pulled her windbreaker up over her head to hide her blushing cheeks.

"In all seriousness, I'll head back after I make the girls a fire, and I'll scoop up Becky in the morning." Finn peeled off his raincoat. "I'm well aware that the last thing a mother wants is some strange man under the same roof as her girls."

"No, stay in the carriage house—*your* house. If I had any idea that people were living there, I wouldn't have asked you to go."

"That's very cool of you, but I really don't want to be a burden."

"Honestly, I've been pretty spooked since I got here last night, and I wouldn't mind another adult around here during the storm," Lori admitted. "Plus, ya know. Hammer to the skull if you try to get cute."

He chuckled. "True and noted. You let me know if there's anything you need, okay? I'm a light sleeper. I'll check on you guys in the morning."

"I will."

They left their muddy shoes behind in the foyer and headed into the parlor where the girls had taken root. Kellie was in the midst of chattering Becky's ear off, her dolls in arm, while Nikki had resumed her magazine reading, curled up in one of the chairs like a graceful cat.

"We're baaack," Finn said pleasantly. "And I come bearing firewood."

"Are you okay with spending the night here, Becky?" Lori asked the young woman as Finn set to work making a fire. "I'd hate to have you and Finn walk home in this. Especially down that mud slide of a driveway."

"Oh, sure," she said easily. "That would be nice, thank you."

"You're letting him stay here?" Nikki asked over the top of her magazine.

"In the carriage house. He used to live there with his grandpa before we even got here."

Nikki's expression let Lori know she was not impressed.

Trying not to blush again, Lori turned back to Becky. "We only have three beds set up, so you can sleep in my room. I planned on camping out in my tent tonight, anyway."

"Sounds good to me."

"Let there be fire," Finn announced, standing as the pile of wood caught with a series of crackles and pops. Kellie clapped her approval. Soon, the dark parlor was filled with warmth and light, a welcome respite from the howling nightmare outside.

"And with that, I'm out," Finn said. "You can keep adding logs until you're ready for bed, then it'll go out on its own. You make sure to get me if you need anything else. Don't let the storm scare you. We don't get tornadoes in the valley, even in March."

"Thanks again," Lori said.

He gave a nod and was off.

Lori turned back to the girls, who seemed pleased by the fire. She knelt down to sit cross-legged next to Kellie, enjoying the warmth on her skin. "This isn't so bad," Lori said. "It's almost like we're camping."

"I hate camping," Nikki said from her chair.

"Oo, let's tell scary stories!" Kellie perked up. "I wish we had marshmallows for s'mores."

Nikki made a sound of disapproval. "Do you ever stop eating sugar?"

"I don't know any scary stories," Lori said, though her mind recalled the letter she just read. *This house is a scary story.* She looked at Becky, who had been quietly staring into the flames. "Maybe Becky knows some?"

Becky looked thoughtful. "Do you know the story of the first settlers here? Not the Stanfords who founded Boston Village or even the settlers in 1796. I mean the ones before *that*. The ones erased from history."

Kellie looked skeptical. "Is the story really scary?"

"I'll let you decide." Becky shifted into a cross-legged position.

"Come on, Nikki, come sit with us," Kellie demanded.

Her sister sighed and closed her magazine. She stood and folded up next to her sister, tucking her legs under the blanket.

"Long before America was a country," Becky began, "England set up colonies along the east coast. But that wasn't good enough for the men—they also had their eyes set on the west. Especially when they heard stories about the lush, fertile land below what we now call Lake Erie. King Charles II granted the Colony of Connecticut the land we're sitting on right now, which was eventually called the Connecticut Western Reserve."

"Even though it's Ohio?"

"It would be a long time before it became Ohio."

"This doesn't sound that scary. It feels like school."

"Colonization is always scary," Nikki pointed out.

"Yeah, so is school."

"Girls, let her tell it," Lori said gently as she stoked the fire with a poker. "Go on, Becky."

"The scary part of the story is that they sent five families to settle in an unknown land, but none survived."

Both girls grew quiet.

"The year was 1703, and the very first families arrived in the late spring, when the entire world was in bloom and filled with hope and promise. They were excited to find such perfect land. The whole thing seemed too good to be true—they survived the long journey from ocean to lake with no native or animal attacks. They were able to build homesteads and plant crops in time for harvest. The nearby river provided plenty of fish and fresh water, while the forests had plenty of game. The families thanked God for all His blessings, and they decided to call their town the Towne of Hope, or Hope Towne. But then winter hit."

For emphasis, the fireplace let out a loud pop.

"The settlers were used to New England winters, but they hadn't anticipated just how much snow the Great Lakes could bring in November—what we call lake effect snow. For weeks, the families battled heavy snow and terrible winds, watching their rations dwindle. Soon, only three of the families were left alive; the others starved. They couldn't even bury the ones who'd passed away in their homes. Their bodies were left there, frozen."

"Why didn't they hunt?" Kellie asked.

"There was too much snow to get through," Becky explained. "Soon, it piled up higher than their doors, making it almost impossible to open. It was a struggle even to get firewood. The three families—the Goodemans, the Aldens, and the Cranes—eventually came together to share the last of the supplies and body heat in the Cranes' home. It was the biggest and warmest because Samuel Crane was the leader of their party."

"How do you know all this?" Lori interrupted.

"It's a legend in these parts," Becky replied. "An oral tradition passed down from generation to generation."

"We learned about that in school," Nikki said, surprisingly engaged.

Becky continued, "The second group of settlers found them the following year, but what they found was so awful, it caused them to scrub the entire account from written history. Ruth Alden kept a journal of their final days, but they set it to flame."

"What did they find?"

"Two of the men, John Alden and Matthew Goodeman, were found frozen near the river with their hunting rifles. They'd tried one last time to hunt before starvation took them all. As far as children, the Aldens remained childless, Goody Alden having miscarried the previous month. The Goodemans were an older couple, but had two daughters —one who died early on in the winter from an unknown disease, and the second from starvation. They left her behind in the cabin before moving in with the Cranes."

Lori snuck a glance at Kellie, hoping it wasn't too much for her. "What about the other family?"

"The young Goody Crane was with child."

"She was pregnant?"

"Yes, which meant she needed more food than the rest, and the other wives grew resentful over the favoritism. But that would be short-lived, as they were all forced to bind together as they watched Mr. Crane grow mad." Becky smiled at Kellie. "This is the part where it gets spooky."

Kellie scooted closer to where Lori sat, her little eyes wide.

"Again, we only have bits of information from Goody Alden's journal and what the second group found in the Cranes' cabin," Becky continued. "But the story goes: as the days grew longer and there was no sign of either man who left to hunt, the true hopelessness of their situation became apparent. A final storm made it impossible to leave the cabin, covering the roof with almost a foot of heavy, wet snow. Their last days were spent huddled together near a weak fire as Crane read the Scriptures aloud from his Bible. But verses that once brought them hope soon brought terror. Crane began to talk of sacrifice, twisting the passages to make them fit a strange new narrative, telling the frightened women that they must be willing to give of themselves to let others live. The women realized he wanted them to give up their flesh to feed him and his soon-to-be-born son."

"Maybe this is a bit too morbid..." Lori said nervously.

"I love cannibal stuff!" Kellie protested.

"How do you know what cannibals are?"

"I wasn't born yesterday."

"It's actually getting interesting now," Nikki said.

Lori sighed. "You can continue."

Becky nodded. "Goody Alden's last journal entry described Goody Crane's miscarriage. Samuel Crane completely unraveled at that point, rocking the dead child in his arms and quoting scripture to him as if he were still alive. He completely ignored his wife, who lay dying on her birthing bed. The other women threw their resentments aside and worked together to try to keep her alive. We don't know what happened after that. The last thing Goody Alden wrote was how the Devil Crane intended to kill and eat them all." Becky paused to unfold her legs.

Lori tried to read her expression, but the bright flames reflected in her glasses obscured her eyes, casting shadows along her face.

"The settlers never found the bodies of the women," Becky continued. "Only a cabin drenched in blood. They did find Crane's rotting corpse, however. All his arms and legs had been broken so they could be threaded through and tied to a large, wooden spoked wheel. He stayed alive for three days like that, howling to God to spare him his torment."

Lori involuntarily shuddered.

"A breaking wheel," Nikki said quietly.

"How do you know about medieval torture?" Lori said in surprise.

"Everybody knows about that stuff." Nikki shrugged. "But how did the women do it? Weren't they all weak with hunger?"

Becky nodded. "That's what makes it so mysterious. How did he get like that? How could three docile Puritan women know about medieval torture? According to Goody Alden's journal, no one could go in or out of the cabin, let alone haul in a wagon wheel. So what happened? Why was the cabin covered in blood, but there was no sign of leftover viscera or bones? And that's not even the worst part."

"What is the worst part?" Kellie demanded.

"What they found in the pot over the stove—"

"Alright, that's enough," Lori quickly said. "It's time for you girls to go to bed."

"What does she mean? What was in the pot?" Kellie protested as Lori picked her up. She could feel her little heart pounding through her chest.

Nikki shook her head, a look of disgust on her face. "That's one messed up story, Becky."

"It's not real," Lori told them both, mad at herself for letting the tale go on so long. "It's just a story, and we don't have to worry about any of it."

"Oh, it's quite real," Becky said, missing the hint. "Legend says the Sisters Three still haunt these woods, trapped in the space between life and death, longing to go home. Some say you can hear them howling in the night."

Lori stopped in her tracks, the hair raising along her arms.

"The woods here? These woods?" Kellie cried tearfully.

Becky nodded. "Haite House was built over the Hope Towne ruins. They built the original settlement high up on the hill so the river wouldn't flood them out. A lot of good that did."

"Lori, I'm scared."

Kellie buried her face in Lori's chest, jolting her from her stupor.

"Shh, don't be scared. I'll sleep in your room tonight, okay?"

"Quit being such a baby." Nikki stood to gather up the sleeping bags and blankets. "I know you stay up and sneak when me and Dad watch scary movies."

"No, I don't!"

"Girls, please," Lori pleaded. "Becky, thank you for the story. And for all your help. I'm gonna stay with Kellie in her room tonight. Make yourself at home in my room, the big one all the way to the left. You can't miss it."

"Okay, thanks, Mrs. Greene."

"It's Miss," Lori said as she hoisted Kellie up the stairs.

"Lori, I want Nikki to sleep with us, too."

Nikki let out a sigh as she trailed behind them, a sound of acquiescence before Lori even asked. The wind screamed outside as they climbed, and Lori fought the gooseflesh that stubbornly refused to let go of her skin. Her mind spun, thinking back to the letter: *There is no God in these lands. Only three... the scalpless, blood-thirsty, demonic three. Heed my warnings! My time here is brief. Either the men in their coats or the Sisters Three will take me.*

Luckily for all involved, Kellie was falling asleep in her arms.

"You good?" Lori whispered to Nikki.

"Yeah, I'm fine. But that Becky girl's got to go."

Lori nodded, but she wasn't sure Becky was the issue. It was the entire house—the town. Regardless of their accuracy, the many stories swirling around it lingered like ghosts trapped in an endless corridor.

Nikki spread out their blankets and pillows so Lori could set the now snoring Kellie on her little trundle bed. A nice thing about Kellie was how soundly she slept—for all her high energy during the day, she burned out like a firework at night. Lori wouldn't have to worry about her waking up in the middle of the night, terrified.

"Are you gonna sleep downstairs?" Nikki asked her casually.

"No," Lori said as she unceremoniously fell into Kellie's beanbag chair. "If a tree falls on the house, I'm dying with you two."

"That's reassuring." Nikki tossed her a blanket. "You're gonna wake up with a backache."

"There are worse things."

Nikki went quiet, and soon Kellie's steady snores were the only thing fighting the moaning storm over who should be heard. It created the perfect white-noise effect that tended to knock Lori out, no matter how anxious her mind was. She kept an eye open to make sure Nikki fell asleep completely before she finally gave in herself, collapsing into a deep and heavy sleep the instant she heard her snore.

The sound of humming woke her.

It was pleasant at first, a reminder of times long past, when a mother's song brought comfort. But as the grip of sleep loosened its hold on Lori, she realized how unusual the sound currently was. She shot up from the beanbag chair, her bones creaking in protest. But she was too alarmed to worry about her back or her joints—it was the dead of night, and an ethereal sound of an unknown woman's voice was wafting from the other room.

Lori felt around for something to use as a weapon and clumsily wrapped her fist around one of the flashlights. It would have to do—the weak plastic cylinder would make bludgeoning an intruder to death a bit difficult, but she hoped the weird humming had a better explanation than that.

Beneath Kellie's door glowed warm light from the hallway, and as Lori opened it, she found the source of both it and the humming. *Becky,* she thought with relief. But her ease was short-lived. Because even though she now had a logical explanation, it didn't explain why the young woman was still awake in the late hour, humming to no one. It was a tune Lori didn't recognize, one of those old songs that sound familiar but you can't quite place.

Lori decided to check on her.

The storm still screamed outside, whipping branches and what sounded like pellets of hail at the old house. The racket had drowned out Becky's voice, but as Lori got closer to the bedroom, she learned Becky wasn't humming, but singing in a different language.

"Sa koyrde han kraka pa lavegolv..."

Then she switched to English.

"And drove the Crow to the barn floor..."

The hair on Lori's arms rose in a prickling shiver, but she continued to walk forward. The closer she got, the more the voice didn't sound like Becky's at all, but mature and old-timey, like a starlet in an old movie. It was hard to picture it coming from the young college girl she'd met in the hotel.

"Sa flädde han kraka og lema ho sund..."

Lori reached the bedroom door, which had been left open a crack. A fire had been lit, and her bedroom glowed with its warmth. She hesitated, unable to muster the courage to push it open. Something didn't seem right. She knew she wasn't dreaming, yet she felt as if she were walking in one. There had been a shift in energy, like the unsettling quiet just before a solar eclipse. A liminal moment, trapped in the linear flow of time.

"Then he skinned the Crow and cut her in pieces... Hello, Lori. You may come in."

Lori shoved the door open, then abruptly stopped, her mouth trapped open in disbelief. Her room, though never used, was not how it should have been.

Chandeliers alive with electricity sparkled above her. The walls were covered in fresh wallpaper, its soft floral pattern more Art Nouveau than Victorian, stretching past the ornate crown molding and onto the ceiling. Tables, desks, and a wardrobe cluttered a floor covered with new rugs, and fires burned low in the dual marble fireplaces. But what was more curious than the completely renovated bedroom circa 1910 was the woman seated on the four-poster bed.

Her head turned toward Lori at an uncomfortably slow pace. Dressed as if she'd stepped right out of the Edwardian era, the woman's soft blonde hair framed what should have been a beautiful face. But she looked strange, uncanny even, her lips pulled into a smile under blank, empty blue eyes.

"W-what—"

"It's an old song from my homeland. It's called Kråkevisa, The Song of the Crow. It reminds me of Norway."

"Who—"

"Lovely to meet you. My name is Ada. Ada Haite. I've been waiting for you."

CHAPTER TEN
Ada, 1910

All she felt was cold.

Her eyes fluttered open. She was standing barefoot in the middle of a dying cornfield, acres of woods stretching out in the distance. Her panicked breathing let out quick plumes of vapor as she frantically searched for an explanation. *What is happening? Why am I here?*

Then it hit her. She'd been sleepwalking.

The realization broke her from her stupor, and her body responded by dissolving into a violent mess of shivers. Her chemise clung weakly to her body, a pathetic shield against the howling wind and snow that bit at her bare feet and ankles. She attempted to hug warmth back into her bones before turning to run home, but a horrible scream ripped through the air.

She froze.

It came again, an unholy shriek that could only exist in nightmares. Not quite animal, but certainly not human.

Ada slowly turned in its direction, seeing nothing but empty, endless woodland. The clouds parted, revealing a plenilune sky, and the exposed moon cast pale light down upon three overgrown birches at the forefront of the trees. Twisted, skeletal giants swaying in the breeze, their jagged white flesh glowed against the black expanse behind them. Another shriek pierced the quiet, and Ada squinted to see better.

They weren't swaying in the breeze. They were moving—dancing, gliding, twisting—right toward her. They weren't trees either, but grotesquely tall women with narrow, elongated bodies and spindly arms. Their heads were completely shrouded in flowing white linen that reached down to the forest floor, sweeping it as they advanced, their bodies bound tightly with rope.

They will lock you away, Ada. This is not real.

Ada struggled to move, her heels sinking deeper into the mud as the creatures advanced. It was as if they put a spell on her, forcing her to bear witness to their monstrosity. Soon, she realized that their shrouds were not clean, but rather drenched in a sticky crimson that dribbled down from the tops of their covered heads. It was blood streaming from their peeled away scalps, their pained expressions poking through the drenched cloth with mouths stretched open in perpetual anguish.

"Mrs. Haite!" a voice called out. "Ada!"

Tom.

The three monsters screeched back, but their spell on her had been broken. Ada bolted toward the sound of his voice, fallen cornstalks whipping at her bare legs as she tore through them. She ran as fast as her limbs could move as the icy gales roared around her. She didn't want to stop and look back, lest the horrible creatures snatch her with their gnarled white hands. The dim glow of the house appeared in the distance, a beacon of light driving her to move faster.

"Ada!"

"I'm here!" she cried as she tore across the lawn. She flew past the lake and then the conservatory as frozen earth and rocks ripped the soles of her feet. Finally, Tom surfaced from the shadows, holding a shotgun. Behind him, the house radiated lamplight, creating a halo around his head.

"What is it? What is after you?"

She collided with him, and he gripped her tightly with his empty arm.

"I don't know, I don't know—"

He squinted into the dark mist beyond. "Let's go inside."

"Please don't tell Charles," she begged him. "Oh, please, please don't tell him."

"Hush now, you know I won't be doing any such thing," Tom soothed as he guided her into the house.

The door had been left wide open, and Rebecca stood on the veranda with wide eyes. Ada struggled to collect herself, reluctant to appear unwell in front of her new hire. "Where are the girls?"

"They are sleeping sound, ma'am. I awoke to the sounds of screaming."

"There's nothing to worry about, Rebecca," Tom assured her. He guided Ada into the parlor where she had once carried Maggie, positioning her on the same rug before the fireplace. The dark stain left from Maggie's bloody legs caught and trapped Ada's eyes; she squeezed them shut, not wanting to remember the sight of the scalpless creatures coming toward her.

"Ms. Rebecca, ring for Ms. Elena."

Ada put a hand on his arm to stop him. "No, please. She could tell Charles—they were all hires suggested by him."

"I've already brought warm linens for her, Mr. Garvey." Rebecca approached to show the stack of blankets and a clean nightdress in her arms. "I wanted to be prepared when you brought her back in."

"Very good. Stay here with Mrs. Haite while I check the perimeter. I need to make sure we are secure."

"Yes, Mr. Garvey."

No part of Ada wanted him to go, but she remained acutely aware that she ought not dissolve into hysterics in Rebecca's presence. Fear had coiled itself around her body and settled unpleasantly in her stomach, but she forced her breathing to remain steady. Her limbs tingled back to life in the hearth's warmth, creating shooting pains that radiated up her legs.

Rebecca came closer with a hesitancy one might apply to a wild animal. "Can I get you anything else, ma'am?" she asked, handing her the linens.

"No, thank you." Ada hurried to wrap her shivering body, wishing Tom would hurry back.

"Don't worry about Mr. Garvey," Rebecca offered. "They don't hurt the men. Men are the purest children of God, after all."

Although Ada was slowly thawing, her skin prickled as the hair rose on her arms. "What do you mean, they?"

Though Rebecca had folded herself neatly beside Ada, the shadows kept their hold across her face. The moving flames only touched her eyes, settling in their empty voids. "The Sisters Three," she explained softly. "That's who you saw in the woods. We all hear their calls. You should consider yourself lucky; they only reveal themselves to a chosen few."

"You should not speak of such things, Rebecca," Ada tried to scold her, although the fear lodged in her stomach began to slither awake. "Are you not a proper Christian?"

Rebecca's lips turned up, which should have been pleasant on the soft, round face of a child. But the smile seemed sinister beneath her glowing eyes. "The Sisters Three are chosen by the Lord, and they have chosen you. You, Maggie, and Josephine all hear the Sisters' call. That is why you and Maggie walk while asleep. This house is blessed by the Lord, indeed."

Tom re-entered the parlor, snowflakes gripping the shoulders of his housecoat. "We are safe for the night, and the snow has begun. We should retire, lest we wake the rest of the household."

"I wish to change from out of my wet clothing," Ada said, unable to look away from Rebecca, who now seemed perfectly ordinary under the glow of Tom's lamp. "Please accompany Rebecca and check on the girls in their room."

He looked hesitant, but nodded.

The moment they left, Ada hurried to the window. There was no arguing that the snowstorm had arrived, the swirling white obscuring her vision as she squinted into the woods. Finding nothing that would confirm she hadn't been dreaming, she went back to the fire to peel away her nightgown.

After the conversation with Rebecca's grandmother, she didn't want to believe that Rebecca was also a religious zealot. But she should have known better. Those who recite Bible verses so seamlessly with their everyday speech indoctrinate everyone around them. Her uncle was one of those very people.

Rebecca was still a child, however, and perhaps being in a less rigid household would do her good. It was not that Ada had little faith; she'd been brought up Lutheran, as many of her people were. She'd just seen too much pointless, painful death to believe any benevolent force cared about her.

She hung her damp clothes on the table closest to the fire, staring again at the blood-stained rug under her feet. She frowned, deciding she would be rid of it as soon as day broke. Elena should have alerted her the moment she saw the stain and found she was unable to scour it from the fabric. Ada squinted, noticing something amiss with her foot.

Her toenail was missing.

She bent down to check to make sure her eyes were not deceiving her. Sure enough, where her big toenail should have been was simply pulpy flesh. She felt absolutely no pain; it was as if someone had just removed it without her knowledge. No pain, no blood, nothing. Just a missing toenail.

She stood back up, horribly confused, when she heard a loud clatter. She jumped, then whipped around to see Tom fumbling to upright the table he'd just run into. Ada hurried to slip her clean nightdress over her head and wrap herself back up in the blanket.

"I-I-forgive me, ma'am, I—"

"You seeing me wet, cold, and indecent is becoming quite the regular occurrence as of late," Ada said playfully. She was pleased to see a blush creep along his gently freckled cheeks.

"I-I should have given you more time, more privacy," he stammered. "I was just worried about leaving you."

"Are the girls safe in bed?"

"Yes, ma'am," he replied, composing himself. "And Ms. Rebecca has retired to her room."

"Good," Ada said. "I'm beginning to hate this parlor. Is there a fire still lit in the front room?"

"I can stoke it to a proper flame." Garvey nodded.

The two reentered the hallway, and Ada felt the Blessed Virgin's judgmental eyes boring down on her as they walked. She kept her eyes cast ahead, struck by the irrational fear that she'd look up to see her veil covered in blood, her mouth twisted into a scream.

They entered the ladies' parlor, and Ada settled on the loveseat. She watched as the fire grew easily at Tom's coaxing, the pleasant orange light casting out the shadows. Outside, the storm whistled as snow built up along the window panes. She pulled her blanket tighter, grateful for the sturdy house around her.

"Is there anything I can get you? Tea?"

Ada shook her head. "Noise in the kitchen will wake the maids."

"Something stronger, perhaps?" Tom grinned as he pulled a flask from his pocket. "Zanski added a pint of vodka to the grocery order."

Ada accepted it gratefully and took a generous swig. She cleared her throat as the intensity bit, but she relaxed to let it travel down and burn away the fear in her stomach.

"I heard the screaming," Tom said quietly as he settled onto the floor. "I don't think it was just you."

"Something isn't right in the house, Tom," Ada whispered. "Charles's first wife died here, and his second wife went mad. I am seeing things that should not be..."

"What did you see?"

Ada hugged herself under the blanket, feeling more like a young child than a proper lady. By all accounts, she must have looked like one with her unkempt hair, bare legs, and thin chemise. "Things of nightmares."

"In my homeland, those who screamed in the night were called banshees. Those who heard a banshee's mournful keening knew their loved ones were soon to pass."

"There were three," Ada admitted. "Three horrible, giant women whose limbs look like knobby, twisting birch trees. Their bodies are cloaked in white, but their heads..." she faltered. "I cannot speak of it. You must find me mad."

"I do not," he replied earnestly, looking up at her with kind eyes. "You said it yourself, there is something not right here. I can feel it too."

"Rebecca called them the Sisters Three."

"You told her what you saw?"

Ada shook her head. "While you were outside, she spoke of them.

She said that it's why Maggie and I sleepwalk—we're hearing the call of the Sisters Three. Apparently, it has happened to Josephine, too."

"So it's a local legend then."

"If she speaks of the creatures I saw in the woods, they are not of God but something else entirely." Ada took another grimacing sip from the flask. The room grew quiet, the sound of thick, wet snowflakes nearly audible as they piled about the manor. The fire rudely interrupted with a pop.

"I forgot to thank you for your discretion and kindness in town," Ada said.

"Whatever do you mean?"

"With Rebecca's grandmother, that horrible Ms. Amity," she explained, taking another gulp for courage. She leaned forward to hand the flask back to him. "I assume Charles told you of the predicament that brought me here."

"He did not, but I drew my own conclusions when that woman began poking at you." He took his own generous sip from the flask. "Years ago, my late wife... She miscarried before the second child took her to Heaven. The mental agony of it troubled her so deeply that she walked while asleep."

Ada stared, emotion in her throat. "Tom, I am ever so sorry."

"I like it when you call me Tom." He gave her a sad smile. "Don't be. All my girls are in Heaven together, as they should be. When they're ready for me to join them, they will let me know." He took another swig and passed the flask back to her.

"Maybe they met my son," she said softly.

"That's a lovely thought indeed," Tom said. "Perhaps it's what that crazy old coot said—your purpose on this Earth is greater. There are two sweet girls upstairs in desperate need of mothering, and you've stepped into the role without a second thought. If God's got a master plan in all this mess, it certainly seems like you found it."

"I can say the same about you," Ada said. "Your presence has brought me a sense of safety I've had yet to feel since I arrived in this country. The girls feel it, too."

"Bah." Tom humbly shrugged off her words. "I'm far from a decent man. I just don't want harm coming to you, job or not." He shifted, suddenly appearing uncomfortable. "In fact, I hope I don't seem too forward, but I would feel better regarding your well-being if I slept up here, in one of the main rooms. Even if I'm holed up in the old study. I want to be sure no one else leaves the house when she is in the midst of sleepwalking."

Ada took another sip, then knelt down on the floor to hand it to him. "You will take the room next to mine."

"Are you certain?" He met her eyes as he took the flask, his fingers brushing against her skin.

"Yes, I am. I will deal with the servants and their gossip. And if Charles ever... I want—I want you close to me."

Her words hung in the air for only the briefest of moments.

They moved in unison, meeting each other's lips with a crackle of fire. The world around them fell away as Ada's body relaxed into his steady embrace. It was as if the horror around them no longer existed, and it was just them, Tom making soft on her body, the places Charles had made tense. If guilt or worry vexed him, Ada did not know, for he breathlessly removed her chemise with the same frantic movement as she removed his shirt. Scars and tattoos crossed his warm, freckled skin, marks of a man who had once lived harshly, and she longed to kiss every one before he pressed his body into hers.

Her moment of bliss came not long after he entered her, for she was entranced by every caress of his hand along her curves. She was glad to have held it, however, for they shared the moment together—a fervent, heated crescendo that forced a soft cry from between her lips.

Then the room was still, peppered with the sounds of them catching their breath as the fire hissed and popped.

"Well, that was...unexpected," he finally whispered with a chuckle.

Ada drew away with a smile, enjoying the bliss lingering all over her body. She longed to stay in that moment forever, safe from all horror. But she wanted to protect him—protect them—from prying eyes and curious children. She started to slip away, but he grabbed her face with his hands.

"Don't you dare let regret darken those beautiful eyes," he whispered before pressing his lips against hers. "I will take care of you always."

She pulled away to look into his. They spoke truth, and she smiled and kissed him again. "I regret nothing," she said as she slid from his lap and quickly redressed.

"Ah, so you seduced me then," he said playfully, reaching for his own clothes. "The creatures in the woods were all a ruse."

"I wish that were so," Ada replied honestly.

"Come," he said, rising to his feet. "Let us get some rest. There's nothing to be done tonight with the storm blowing in. I'm not going to let you out of my sight ever again."

Ada smiled, then her face fell when she thought of Rebecca sleeping nearby. The unease the young girl's words created crept in as the warmth of lovemaking faded. "I deeply regret inviting Rebecca into this home."

"We should have pressed the grandmother more," Tom agreed. "There seems to be more to their story."

"Do you recall when you asked me how I saw Maggie by the lake? I *did* enter the tower. I don't know how, but I did. And when we went up later, do you remember that Bible I opened? It had a written book glued inside it. I didn't get a chance to examine it, but I saw it spoke of the Sisters Three."

"We must take a look then," Tom said. "Tomorrow."

"I am the bravest I will ever be in this moment."

He shook his head with a smile before putting his hand on her face. "Then sleep shall have to wait."

Tom fetched a lamp to light their way, and they ascended the stairs in quiet footsteps. When they reached the second floor, Ada slipped into her bedroom to check on her sleeping stepdaughters. She was pleased to find them undisturbed, their soft snores rumbling through the room. She shoveled another bit of coal onto the closest fireplace and quickly fetched a pair of stockings and a robe. Then she hurried to meet Tom back in the hallway.

"After you," he whispered, holding the lamp high.

The winter storm roared loudest the closer to the heavens they climbed, and Ada gripped her robe tighter, wishing she were still lost in Tom's embrace by the fire. He seemed to share the sentiment, following so closely behind her, she felt the warmth of his skin and breath on her neck.

They greeted the tower as they'd left it, this time, with snow obscuring its windows. Far from a heat source, the tower was as cold as the air outside it, and their breath turned to vapor.

Even Tom shivered. "Let us be quick."

Ada took the lamp from him and pointed it back at the bookcase. She found what she sought immediately and tucked it under her arm. "Come, let us read it in my room."

With a clattering jaw, Tom nodded his agreement.

Her bedroom was a welcome reprieve, and they hurried to settle around the fireplace farthest from the sleeping girls. Once settled, Ada opened the book, struck by the same unsettling feeling she had when she first discovered it.

Tom seemed to notice, for he drew closer. "You'll have to read it to me," he whispered. "My eyes give me hell in the dark."

Ada swallowed closer, grateful he was with her as she began to read.

The Book of Ruth. Towne of Hope, 1703. Take heed the Sisters Three...

1. And as the Lord hath provided Cherubims at the garden of Eden, so too does the Lord bide them guard his men on earthe. 2. For the Lord hath said, ye should not company together with fornicators or the unclean, for then ye must go out of the world. Those ye knowe corrupt amongst ye must be punished by Council. 3. And ye who are unclean must be bringeth to the earthly altars, so Cherubims may judgeth as the Lord doe judgeth them that are without. 4. Put away therefore from among ye the unclean that the Lord God shall make them clean with hellfire.

Below, there was another part written out in a different handwriting. She cleared her throat and continued.

5. And so sayth the Lord, "Take the unclean mothers to the fields where they shall meet their Judgment by Seraphim and ask that their sons be spared. As Abraham was once tested before God, so too shall the unclean woman. 6. And if the unclean mother lives and her child dies, her sacrifice shall act as her baptism, as she will be spared hellfire. If the child lives and the mother dies, the child is baptized and a child of God. If neither mother nor child lives, their cleansing will be only by hellfire.

She threw the book away from her, an instinctual reaction. Her entire being recoiled, her mouth dry like she'd swallowed ash. "Those words are not of a benevolent God," she whispered, "nor are those creatures angels."

Tom pulled her close. "There is nothing to be learned from the ramblings of the disturbed. Let's put these terrors to rest for the night."

Ada nodded and let him guide her to bed. She slipped under the covers, soothed by the feel of the girls. Tom planted a kiss on her cheek and lingered near the hearth until she drifted off to sleep.

INTERLUDE

New Hope Towne, 1820

The full moon burned low and copper in the evening sky as they dragged the girl up the hill. The cornstalks crackled in the summer wind, and the cicadas screeched, fighting to be heard over the sound of her screams. Amity had been anticipating this moment the entire day, struggling to contain her excitement as she peeked out the window in intervals. Her very first Culling, something she and her siblings only whispered about. It was the day she evolved from a girl into a woman, no longer shielded from their traditions. She felt her mother's comforting hands on her shoulders.

"Reverand Wolcott will be joining us soon," Agatha whispered, her eyes shimmering in the torchlight.

"Will we see the Sisters Three, Mother?"

"Amity Goodeman." Her mother's chastising whisper nipped like the wind. "Take heed of your fervor. We shall not worship false gods, only He. The Sisters Three are simply his angels who enact His Divine Will. We must not let them take from His glory in our minds."

Amity looked down, ashamed. "Please forgive me, Mother."

Agatha nodded and gave her hand a squeeze.

Amity looked up and recognized the girl ahead as the Brannons' daughter from her shock of red hair. She was surprised how quickly the babe in her stomach grew; it seemed almost yesterday she noticed the swell during her errands in town. A flash of sympathy overtook her suddenly, which was quickly followed by the relief that neither she nor her sisters would ever have to endure such a trial. The Culling was reserved for those without the blessing of God's protection and love. The Brannons were outsiders, having just moved to New Hope with others to build the new mill. Amity knew they had been warned what would be required to live and work amongst them, and she discovered later that William Brannon had no qualms regarding the agreement— the Brannons were destitute, and he needed the job. It was quite a different story to witness a culling, however, and Amity's father stayed behind with other council members to ensure there weren't any problems.

With a rumble of hooves, Reverend Wolcott appeared from the shadows, joining the crowd where they stood at Corn Hill. Amity's heart jumped with joy as her mother let out a happy gasp. Directly descended from the man who pioneered their land, the Reverend cut a handsome silhouette in the night, one of strength and power. Radiant beside the rest of the council, the villagers knew his godliness alone allowed their town to flourish, and they treated him accordingly.

The gathered crowd murmured their respectful greetings as they waited for the beloved Reverend to dismount. His footmen assisted, and after his boots had cleanly hit the earth, he marched to the precipice set up for him, his long cloak fluttering in the breeze.

"Good evening, citizens of New Hope!" His voice boomed loud enough that it muffled the young woman's pleading cries. "It is on this fine evening that God has called us to bear witness to one of His great mysteries. We have survived and flourished because we honor those who have come before us. Because we obey our righteous Father, who has gifted us this fair land of bounty. Eve's Daughters must bear the burden of her corruption, and each time a child is conceived, God and God alone must decide if they are worthy of His gifts. The gift of Life. As it has been since my father first arrived in this land, we will await and bear witness to His decision."

"Amen," the crowd said in reply.

The laboring young woman let out another sob, and water immediately poured from her womb, soaking the dirt beneath her.

"It has begun!" Reverend Wolcott called out.

The congregation let out sounds of worshipful jubilation as building bonfire smoke seasoned the air. Amity's stomach growled in response. "Mother, will we roast the pig soon?" she whispered.

"Patience is a virtue, Amity," her mother reminded her.

Amity caught the eye of Sarah Duncan, who had been standing quietly near her own parents, and the girls shared a knowing smile. Their fourteenth birthdays were only a few days apart, and Amity had found comfort knowing she'd share her first culling with another. But now she knew there was nothing to fear.

The men began to drag the Brannons' daughter into the cornfields, and Amity's eye caught the spit pig turning over the fire. They would feast as they waited, a time-honored tradition, while the laboring girl bore her birthing pains alone in the fields. They would celebrate if two came back, spared from God's fury. They would also celebrate if either or both of them died, for that meant their blood soaked the earth, and the Sisters Three would feed.

"Dearest Father, we pray that our sacrifice be accepted into Your merciful hands. That where the blood of Eve soaks the earth, there will be bounty. That your angelic guardians spare us from Your Wrath."

"Amen!"

"Let us now partake in God's bounty as we await His Holy Decree."

The villagers moved in a delightful unison as each family retrieved their prepared dishes from the wagons and placed them around two long tables that had been laid out in preparation. Amity took her seat next to her mother and the other women whose husbands had remained behind to look after the Brennans. It brought Amity such joy to see them all gathered outside of their homes, partaking in the only celebration outside of mass. Cullings were sacred, yes, but they were far from solemn. Their many days of work, fasting, and purity allowed them these days. *God's love is so good*, she thought as the roasted pork melted on her tongue.

The next few hours seemed to fly by as the women seated around her spoke freely amongst themselves, something she had never witnessed before. She was even allowed a sip of the wine passed around the table. *Is this what being an adult is like?*

"John said the Catholics were invading Stanford Towne up north." Her mother told Mrs. Abbott, who sat nearby.

Mrs. Cutler shook her head. "This is why we must keep our traditions. These religions cannot be allowed to undermine all that our fathers have built."

"Hear, hear," Mrs. Abbott replied. She turned to look at Amity. "My, how quickly you have grown."

Mother swelled with pride. "Our Amity is the greatest example of God blessing our most pious. The Council has already arranged her marriage to the finest man a mother could hope for."

Amity couldn't help but steal a glance at Reverend Wolcott, who returned her gaze with a smile. She quickly looked down as warmth rose in her cheeks, but it was too late not to be noticed by the women around her.

Mrs. Cutler let out a gasp. "Is it true?"

Agatha hushed the erupting women at the table with a cluck of her tongue. "Ladies, please. We must not let the uplifted spirits of our celebration distract us from remembering we are proper women of God."

The women immediately hushed, casting their eyes down to their plates in obedience.

"It will be announced soon," Agatha said softly, giving Amity's hand a gentle squeeze.

In the distance, there was a shriek.

"The Sisters..." Amity murmured, struggling to hold back her excitement.

"Is it time already?" Mrs. Cutler wondered aloud.

"That is the quickest birthing we've witnessed in years," another woman remarked.

At the head of the table, Reverend Wolcott stood. "Good townsfolk! Let us now cease our festivities and gather to learn His will."

Cups and plates were left behind as the crowd thickened near the entrance of the cornfield. They grew silent as screams from the Brennans' daughter devolved into the low, guttural moans of a laboring woman's final hour. Amity felt breathless, exhilarated even, as plumes of vapor escaped her mouth. She prayed she would get a glimpse of the Sisters as they came to collect their bounty. Several minutes passed, and neither the mother nor the babe could be heard.

"Mr. Duncan and Dr. Mather," Reverend Wolcott's voice interrupted the silence. "Please verify if the young woman has been spared."

The two men disappeared between the rows of corn. Amity searched the skyline, looking for any sign of gnarled, birch-like limbs. There was a rustling, then the two men returned, Mr. Duncan carrying an unconscious woman in their arms. Blood poured from her onto the ground.

"The woman lives!" Dr. Mather announced. "But the Sisters have taken the babe. God is good!"

"God is good!" The crowd erupted in happiness.

"God is good, indeed," the Reverend echoed. "Put her on the wagon and take her to the doctor's office. Duncan, please let the Council members and family know the mother has survived."

He turned back to face the Congregation. "May you now retire to your homes and sleep well with your bellies full and the promise of a bountiful harvest on your lips. God is good."

"Amen."

Amity watched Reverend Wolcott remount his horse, wondering what it would be like when they were wedded and she mounted behind him. She would soon be the envy of every woman and child in New Hope, and though she knew those were sinful thoughts, she found in them great joy. She smiled to herself as she hurried to catch up to her mother, who walked with the other women back to the village.

Sarah Duncan fell into step beside her. "That poor baby," she said after a pause.

"None of that talk now," Amity hissed. "The baby's soul will be delivered straight to Heaven, and the Sisters Three will have their blood. Our harvest will be bountiful, and our village will continue to thrive. These are all wonderful things."

A flash of fear crossed Sarah's eyes. "Oh yes, of course. I-I didn't mean to imply otherwise."

Amity gave her a curt, but forgiving nod. "I do not feel poorly for any babe offered to the Sisters. They are the lucky ones. In fact, I don't even see the need for the birthing mother. She is simply a house for the Sisters' gift."

Sarah was silent.

"It seems an insult to continue to offer the Sisters the worthless mothers," Amity continued her quiet muttering. "Like rotten potatoes served with spring lamb."

"I hope to be as pious and good as you someday, Amity," Sarah said quietly. "God has blessed you with much of His wisdom."

There was a shriek in the distance, followed by two more.

"Yes," Amity said with a smile, casting a final glance at the woods behind Corn Hill. "God is good, indeed."

CHAPTER ELEVEN
Lori, 1981

Lori continued to stare dumbfounded at the strange woman who called herself Ada Haite. Everything about the situation she currently found herself in was impossible—the roaring fire, the perfectly reconstructed bedroom, the proper Edwardian lady addressing her as if they knew each other. And yet, it was real. It was happening, whether she liked it or not.

"Don't be frightened," Ada said, though her expression did not change. It was as if she wore a mask of her own face, trapped in an empty slate expression like the creepy Halloween masks Lori saw in old photographs. "I am just here to help you. To explain how things work here at Haite Hill. Please, have a seat."

"I-I'd rather stand."

"Suit yourself," Ada said, unmoving. "I shan't keep you long, as I know you must return to your daughters. I've never seen skin that shade before. Such a lovely caramel, like candies."

Lori's cheeks burned with anger. "Look, I don't know who you think you are—"

"Ah, you've discovered my ruse," Ada interrupted calmly. "I must admit, I do like to wear Ada's face. I do not have a body of my own, as do my sisters. Rebecca grew her own, and Theodora was gifted hers through Amity's honorable gift of self-sacrifice. There has yet to be a suitable match for me, so I borrow Ada's visage from time to time. She's not using it anymore, anyway."

"What the hell are you talking about?" Lori demanded. She wanted to run across the room and slap the smug expression right off the woman's face, but her feet felt glued to the floor.

"I will be succinct. We will first require a demonstration of your willingness. Both girls—the young one and the seasoned one, though if you wait too long, we will require a younger one to take her place. We were once offered sacrifices that were too old, and we left them to rot in the stale waters below. You should be grateful we are not so picky now."

Lori found herself speechless. The world around her started to sway as if she'd been drugged, and she struggled to stay focused on what could only be an apparition before her. An apparition or a nightmare.

"You will feed their blood to the fields as is our tradition, or preserve them in the lake as Julianna, your predecessor, has done. How disappointed was I that she proved unsuitable for my needs. But her womb was not marred, you see. Nor Eleanor's, nor Ada's. Yours, however, will be sufficient. Which is why we will require you as a sacrifice as well."

The scent of decay hit the air then, biting at Lori's nose. The illusion of the aptly decorated bedroom began to fade, the fireplace growing cold, the wallpaper peeling, and the rugs starting to fray. It seemed Ada, or what called itself Ada, was fading along with it, as what once presented as supple skin now fell slackly from her facial bones.

"If you do not do as we ask," she continued, "you will become part of the house, like Ada did. And I will use your face regardless." As the last word rolled off her tongue, Lori watched a single drip of blood roll down her forehead to her nose. Then another down her cheek, then another, all coming from an unknown wound at her hairline. The skin of her face slackened further, ruining the upturned muscles of her forced smile. It now appeared like she was scowling.

"We do not know how the house will take you, for there are things unknown even to us. Perhaps it will start with a tooth, or an eye, or your liver. Your spleen. Your tongue. It does not seem to be a pleasant transformation. Rebecca will gather the children for us, regardless. Becky, as you call her. It is best to simply accept and honor our terms, as is the tradition."

Lori stood paralyzed as the room continued to fall back into a ruined state. Her eyes were hopelessly fixated on the woman—the creature—as she spoke through slackening lips. The wound at her hairline slid open into a horrible red grimace, widening as her skin continued to melt from her face. Her hair won the race, however, and her scalp and blonde braid fell back from her head and landed on the ground with a sickening splat. The front of her face followed suit, the bloody musculature staring at Lori with its authentic smile as she swayed, trying not to faint.

Horror screaming from every pore in Lori's body, she understood the creature was once a woman who had been scalped before her facial skin was removed. A part of Lori's mind fought the revelation—*this is only a nightmare like before—Lori, wake up*—but it felt so real. The smell of wet blood, the way the woman opened her lipless smile to shriek, the way she let out a sound similar to the one they heard in the forest. Lori felt her eyes roll back, her body no longer able to stay upright. She hit the ground as the vision faded to black, and all she was left to perceive was the sound of screaming.

For the second time since she arrived at Haite Hill, Lori woke drenched in sweat. This time, she did not pause to shake off the nightmare. Her maternal instincts decided the message—even if it was fictional—was received. After a quick check to make sure both girls still slept soundly, she grabbed her flashlight and raced back to the bedroom. As bad as she felt about sending a young woman home at night during a storm, the creature from her dream made it quite clear that the young woman sleeping nearby was not to be trusted. She'd deal with the question of whether she was really a college student named Becky or some mysterious being called Rebecca Crane later.

Lori pushed open the bedroom door with both hands.

There was no one there. No young woman sleeping in a room that needed renovations, no human-looking thing speaking to her calmly from a four-poster bed. She checked the fireplace and determined it was empty, any leftover ashes long gone cold. She shuddered as she looked over the dark room, remembering the horrible vision of a face melting off its skull. A violent crack of thunder pushed her out of the room.

"Becky?"

She made a quick sweep of the other room, which also turned up empty. Prepared to continue her search below, she nearly fell backward when Nikki met her groggily at the doorway of Kellie's room. "What's wrong?"

Lori forced herself to be calm. "Oh, nothing big. Becky isn't in her room, and I want to make sure she's okay. Just hang with your sister, okay? I'll be right back."

Nikki looked skeptical but let out a yawn as she nodded and shuffled back to bed.

Clear-headed thoughts came back to Lori as she went down the stairs. It had been a nightmare—this house gave her nightmares. She had been listening to whispers of houses since she was a teenager, and this one was no different. It simply had teeth.

Her stomach did a somersault as the thought made her remember the contents of her pocket. *If you do not do as we ask, you will become part of the house, like Ada...*

"Becky?" Lori called again, this time softer. The power was still out, and her flashlight was weak, making navigating the house that much harder. But she continued her search of the first floor as lightning lit up the house in small bursts.

Still no Becky. Every fireplace was out and positioned as they'd left it —not even a candy wrapper had moved. Lori paused in the grand parlor and stared out the dark bay windows, considering her options. If the dream was not prophetic, Lori had still taken the girl under her care for the night. Her leaving was suspicious and potentially could mean something tragic. Even if Becky had just walked back to the hotel and something had happened en route, Lori would've felt responsible. Blurry yellow light caught her eye in the darkness, and suddenly she remembered—Finn.

"Ms. Greene?"

Lori whipped around to see Becky yawning as she fumbled to put on her glasses. She looked every bit a regular nineteen-year-old girl, and suddenly Lori felt very dumb. Her hair was ruffled from sleep, and she was wrapped in one of Lori's camping blankets. She realized Becky had been sleeping in her tent in the study.

"I didn't see you in your room."

Becky smiled sheepishly. "Yeah, the wind scared me. I didn't think you'd mind if I crashed down here. I didn't want to wake you up. Is everything okay?"

"Oh, yeah." Lori's cheeks burned with embarrassment as she scrambled for a story. "I-I just wanted to see if you were still up. I saw the carriage house lights on and wanted to check to make sure Finn is okay." She winced; even as she said it, it sounded ridiculous. And desperate.

Thankfully, Becky seemed to buy it. "Oh yeah, I'll listen for the girls. Can I stay in the tent, though?"

"Of course. I'll be right back."

"Okay, be careful."

Lori hurried out the front door.

She didn't realize she'd forgotten her windbreaker until she was halfway there. The brutal wind battered her face as she jogged, pulling her fully back into her body. The house was getting to her, and she knew it. She almost believed that the poor college student was some demon come to sacrifice her daughters. And now she was stuck having to figure out an excuse for why she was showing up at the door of a man she'd just met in the middle of the night. During a storm.

Generally speaking, she was awkward enough when it came to men in a romantic sense. It was so much simpler when the roles were clearly established—working a job, managing a project. She knew what was expected, and if a guy got weird, well, that was on him. In fact, it took her a full year to realize Sean was into her. She had a strong sense that Finn was trustworthy; she had worked with many guys in her lifetime, and the quality of their character always shone through, whether they liked it or not. But she was pretty sure any man—trustworthy or not—might scratch his head at some woman ranting and raving about nightmares.

She reached the carriage house and paused at the door, still trying to gather her thoughts, when it burst open.

"I saw the flashlight—is everything alright? Jesus, where's your coat?"

"I need you to tell me what the fuck is going on with that house," she blurted out as she walked in, and immediately winced. So much for calm.

Finn frowned. "Are the girls with you?"

"They're still asleep in Kellie's room." Lori felt another blush creep from her cheeks to her chest as Finn shut the door behind her. Her eyes caught the glow of the TV, the picture struggling to stay clear on the screen as service flickered in and out. In front of it was an armchair draped with a rumpled blanket and a table holding a bottle of Jameson and an ashtray. She realized Finn was shirtless, his dark hair unkempt from sleep. Embarrassment burned in her cheeks, and she wrenched her gaze away from his tattooed musculature. "Oh God, I woke you up. I'm so sorry."

He chuckled. "Nah, I told you to come here if you needed something. It's your property, remember? Let me get you a towel and a clean shirt. You're drenched."

Lori's anxiety babbled. "I-I know it sounds stupid, but Becky told us this story and then I had a wicked nightmare... Earlier, I found this old letter written by a woman who lived here, raving about these sisters... I saw you were still up, and I couldn't sleep—"

Finn popped back out with a stack of clean laundry, which he thrust into her arms. "Quit trying to apologize. I'm glad you came over. Here. The bathroom is clean, I promise."

Lori was beyond flustered, but the thought of pulling off the cold, soaking sweatshirt she'd been wearing for two days sounded too wonderful to pass up. She headed into his bathroom, immediately overwhelmed by the scent of his soap and aftershave. The clean shirt he'd handed her also smelled wonderful; a man who was handy, rugged, and took the time to groom himself seemed too good to be true. He had to be a serial killer—it was the only explanation. He was planning to murder her and dump her in the woods somewhere. Feed her to the Sisters Three.

Lori took a deep breath to slow her wild thoughts and faced the mirror. As expected, she looked an absolute mess. She peeled off her sweatshirt and quickly washed her face and under her arms with hand soap. A whore's bath, Janet used to call it. Then she pulled on Finn's shirt, which hung loosely around her curves. She tried not to think about how wonderful it smelled as she began hunting for supplies. After finding a comb, she was able to tame her waves, rendering herself acceptable for a conversation with someone she was finding herself increasingly attracted to, despite the confusing horrors of her current predicament.

She exited the bathroom to find Finn fully dressed and waiting for her in the living area. He'd turned off the TV and lit the fireplace. "I have coffee or booze," he said. "Or both—the drink of my forefathers."

"Irish coffee does sound pretty good," Lori admitted.

"I was hoping you'd say that." Finn darted around his kitchen. "I make a wicked Irish coffee—it's Granddad's favorite. I even have cream that hasn't expired yet. Take a seat wherever."

"Sorry again for disturbing you," Lori said as she settled onto his couch. As time passed, she felt more and more ridiculous for running over to his house after having a nightmare.

"You better quit that apologizing, or I'll send you back out in the rain." He started the coffee maker, and soon the aroma of freshly brewing beans wafted pleasantly through the air.

"This really is a cozy place," she said awkwardly. She was never good at small talk to begin with, and definitely not now.

"Yeah, it's a lot more so without a cranky old man barking orders at you. But Haite Hill has always been home, in different ways. I used to sleep there, you know. When it belonged to Ms. Josephine."

"Oh, really?"

"Yeah, usually when the old man and I were arguing. I'd pitch a tent in the foyer right under that creepy old Mary and Jesus painting on the ceiling. Call me crazy, but it made me feel calm. I feel my grandmother there."

"Your grandmother?"

"Yeah." Coffee and whiskey poured, he added a spoonful of sugar to both mugs, then topped them off with the cream he pulled from his refrigerator. He stirred both and brought one to her. "Sorry I don't have those fancy glass mugs."

"I'm not picky." Lori took it gratefully, taking a generous gulp without pause.

"She was married to the man who built that house," he continued, "before she fell in love with my granddad. Her name was Ada."

Lori nearly spit out her drink. "I'm sorry, what did you say?"

Finn winced. "I'm getting ahead of myself. There's a lot to explain."

Gooseflesh returned to Lori's skin as she stared at the man across from her. "I just had a nightmare about a woman named Ada Haite."

"Ah, so you're seeing her, too... Okay. So what I'm about to tell you is gonna sound really crazy, okay, but please give me a chance to get it all out." Finn took a sip of his drink, as if steadying his nerves. "I'm not the best at explaining things."

Lori followed suit with a generous swallow of her own. "Give it to me straight."

"I probably should start at the beginning," he began. "The man who built Haite Hill was a really nasty guy named Charles. He had three wives—the first two each had one daughter, Josephine and Margaret, before they died. My grandpa worked for Mr. Haite and was supposed to look after the girls, plus Charles's new wife, Ada, when Charles abandoned them here. I think it was in 1910, or something real early like that. Well, Granddad fell in love with Ada, and they ended up having my dad, but not before some crazy stuff happened. Charles ended up dying, and Granddad took in the two daughters—one being your grandma."

"What happened to Ada? Did she pass away here?" Lori asked the question, but wasn't exactly sure she wanted to hear the answer.

"So there is an untold history in these parts—"

"Oh, yes. Becky told us all about it," Lori said with a shudder.

"Wow, okay, so what did she tell you?"

"She told me and the girls the story of the original settlers who froze to death here in the early 18th century. The women who survived were murdered by their leader, whose death remains a mystery."

Finn nodded. "That very bloodshed fed an ancient darkness that already existed here. The second group of settlers who came after were drawn in by it. They believed the words Ruth Alden wrote in her journal. All kinds of crazy shit. Even though they burned it, the Congregation—as they called themselves—thought of it like a newly discovered book in the Bible."

"Like the Mormons."

"Exactly. They rewrote what they supposedly read and claimed it was scripture. They believed God would bless them with prosperity and riches if they followed what it said...which devolved into the ritual sacrifice of young mothers and their children. Whether Ruth actually wrote all that in her journal or the Congregation just said she did, we'll never really know. Ready for a history lesson?"

Lori gave him a weak smile. "It's what I went to school for."

He lit up. "Beautiful *and* smart. Nice."

She took another sip of her drink, tipping her cup up to hide her reddening cheeks.

Finn continued. "Crane's brother, the town's reverend, changed his name to Wolcott to distance himself from his brother and still keep power over the settlers. Under the guidance of the Congregation, who wanted to ensure the religion stayed strong, he married Amity Goodeman, who was related to Theodora Goodeman. That was the name of one of the murdered ladies from the cabin. But it didn't matter—the Congregation's luck wore out. Rumors spread about the town and its creepy cult, and the Reverend fell victim to a 'mysterious illness.'" Finn made quotation marks with his hands. "Then, in 1821, a man called Stanford, who ran the town up north, swept in to take over and build a mill. You with me still?"

Lori nodded.

"Stanford ends the Congregation and renames the town Boston Village. He creates a new organization called The Boston Moral Society —he told everyone it was to create an official cemetery and build a Presbyterian church, but it was really to get rid of that weird Puritan shit. And it worked. The Congregation was forced to either convert or move. The only problem was that the gods the cult worshiped stopped getting fed."

"But Puritans worship God."

Finn set down his mug. "Do you want to see some crazy shit?"

"Sure, why not?" Lori said with a sigh.

Finn stood and walked over to a space behind the fireplace. Lori craned her head, pleasantly surprised to see a little makeshift reading nook. He scanned the books in the bookcase before carefully selecting an old, faded leather book preserved in a special casing. He handed it to her. "Granddad likes to keep things nice," he explained.

Lori took it from him, realizing it was the Geneva Bible, the version the Puritans used as their attempt to purify the King James Version circulating at the time. "I should be wearing gloves," she murmured as she let the book fall open. She was surprised to see that the original pages had been torn out and reglued so that between the Old and New Testaments was a written-out section: *"The Book of Ruth. Towne of Hope, 1703. Take heed the Sisters Three."*

Lori shuddered and looked up at Finn. "I found an old letter in the tower that warned of the Sisters. So they considered them connected to God, like some kind of angels?"

Finn nodded grimly. "Exactly. To appease the Sisters Three meant you appeased God. So while Boston Village thrived and grew during the days of the Ohio & Erie Canal, when it started to decline in 1860, whispers claimed its cause was a lack of faith."

"When, in reality, it was the railroad ending the need for canals."

"I love talking to you." Finn smiled. He looked at her empty cup. "Want another drink?"

"Just coffee this time, please."

"Coming right up."

He rinsed out her mug and filled it with fresh coffee. It seemed the storm had quieted, reduced to a gentle drizzle. It softened Lori's fear of a tree falling on the house and hurting the girls.

"Where was I? Oh yeah, the town going to hell." Finn settled back into his seat. "Okay, so the Congregation members who were left, including old Amity, knew they needed help. Apparently, she petitioned the Sisters—no one really knows how, but we can all guess—and Charles Haite arrived in town like he had been summoned from Heaven itself. Haite buys the mill from the Stanfords, convinces lawmakers to run the railroad through the valley, and turns Boston Village into a company town. He also built your house for his first wife, Julianna."

"My great-grandparents."

Finn nodded. "And guess who eventually becomes best friends?"

"Julianna and Amity," Lori murmured, staring at the cup in her hands. She was quiet for a moment. "I found a letter from Eleanor in the tower. It was stuck in one of the old books. She said the town called Julianna the Saint of Orphans for her work running an orphanage out of her house. But Eleanor thought she was murdering them. Now I know why..." She took a sip. "It's horrid to think I'm related to such a monstrous woman."

"Well, I was gonna save that part for the end, but that's not *quite* correct."

Lori met his eyes.

"Josephine owned the house, but she's not your true grandmother. You don't come from Julianna. You come from Eleanor. Eleanor's daughter, Margaret, is your grandmother."

Lori blinked. "Eleanor, the woman who wrote the letter?"

Finn nodded.

"That doesn't make any sense. Why wouldn't Josephine just say she was my great-aunt when she gave me the house? That shouldn't make a difference in anything."

"...and that brings me to what is wrong with Haite Hill. It's important that the house stays in your family to protect... How open are you to the supernatural?"

A piercing shriek rang out from the woods.

"The girls." Lori jumped to her feet.

"Wait, I'll come with—" Finn started, but she was already out the door.

CHAPTER TWELVE
Ada, 1910

Ada's eyes drifted open to greet a soft and pleasant darkness. Slumbering soundly beside her were both girls, slips of white lace from their nightgowns peeking out over the blankets. She looked across the room to see Tom snoring in an armchair by the fireplace as the coal's dying embers flickered into tendrils of smoke. Although the previous night's events left her with an uneasiness that stubbornly clung to her bones, she smiled when she recalled the way Tom's gentle hands caressed her. With all the terror surrounding her, he was a shining beacon in the storm. He and the girls.

She slipped out of bed to peek out the window. The turbulent weather had passed, leaving behind a sparkling blanket of snow that coated every lonely branch and bulbous bush. The rising sun created a portrait of winter splendor.

Not wanting to wake Tom, she decided to dress herself and greet the help before they came to her room. She went to the bathroom to wash and fragrance her skin, then pinned her hair into a quick chignon. She donned a simple day outfit—blouse, wool skirt, and winter stockings—then dabbed her wrists with violet perfume. She paused for one final examination in the mirror when she realized with a start that one of her teeth had fallen out.

Alarmed, her tongue sought and found the gum socket and was shocked to discover she felt no pain. She looked down at her toes, still aware that although she'd kept her feet covered by stockings, her toenail was still missing. A slow feeling of dread coursed through her body. *What was happening to her?*

Ada pushed away from her vanity and stood, preparing to head down the stairs to the kitchen, when she heard the sound of footsteps above. She froze, but it was not coming from the tower—it was coming from the third-floor nursery. Perhaps one of the maids had risen early and thought to get a start on the chores, she told herself, desperate for a logical explanation to yet another odd occurrence.

She debated whether or not she should wake Tom, but she felt it best if he stayed near the girls in case they woke. She gathered her wits about her, trying not to think of the strange Bible verses and bloody monsters, and left the room. After all she had seen and experienced, she could handle whatever was thrown her way. She was mistress of Haite Hill, after all.

As Ada grew closer, she heard gentle, hurried footsteps tap above, almost like the happy feet of small children. She frowned. She didn't know any of the maids were mothers, and even so, she couldn't imagine anyone bringing children to the manor during such heavy snowfall. If it had been this morning, she would have heard their arrival.

Ada reached the stairwell and began to climb. "Hello?" she called softly.

The footsteps stopped.

"Hello? I am Mrs. Haite..."

Ada reached the short, third-floor corridor. To the left, two doors led into a large nursery, and to the right, there was one door to the nanny's room, a space no bigger than a modest closet. All three were shut, which cloaked the hall in total darkness. Ada felt along the wall for the first door, and when the smooth iron of the handle found her skin, she turned it.

"Hello—"

Like her experience in the tower, the room had been altered. The nursery she stood in was not the girls' as she remembered it, but entirely remade. The room was the size of the grand parlor and halved by a set of swing doors, with the first part set up like a sitting area with chairs near the fireplace and bins holding the playthings of children. But behind the separating doors, where Jospehine and Maggie once slept in a grand four-poster bed with fluffy pillows and quilts, were several old cribs and child-sized beds. There were no rugs or open windows, and though the wood floors were swept, the stench of excrement and sickness lingered. The repugnance caused her to jump back, but she found her footing as two small children appeared before her, seemingly out of thin air.

"Sorry for waking you, Ms. Ada."

"How–what—"

Both children wore tattered clothing, hanging from bodies ravaged by an unknown sickness. Behind them, other malnourished children lay in their beds, a few bundled infants nestled in the cribs. All around the room was equipment and the tinctures used by hospital doctors, but there were no nurses in attendance.

"What is the meaning of this—"

"Now, children, you must leave Ms. Ada be. She has plenty to do before this month's Culling."

Ada's mouth dropped open.

Standing before her was none other than Julianna Haite.

The raven-haired, hook-nosed woman ushered the children back into their beds before securing the double doors behind them. "I apologize for the noise. They are not permitted to leave their beds until I fetch them, but you know how children can be."

Ada struggled to make words. Of all the things she had experienced at Haite House, this shook her down to the bone. She wasn't sleepwalking this time—she felt fully conscious and in her body, which had succumbed to trembling. She tried not to gape at the dead first wife of her husband as she flitted around the room, drawing back the shades and tending to the fireplace. As if it were the most natural thing in the world.

There was no question of the woman's identity—before her was the exact replica of the portrait hanging in the Haites' Cleveland manor. The same tight lips, the same dark velvet green dress. The cold, dark eyes only softened by a child's innocence in Josephine.

"J-Julianna Haite?" Ada finally managed. "I-I thought you were dead."

"Of course I am. Please, do sit." Julianna settled into an upholstered armchair and gestured to the one across from her. "We have much to discuss. How is my daughter? Is she well?"

Ada fell helplessly into the chair. "What is happening?" she whispered.

"Oh, come now, you cannot be so surprised. Have you not experienced enough to understand what is happening to you?"

Ada swallowed, but her mouth had gone dry. "Forgive me. It is still quite a shock."

"I understand," Julianna said, though her expression was not understanding. "I will need you, however, to gather your wits about you and listen to what I have to say. Do you believe you can manage to do so?"

Ada nodded.

"Charles has the brains for business, but he does not have them when required to find a suitable mate. Besides myself, of course. I had high hopes for the wife before you, but her 'brilliant ideas' fell short."

"Eleanor."

"This means it now falls into your hands. You cannot let us down."

"You and the children in the nursery? In the lake?"

Julianna grew still, her expression sharpening. The look in her eyes caused a shiver down Ada's spine. "You have seen the children in the lake?" Her voice was acidic.

"Yes," Ada said quietly, her face draining of color.

"I did try to stop it all, you know." The late Mrs. Haite pulled her gaze away from Ada and looked out the window. "They would have ruined us—the entire Haite fortune, lost to the wind. Though little good it does me now."

Ada wasn't sure how to respond. She watched as Julianna stood and walked to a cabinet along the wall. From a thin drawer, she retrieved a book of matches and a half-smoked cigar.

"Forgive my indulgence. Bad habits seldom absolve, even in death." Julianna stuck the stub between her teeth and lit the match.

This can't be real, Ada thought, even as plumes of cigar smoke filled the room. It was merely a convincing dream—perhaps someone was smoking tobacco near where she slept. *Tom, wake me, please.*

"What do you know of the Congregation?" Julianna asked as she settled back into her chair, smoldering tobacco in hand.

Ada thought of the old Bible she'd found with Tom and its strange verses. "I know nothing of what you speak," she half-lied.

"The Congregation settled in this land long before anyone else," Julianna explained. "But rumors had spread to neighboring towns of their rather unconventional practices, and when the Standfords swept in to reclaim it as Boston Village, the fellowship was forced to disband. The Sisters were violently displaced."

The Sisters... Every hair along Ada's skin stood erect as it all finally came together. "Those ghastly demons in the woods?" she sputtered.

Julianna nodded. "The Sisters Three."

Ada squeezed her eyes shut, trying not to envision the screaming, bloody mouths looming over her like evil, twisted trees. She couldn't understand how any religious group could revere such creatures.

"The Congregation was forced to find a way to practice in secret to appease them. A descendant of one of the founding fathers, Dr. Mathers, posed as an abortionist. Young, unwed women traveled for miles to receive his procedure. It is the lifeblood the Sisters thirst for, you see. It is only found in infants and young children, though they've been known to take them older when in desperation. It worked for a time, but the Sisters eventually grew tired of consuming birthing waste and demanded more. The Congregation was unable to provide lest they be caught, and the town fell into ruin." Julianna took a long drag from her cigar and swept the fallen ash from the ruffles of her dress with her finger. Without any windows open, the air quickly grew dense with its smog.

"The Stanfords eventually moved on, but our Charles came to the rescue. By now, you should well know of his greed. He saw this location for the goldmine it was, so he bought it for next to nothing, agreeing to let the Congregation bring the old religion back. You see, he, too, had heard the rumors and wanted the Sisters' favor. As his dutiful wife, it was up to me to ensure the sacrifices resumed as before. In return, I could build this beautiful home and do whatever I wished with it." She leaned forward, her dark eyes burning. "You must understand how appealing this was for me and how desperate I was to be rid of high society, of Charles and his *ways*. My heart holds love for him, as all wives have for their husbands, but I am not made to be some man's counterpart. I was destined for more. So I agreed."

"You sacrificed the children," Ada whispered.

Julianna pulled from her cigar. "At first, I tried by using the maids, drowning them in the lake. But they were too old, and the Sisters were unimpressed. They sent a wildfire in response that destroyed Charles's newly constructed mill, killing dozens of workers and costing him thousands. Naturally, he was furious, and, naturally, he took out his anger upon me... That was when I met Amity Goodeman."

Ada recalled the ancient, pipe-puffing woman she'd met in town. It was not difficult to picture the two of them as friends.

"Amity was one of the Congregation's long-standing members. A strong, proud woman whose qualities she saw reflected in me. She suggested we open a children's home at Haite Hill for the mill orphans, which I found strange until I realized what she intended for me to do. We'd also take in the sickly children from the city orphanages, as a healing country retreat... It was the perfect plan. The sickly orphans were gladly given, and they were nearly ready to die, so I thought nothing of offering them to the Sisters. I gave them baneful herbs, grown right in our conservatory, to put them into a deep sleep. They felt no pain, even as they drowned. Their deaths were merciful."

Ada closed her eyes as nausea bit. *Those poor children.*

"Yet still, murder is a sin, and for it, I am trapped for all eternity in this house as my punishment. I will never feel the warmth of the Creator nor see my Josephine, or the two sons I left behind."

Ada fought the urge to tell her she deserved every moment of suffering.

"The sacrifices did not matter," Julianna continued. "The Sisters were insatiably greedy—they wanted more. More than I could give without raising suspicion. During this time, I occasionally returned to our Cleveland residence to fulfill my duties as a wife while Amity ran the orphanage in my stead. Once, I came back with Josephine growing in my womb. How they discovered what I did not even know is beyond my imagination, but they demanded I offer my infant to them as a sign of my devotion. Amity explained that I must endure the pain of childbirth alone in the fields, as is their ancient custom, feeding the crop with lifeblood. The Culling, she called it. You see, although I provided for them, I was not officially part of the Congregation, and all pregnant women must be tried before them."

Nausea firmly seized Ada's stomach.

Julianna ground her cigar nub into the table next to her. "I tried everything to dissuade them. And that was when the solution came. You see, the Sisters long to move about this world as we do. Rebecca was able to manifest a human form beyond the horrible, bloody visages you've seen—you know her now as a young girl. But the other two cannot. At some point throughout her life, Amity gifted her body to Theodora, a heartfelt self-sacrifice. The human has long since died, but her body lives on. Ruth, however, was never able to find a worthy vessel like her sister. She remained without a face, and it caused her great agony. So I offered her mine."

In the distance, Ada heard a woman's voice.

"Kellie?"

"Who is that?"

"Ignore her, she is not of our time. The veils that separate us are thin, and we do not have much time. You must listen to me."

"Kellie!"

"The Sisters accepted my offering, and I was allowed to keep my child," Julianna spoke more quickly. "As soon as I had their blessing, I stole away to the city, where I birthed Josephine and left her with a nanny named Eleanor. When I returned to Haite Hill, Ruth tried to take my body as discussed, but it was a failure. You see, she is barren, and I was not. Unbeknownst to us, she needed a perfect match. I died during the attempted transition, and the Sisters grew so incensed that they released from the skies the heaviest rains this land has ever seen. The river flooded and devastated the town."

"Kellie! Where are you?"

"After my death, Charles hurried to marry Josephine's poor nanny," Julianna continued, "whom he impregnated immediately. He moved her here with my daughter—a double offering for the Sisters." Her eyes went dark. "The Sisters tried to convince her to give up her child willingly, but Eleanor is a different breed of woman. Wise beyond her years and unable to be persuaded, she feigned insanity, writing letters to newspapers and threatening to expose the Congregation. Charles was mortified, and his solution was to send her away to an asylum. Which brings us to you. Wife number three."

Although her cigar had long been extinguished, the room felt different, like all the air had been choked from it. Ada's vision wavered, the furnishings fading in and out like the flickering of light as distant screams echoed from beyond. She looked at the door that separated them from the children, seized by the sudden urge to open it and free them all.

"Have you birthed a child yet?"

"N-no. I care for my—your daughter. And Eleanor's."

"Woman, listen to me," Julianna said sharply.

Ada struggled to keep focus. It was as if the room—the world around her—was rejecting her, like a stomach heaving out spoiled pork. Pressure squeezed her head and chest, demanding she leave.

"The Sisters are starving, and Charles knows it. They will ruin him. That is why you've been left here. To sate them. If you have a child in your womb, they will demand it. They will demand my daughter, too."

"I will not give my children to those horrid creatures," Ada gasped, trying to sound firm as she fought for air. "I am not like you."

Julianna merely smiled. "Then you must find and release Eleanor. Before she was sent away, she forged an amendment to Charles's will—she has full guardianship over the girls in the event of his passing. The documents in his Cleveland safe are blank. His actual will is here, in his desk drawer. I know you have the key."

Ada climbed to her feet, determined to flee no matter how badly she trembled. "I must leave this room..."

"Woman, listen to me! I am telling you there is a way out. Find and save Eleanor. When she is released, be rid of Charles. Eleanor can take the girls far away from this place."

"I must go—"

Julianna leapt to her feet. "Do you not hear me, you stupid girl? Josephine cannot die by their hand! Or she will never find rest. All who are killed by the Sisters are cursed to be trapped here. We are all trapped by their pain."

The world began to sway, turning upside down, then right side up again as Ada remained planted firm, like someone was spinning a painting before her. A sound roared in her ears like a train as an invisible vise grip clenched her, digging into her bones. She thrust her body against the door. "Where is Eleanor?" she gasped.

"The Cleveland State Asylum."

Ada bolted upright.

Her heart hammered her ribs, the pumping blood muffling out all else from her ears. Her eyes flitted back and forth as she took in her surroundings. She was still in bed. It was daybreak. The girls slumbered soundly beside her. It had been a nightmare after all.

And yet...she was fully dressed in her day clothes.

Confused and relieved to be firmly planted back in reality, she slipped out carefully from beneath the blankets. She promptly gasped, realizing a small pool of blood had gathered on the bedding. Josephine's eyes shot open.

"I don't feel right, Ms. Ada..." The girl looked down to see the blood beneath her, spotting her nightgown, and promptly shrieked. "Am I dying?"

Ada quickly figured out what was happening and hurried to her side. "Hush now, Josephine, it is nothing to fret over. You are a woman now, is all."

Tom appeared at the door, breathless. "Is everything alright?"

Ada adjusted the blankets to conceal the spot. "Yes, she just had a nightmare, is all."

Tom let out a deep breath. "You women will soon be the death of me. I found you this morning, collapsed in the third-floor stairwell. I thought you were sleepwalking, so I carried you back to bed. And now poor Miss Jo."

"How are the roads, Mr. Garvey? Do you think they are suitable for travel into the city?"

A moment of confusion flashed over his face before he replied. "The storm has passed, and the sun is slowly making work of the snow. I can't say I trust the Model T down the hill, however. Do you have errands to run, ma'am?"

"Perhaps we can borrow a horse-drawn carriage from someone in town, then, so that we may get to the nearest train station. It is imperative that the girls and I go to Cleveland immediately."

"To visit Mr. Haite," Tom said loudly as he met her eyes.

"Yes, and I wish it to be a surprise." Ada raised her voice as well, playing along.

"Very good, then, ma'am. I will see to fetching a proper carriage for your travels and plan to accompany you as an escort."

"And please tell one of the housemaids to come here with fresh linens," she added.

"Will do, ma'am. See you soon." A smile twitched beneath his mustache before he was off, as if knowing that any immediate danger had passed and he could fondly recall their night together.

"Please don't tell anyone about my predicament," Josephine whispered from beside her.

Ada kissed her forehead. "I shall say it was from me."

"Are we really visiting Father?"

"Good morning."

Ada jumped at the voice which came from the body of a young girl, but was not of a young girl at all. She clutched Josephine close.

"Josephine, how are you feeling today?" Rebecca Crane stood in the doorway, wearing a smile that made Ada's skin crawl. She recalled the moment by the fire, when the shadows created otherworldly voids for her eyes, and she cursed herself for not seeing Rebecca clearly for what she was before.

"Your services are no longer needed here," Ada told her coldly.

"Maggie," Rebecca called in a saccharine coo. "Come here, sweet child."

Maggie stirred from beside Josephine, but she grabbed her sister and held her tight. Ada added another reinforcing arm, realizing Josephine saw Rebecca for what she was, too.

"Aw, come now, sweet babe. You don't want to sit in your sister's blood, however sweet it is."

"Be gone from this place, you vile thing!" Ada commanded with a rage she'd never summoned before.

"I'll see you soon, Adaaaa," Rebecca sang as her jaw fell open wide.

The girls cried and pushed their terrified bodies into Ada as Rebecca's jaw continued to fall, pulling at the skin of her face until it ripped and the bone clattered to the floor. Her stomach spilled open as well, pouring pulpy innards onto the floor with a rude splash. The girls screamed, and Ada squeezed her own eyes shut, willing with all her might that the horrid creature be gone.

"Ms. Ada? Is everything okay?"

It took everything in Ada to snap herself back into pleasant formalities, but she succeeded. "Yes, Mary. The girls saw a rat. I will have Mr. Garvey set out traps while we're gone."

"Gone, ma'am?"

Ada rocked Maggie in one arm and hugged Josephine with the other, caressing her hair until she settled. "Yes. I'm taking Ms. Josephine and Miss Margaret on a day trip before the next winter storm. Rebecca will no longer be in our employ, so in her stead, I'll need you to set out clean, warm attire for both girls and me. I will also need our bedding changed."

"Yes, ma'am."

"Come, girls, let's have a bath before breakfast," Ada said gently.

She'd calmed them both down and gotten them settled into the tub when she realized her pinky finger was missing.

CHAPTER THIRTEEN
Lori, 1981

Screams like the ones in her dreams propelled Lori's limbs into a full sprint toward the house. It was all becoming too much—they would leave this hellish place first thing in the morning, storm or no storm. Haite Towne, Haite Hill, Haite whatever the fuck—they could all rot for all she cared. It was time to go back to New York.

She shoved open the front door to greet a dark and quiet home. "Nikki?" she called. "Becky?"

She slipped off her shoes and hurried up the stairs, leaving the door open for Finn, who she knew would eventually follow after her. Halfway up the stairwell, she realized she'd left her flashlight behind, its absence forcing her to squint in the shadows. She tried to suppress her rising worry as she trudged down the corridor, eager to find the girls safe and sound.

She reached Kellie's door and peeked her head in. As she hoped, both girls were still snoring in their sleeping bags on Kellie's bed. She let out a deep sigh of relief. Downstairs, there came a gentle knock on the frame of the front door.

"Everything okay?" Finn called softly.

Lori jogged back down to meet him at the foyer. "Yes, please come in. Sorry for running off like that. And re-dampening your clean shirt."

He shrugged it off. "I have plenty."

"Becky's set up in the study, but there are chairs already set up in the ladies' parlor if you want to sit." Lori pointed to the front room on her right.

Finn chuckled. "Never thought of myself as a lady, but I'm happy to talk anywhere you want."

They headed into the parlor, and through the window, Lori saw the storm had finally stopped. Slivers of light broke through the clouds, letting her know it was daybreak. "Looks like we made it," she remarked.

"Well, for the moment," Finn said as he fell into one of the fancy Victorian chairs. He admired it for a moment, running his hands down the wood, before he continued. "Another one's gonna hit later tonight. Ed says it's gonna be worse. You know, you ought to take the girls down to Carl's. Haite Hill can withstand any storm, but we're gonna get some pretty wicked wind. Better to be safe than sorry."

"That's a good idea. I'll tell the girls when they wake up." She took the chaise across from him, suddenly exhausted after the burst of adrenaline. "Sorry, I don't have any yummy beverages to offer you in return. I'm so damn tired. It's making it hard to process everything you just told me."

"Eh, don't worry. I'll let you copy my paper when you take the Boston Village history test." Finn popped another grin.

"Okay, so my grandmother is Maggie," she said, resuming their conversation. "Which means the madwoman who wrote the letter, Eleanor, was my great-grandmother."

"Correct."

"And both my grandmother, Maggie, and her sister, Josephine, were adopted by your grandparents."

"Yup," Finn said. "We were fated to meet."

Lori looked down at her dirt-streaked hands, then back up at Finn. "Well, since we are practically family, I'm gonna insist that you and my step-granddad resume your jobs as ground keepers."

Delight danced in Finn's pale green eyes. "Granddad is gonna be thrilled."

"I'd love to talk to him if I can," Lori said. "Ask him about my grandmother and maybe get some insight into who Eleanor was."

Finn perked up like he had an idea. "I'll tell you what—you get the girls ready, and I'll grab us a couple of coffees to go. We'll go down to Carl's for breakfast, and you can talk to Granddad. He's as old as dirt, but he's much better at explaining things than I am. Carl makes a mean pancake and puts my omelets to shame."

"Sounds good."

Finn stretched and stood. "Well, I'd call our first night together a success. Looking forward to our second breakfast date."

Lori smiled, charmed by him despite herself. Finn was good-looking, of course, in that rugged, unkempt sort of way, but he also had the type of energy that put her at ease. Like no matter what, things were going to be okay. She never realized how badly she needed that in her life. "See you in a few."

Finn headed out, and she walked back up to the second floor, slower this time. She hit the landing and learned Nikki was already up and moving around.

"Morning." Lori greeted her as she walked into Kellie's Pepto Bismol room. "How did you sleep?"

"Fine, but I kept having weird dreams."

Goosebumps spread up Lori's arms as she remembered her own. "Oh, yeah? Me too. Becky's story got to me, I think."

"Yeah, but this one was different. I had a dream that I was trapped in the basement, like I was locked in there while it was storming. The water kept rising and rising, but no one would let me out—"

"I want pancakes," Kellie interrupted.

They both turned to see she'd bolted upright in bed, appearing to be half-asleep with her braids askew.

"Well, good morning," Lori said as she went over to fix her hair.

Nikki shook her head. "I swear all you think about is food."

"Lori, can we get pancakes?"

"Actually, yes. Finn invited us for breakfast at the hotel we went to yesterday. The storm passed, so we can walk there," Lori said. "Pretty sure the pick-up is still dead."

Kellie wiggled out of her sleeping bag and bounded toward the door.

"Wait—I need you both to pack your backpacks for a night."

"Wait, why?" Nikki made a face.

"We're gonna stay at the hotel for a night or two."

Kellie immediately stomped her foot in protest. "I don't want to stay at that stinky hotel. I want to stay here in my pink room!"

"It's going to storm again tonight, so I was thinking we'd stay there until it passes," Lori told her gently. "I highly doubt your dad will be in any rush to come back. Especially on a weekend. We'll have plenty of chances to stay here."

"I don't want to stay at that hotel either," Nikki said, crossing her arms. "I don't see why we can't just stay here. We were fine last night, and the lights are back on."

Lori gave her a look. "You were sleeping, but the wind was insane. It's gonna be worse tonight. We were lucky to get through last night, so let's not tempt the Fates."

"I want extra pancakes, then. With chocolate chips."

"Deal."

"Morning." Becky appeared in the doorway, looking impossibly fresh-faced for a night spent in a tent. Lori felt another wave of embarrassment for thinking she was anything other than a pleasant college girl. "Feels like it's getting warm out there. Must be all that sun."

"We're getting pancakes," Kellie informed her.

"Oh, that sounds good. My aunt Carl makes breakfast every morning at the hotel. Is that where we're headed?"

Lori nodded. "Just give me a few to pack up the girls, and we'll all go down together. Finn is coming, too."

Lori hurried to help the girls unpack their school bookbags and fill them with their toiletries and a change of clothes. Then she took a moment to dip into one of the bathrooms to make herself presentable with a fresh pair of denim cut-offs and a t-shirt. It seemed the cold front responsible for creating the windstorms still had yet to arrive, but she wrapped a clean sweatshirt around her hips just in case.

"Make sure you bring your windbreakers," Lori called to the girls as she searched her bag for mascara and lip gloss. "It's warm now, but that cold front will blow in before we know it."

Kellie had come prepared for whatever with her pink rainboots, but Lori had to fish out a pair for Nikki. Luckily, she'd packed both her hiking and rain boots, which she handed to her. Then they strapped on their backpacks and greeted an unusually warm spring morning.

Although it looked post-apocalyptic outside with fallen tree branches and broken corn stalks strewn across the lawn, the sun was a welcome reprieve after such a cold, rainy evening. Lori was grateful for its presence; sunshine made it seem like everything was normal—no more nightmarish screaming and things with melting faces.

Finn met them outside the carriage house, holding two travel mugs of coffee. He'd also freshened up, now wearing a fresh t-shirt with his dark, wavy hair combed back from his forehead. He handed a mug to Lori as they all exchanged hellos. "This one's booze-free," he promised her with a wink.

"Isn't there an easier way to get down there?" Nikki asked, eyeing their impending woodland descent.

"'Fraid not," Finn said. "But there are plenty of branches to hang onto and rocks jutting out to stop you from sliding. It'll be fun, like skiing."

"Kellie, hold my hand," Lori instructed her before she took off like a bat outta hell.

"But what if I wanna slide by myself?"

"Absolutely not. You will poke your eyes out with these branches. I scratched mine once when I was your age."

"Oh yeah, pokes in the eye hurt like hell," Finn confirmed, and Lori felt Kellie's little hand slip into hers.

They started down the hill as the light peeked through the branches. As graceful as Nikki was by nature, she seemed unsteady as she tried to maneuver the sloping path, and Lori grabbed her with her other hand. Now, if Lori slipped, they'd all be doomed, but she trusted her hiking boots. They had yet to let her down.

"I did tell Seth I want a driveway laid, but of course, it's gotta dry up first," she told the slip-sliding party around her, but everyone was too focused on their skidding feet to reply. Finally, they reached the pavement, where they met an ear-splitting chorus of chirping frogs.

"What's that sound?" Kellie yelled.

Finn laughed. "Those are peepers! We have a ton down here because of all the swampy marsh."

She clamped her hands over her ears, but she looked excited. "They're so loud! Can I catch some?"

"After breakfast, I can take you," Becky offered from beside her. "I'm the best frog catcher around."

Lori smiled at them before she looked ahead, and was instantly disheartened. The wind had done worse work here, causing an entire tree to block half the road. From the looks of it, it had fallen from her yard. She groaned—another expense to add to the list.

"Don't worry, the Wheatley brothers will take care of it," Finn said as he caught up to her. "It's blocking the road to their barn, but to be honest, they love any excuse to break out the chainsaws."

"Charming."

They reached the bottom of the hill and only walked a short distance down the main street when Carl came out onto the porch. "Well, aren't y'all a sight for sore eyes," she called. "What a motley crew! I see you survived the storm."

"Just barely. The electricity took a shit," Finn told her as they approached the hotel.

"Good thing he went up there to rescue you." Carl slid Lori a sideways smile. "Hi, sweetheart," she greeted her niece.

"Hey, Auntie Carl. Want me to help with breakfast?"

Before she could reply that she'd already cooked it, the smell of food wafted through the air and hit their nostrils. Kellie scurried inside without further prompting.

"I figured ya'll would be coming down here hungry and wanted to have it ready," Carl explained.

"Thank you so much. Actually, we're gonna need a room or two as well, if you can spare it," Lori said. "Just for tonight. Finn said the next storm is going to be even worse than last night—"

"Oh, absolutely," Carl said. "You're making the right choice not to chance it. Haite House is solid, but who can pass up hot water and electricity?"

"Thank you so much. For everything."

"Hey, Comfort!" Carl yelled up the stairs. "Get two rooms set up for Lori Greene and her girls. And come down and get their bags!"

"I'm coming, I'm coming!" came his reply. "It's too early for you to be hollering like that."

"Too early, or you drank too many beers last night?"

Lori and Finn walked into the dining room, where a little buffet had been set up along the bar. Kellie had already created a towering pancake pile on her plate, and she wavered as she tried to get to the table where her sister sat without them toppling over.

Lori topped off her travel mug with fresh coffee and then helped herself to the vat of oatmeal. "Where's your granddad?" she asked Finn as he plated himself some sausage and eggs.

"Probably still upstairs. He'll be down in a few for a coffee and a smoke."

Lori slid into the open chair at the girls' table. From the window, she could see dark blue storm clouds fighting with their soft white counterparts, creating crisscross patterns with the sunlight that broke through them both. Though Lori had managed to shake off the dread from her nightmare, what Finn told her about the town still clawed at the corners of her mind. It was hard to imagine such a beautiful valley, full of sparkling waters and towering trees, could hold such dark secrets, but considering how America itself came to be, it was no surprise. No wonder the people from neighboring cities called this place Hell Town. You could feel it.

After a few tasteless mouthfuls of overcooked oats, Lori put down her spoon. She debated drenching her bowl with Kellie's syrup, but found she had no appetite. She could hear her dad now, reminding her that humans are not meant to survive on coffee and beer alone.

"What's up with you?"

Lori looked up to see Nikki staring at her. "Oh, nothing," she lied, taking a sip of coffee. "Hey, we should try calling your dad later on the hotel phone."

"I don't want Daddy to come yet," Kellie said, her cheeks full of pancakes. "I like it here."

"Well, we should check in with him at least."

A door slammed behind them, causing Lori to jump. She turned to see Finn's granddad shuffling down the stairs and straight to the front porch. "Hey, Nikki, I'm gonna go talk to Finn's grandpa about the house, can you—"

"Watch your sister? Yes."

"Or I can," Becky said across the room, forking up the last of her pancakes. "We still gotta catch those peepers."

"Oh yes, that's right," Lori said, remembering earlier. "Thanks so much, Becky."

Kellie excitedly bounded over to where Becky collected her empty dishes. Nikki, clearly thrilled to be let off the hook, stood as she pulled her Walkman out of her bag.

"I'm gonna go sit by the river."

"Okay, be careful,"—Lori looked from daughter to daughter—"both of you."

Finn crossed her path to the coffee pot. "He'll be a lot more pleasant to talk to if we bring him coffee," he explained as he filled a fresh mug.

Lori nodded, suddenly nervous. She wanted answers, but she was afraid to receive them just the same. They headed out to the front porch, and Lori shivered. The temperature was starting to drop after all; the sweatshirt and jackets had been a good call.

"Morning, Granddad," Finn announced their presence cheerfully. "I got your coffee. Black as your soul. This here is Lori, remember? Lori Greene. She owns Haite House now."

"I know who the hell she is," the old man erupted. "Her last name isn't Greene, either—it's Byrne. Eleanor Byrne was one of my favorite people in this godforsaken world."

Finn gave Lori a sheepish look.

"Why are you bothering me?" the old man demanded from behind his wall of cigarette smoke. Lori tried not to enjoy the smell. If there was any time to pick up the old vices, it was now.

"Well, Grandad," Finn said carefully, "I was thinking you could tell her about Grandma."

"Why don't you tell her?"

"Why you always gotta give me shit?"

"Because you deserve it."

Finn shook his head before he turned to Lori. "Grandma mysteriously disappeared one night, and Granddad says he went out looking for her. He found an infant swaddled on the steps of Haite House—my dear old dad. Grandma was nowhere to be found. I always thought she'd run off, but eventually they told me the truth..." He trailed off.

"What?" Lori asked, thrown off by his nervousness.

"She, uh. She—

"Oh, spit it out, will ya?" the old man croaked.

"She became the house," Finn finally blurted. "That's why we've been caring for it all these years."

"What do you mean, she became a part of it? Like a ghost?"

"You're not telling it right," Tom grumpily interjected.

"Then you tell her! Jesus, Mary, and Joseph, that was the whole point."

Tom turned to face Lori, and she saw what was probably once a set of lovely green eyes like his grandson's now filmed over by cataracts. "She's a part of the house now. Absorbed."

"What do you mean *absorbed?*" Lori nearly laughed before she thought of the teeth and the horrifying rug. The words from her nightmare rudely resurfaced. *"If you do not do as we ask, you will become part of the house, like Ada..."*

She took a step back, jolted to her core. "Wait, so my dream was real?"

"What dream?" Finn asked, concerned.

Lori struggled to control her building distress. "I had a nightmare last night before I came to your house. A creature—one of those *Sisters* or whatever was dressed up like your grandmother, Ada. They said... they said..."

Finn's eyes widened.

"They said if I do not give them the girls, then I will become part of the house, like her," Lori whispered. "That horrible man—Samuel Crane—scalped those women, Finn. During the snowstorm. And he ripped off one of their faces. She told me if I don't give them the girls, they'll kill me and use my face regardless."

Gone was any trace of playfulness in Finn.

"That can't be right. Ada would have told me." Tom smashed his cigarette out. "Boy, you take me up there right now, you hear me?"

"I can't, Granddad. That hill is a mud slick."

"Dammit, boy! Unless…" A strange look crossed over the old man's face. "She knows I'm going to die. And she wants to die with me."

"What do you mean—"

All around them, it went dark like someone had flipped a switch. Lori looked out from behind the porch screens to see that the rain clouds had won the battle in the skies, smothering any hope of sun. Thunder rumbled as it approached, letting them know another nasty storm was blowing in.

"Guess she's coming early." Carl came out to the porch. "Finn, help me pull these chairs inside."

"Shit, the girls are out there."

"I'll help you get them," Finn offered, hurrying to grab the rocking chairs around where Tom sat and hoist them into the hotel.

"Come on, Tom," Carl said, touching his shoulder. "Let's get you inside."

"Nonsense," he huffed. "I'm about to die. I'll do it as I wish." With one still lit, he fished another cigarette out of his pocket.

Finn shrugged at the look Carl tossed his way.

"Don't look at me. He doesn't listen to me either."

Lori opened the screen door and stepped off the porch as biting wind smacked her in the face. "Kellie? Nikki?"

Finn jumped down to where she stood. "I'll grab the teen, and you go after the little one," he called over the rising clamor. "I'll meet you up there with my truck."

Lori nodded and started to head up the street when she noticed Tom had gotten up from his chair. He had pressed his face against the screen, the metal distorting weathered flesh pulled up in fear. "She's back at the house!" he cried. "She's back at the house, don't you see! She's taking her to the Sisters Three!"

Lori did not pause to think or breathe. She burst into a sprint, headed for the place where they heard the peepers in the marsh. "Kellie!" she called, but her voice was immediately snatched by the building wind. Fear, cold and all-consuming, mounted in her chest, catapulting her forward. She wanted nothing more than to reach the top of the hill and see her youngest and Becky—a nice, normal college student—scurrying down to seek shelter. But as she continued beyond the screaming marshes to learn they still were nowhere to be found, she quickly understood that wouldn't be the case. She continued her rapid ascent, her lungs and legs burning as she passed the fallen tree.

She stopped at the entrance to catch her breath, bending over to scoop in deep lungfuls of air. The stone marker reading HAITE HILL stared back at her, and she flew back up, determined to finish the climb. She grabbed the first tree branch, then the next, maneuvering her way up the mudslick hill. Her feet slipped as they found each jutting rock, but her rubber soles fought back, and soon she could see the outline of the house stabbing the swirling, bruised sky.

Lori finally made it to the top.

Haite Hill loomed in the distance, every light turned on to create an ominous, glowing monolith in the storm.

CHAPTER FOURTEEN
Ada, 1910

By the time they climbed into the train car, the heavy press of exhaustion weighed down Ada's movement. But the fires of determination kept her going, even as she met with Tom's worried skepticism. She'd explained what she could during the carriage ride to Brecksville Station, where the only train into Cleveland ran, but she did not want to risk being overheard by Mary. Not knowing what to expect at the sanitarium, and with Elena's gentle coaxing, she'd taken the quiet, young maid along with them.

The girls remained silent for most of the trip, neither breathing a word about what they had seen. It seemed they were all in an unspoken agreement to follow Ada's lead, for which she was grateful. They slept now, lulled by the rumbling train, Josephine's head on her lap, and Maggie curled up against Tom. Mary remained at the far end of the car, focused on the bit of knitting she'd brought along.

Ada stared out the window at the rolling landscape, watching it shift from farmland to city. "I know it is hard to believe," she murmured, resuming their conversation. "But I beg of you to trust me."

"I do trust you," Tom promised. "But I don't trust the ghost of Julianna Haite."

"Shh," Ada warned, glancing at Mary.

"Forgive me, love," Tom whispered. "I just hope we're not tempting fate."

Ada murmured her agreement.

She knew the insanity of it all. For someone so worried about being seen as hysterical, she'd given in entirely to sleepwalking, nightmares, and visions of monsters. She was thankful Tom did not condemn her, choosing instead to protect her and the girls through it all. She could only hope that she was doing right by following her instinct. It had all become so much bigger than she thought—she was not only fighting to protect herself, but her daughters and scores of unknown children, both alive and long passed. She was unsure why, but she knew in her heart that Eleanor was the solution.

Afraid someone might recognize them, she'd insisted they buy a middle-class ticket and kept her tell-tale light blonde hair carefully tucked under one of Mary's hats. She told the girls they were traveling incognito, like a game, but though they humored her, she knew they felt the perilousness of their situation. Tom kept his head down as well, but his eyes were alert, always watching.

It was afternoon when the train pulled into the station, and Ada had a brief flash of worry that they would miss hours of visitation. But she watched in relief as Tom spoke with the taxi driver and slid a few bills into his pocket, ensuring they would get to the hospital in time.

By the time the towering edifice appeared on the horizon, the sun hung low in the sky. Recalling her initial jolt upon discovering Haite Hill, the hospital managed to evoke an even stronger reaction. This vast, three-story building of stone masonry, towers, and gables looked impressive from the outside, but was a prison for those society did not understand. For the outcasts and wayward women. For women like her.

They pulled up to the administration building, an imposing central block flanked by two towers with fourth-story gables and traceried Gothic windows at the front. Each tower spilled out into a wing behind it that seemed to stretch on for miles. As they drew closer, Ada saw that wire mesh covered the windows.

"I don't want to go in there," Josephine said quietly.

"Forgive me for taking you to a place like this, but I couldn't leave you at Haite Hill," Ada told her.

"Perhaps we can have Mary take them for a walk on the grounds?" Tom suggested from his seat beside the taxi driver.

"The main building is full of fountains, parlors, and all kinds of fancy things," the driver said. "She might look scary, but I've made enough trips here to know the only thing to fear is what happens way back in the wards."

His words, however kind, didn't help.

Ada held Maggie in one arm and Josephine's hand with the other as they exited the taxi and began the climb up a steep set of stone steps into the building. She was surprised to see a woman at the front desk, not much older than her, wearing a thick pair of spectacles and a high-collared shirt.

"Good afternoon," she greeted them. "Have you an appointment?"

Tom stepped forward and removed his hat. "Hello, my name is Tom Garvey, and I represent the interests of Charles Haite. I am here as an escort to his wife, Mrs. Ada Haite. We are on urgent business regarding one of Charles's relations stationed in this hospital...an Eleanor Haite?"

"I'm not sure there is anyone with the last name of Haite in this establishment..." The receptionist stood to retrieve a heavy, leather-bound ledger from a stack of files, which she proceeded to flip through as soon as she was re-seated.

"Perhaps it is under her maiden name, Byrne."

"Oh yes, right here. Eleanor Byrne. I'm afraid she has been relocated to the hospice wing. She has been ill for some time, but has taken a turn for the worse in November."

Ada spoke up. "I wish to pay her a visit, regardless. It is an important family matter, you see. One that requires discretion and urgency."

The receptionist's eyes swept over Ada, as if determining the best course of action. Ada wondered if she recognized her from the papers. Society hadn't been favorable to the third wife of Charles Haite, and she held her breath, hoping her reputation wouldn't ruin their chances.

Remarkably, the receptionist relented. "Mr. Garvey must accompany you to the hospice ward, but we cannot permit the children. They can remain in the west parlor with your nanny until after your visit."

Relief flooded over Ada. "Understood."

"Please have a seat, and I will fetch you an escort shortly."

They returned to where the children patiently sat, wearing their Sunday best.

"Mary will watch over you two while Mr. Garvey and I visit Ms. Ada's old friend," Ada explained to the girls. "Would that be alright? Perhaps we can visit the ice cream parlor before we head home."

The girls accepted her terms, and Josephine left her with a kiss on the cheek before they followed Mary into the children's parlor. Ada waited until they turned the corner before she took Tom's hand. "Whatever transpires, I must ask you again to please trust me. I know we have only known each other for a short time, but my soul feels tied to yours."

"I feel very much the same," Tom said gently.

"Good. If there is a God, I believe He gave you and me the girls to care for. And we must promise always to do that, no matter the circumstance."

Tom squeezed her hand. "I will care for the three of you until my final breath."

An orderly clad in hospital whites appeared in the doorway, causing them to hurriedly part. "My name is Bobby, and I will be your escort to Ms. Byrne's room," he said with a voice too chipper for the grim setting. "She is one of the few patients fortunate enough to have a private room, so you won't have to weave through dozens of sick beds to get to her. But you'll still want to use your handkerchiefs to ward off any germs. Right this way."

Ada struggled not to grab Tom's hand for comfort as they followed him down the hall, which devolved into a labyrinth of seemingly endless corridors. Although they were far from where most of the patients stayed, the emotion left trapped in the walls felt almost palpable, an ashy taste on her tongue. It grew even more dismal as they entered the ward where patients were sent to die. She could hear their distant moans and sobs, letting her know that although the floors were clean and the walls painted white, this was a place of utter darkness.

As if he heard her thoughts, Tom pressed a palm against her back as a gentle guide. She focused on its weight as they moved deeper into the building's bowels. It was not so long ago that she worried his opinion of her would send her to such a place. Now he hovered near as if shielding her from it.

Just when Ada felt she could not bear to walk any further, the orderly paused before a room. She swallowed.

"Ms. Byrne," he called as he pushed his key into the lock. "You have visitors."

The door opened, releasing the scent of spoiled roses and melancholia. Ada immediately recognized the curly red hair Maggie inherited, but the waif lying motionless on a medical cot barely looked human, a stark contrast to her portraits. Ghostly pale, she wheezed with every breath, her cracked lips the slightest shade of blue. Ada struggled to keep her emotions tempered as she approached, pulling breath through a handkerchief pressed to her nose.

"I'll be out here if you need me," the orderly chirped before shutting the door behind him.

"Eleanor?" Ada said. "My name is Ada. Ada Haite. I-I am Charles's new wife."

The woman's eyes shifted listlessly from the wall to her.

"I'm caretaker to your daughter, Maggie."

"Maggie?"

Like a reanimated corpse, life sprang into the woman's eyes, followed by tears.

Ada dropped the handkerchief, too moved to care about sickly air. Before Tom could stop her, she sat at Eleanor's bedside, taking her clammy, skeletal hand in hers. Her own tears flowed along with hers. "I am so sorry he has done this to you."

Eleanor's dry lips turned up into a weak smile. "I chose this. For them."

"Maggie is beautiful," Ada told her. "Beautiful and healthy. She's got your hair and eyes, and her laughter sounds musical, like a cherub's giggle. We have come to release you so that you can see her."

"What a lovely thought," Eleanor croaked. "But I am dying, my sweet friend. I have only a matter of days. Hours even."

"Nonsense, we can find you better doctors—"

"Ms. Ada, we must move quickly before we are discovered," Tom broke in, urgent but gentle.

"Tommy?" Eleanor said in wonderment, noticing him for the first time. "Tommy Garvey?"

"Hiya, Ellie," Tom said, sadness in his voice. "Forgive me for rushing you, but we have snuck behind Charles's back to be here. He's left the girls and Ada at Haite Hill."

"What? No—" Eleanor tried to move, the slight exertion causing her to erupt into a fit of hacking. "You must—*ugh, ugh*—keep them—*ugh*—away!"

Ada watched the black globs fly from her mouth and realized Eleanor was right—she was dying. She'd seen such sickness before... when her sister died. She collected herself, determined to make their visit worthwhile. "I intend to protect Jospehine and Maggie, but I need to know how. I had a dream—a vision—of Julianna. She told me the only way to stop this madness is to find and release you, and then be rid of Charles. She says in the event of his death, the girls and that awful house become yours..." She withdrew the folded will from her purse.

Eleanor's coughing subsided, replaced by a flash of somber strength. "Tommy, have that young orderly fetch me Father Connor. Tell him it's urgent—accompany him if you must."

Though Tom looked concerned, he bobbed his head and withdrew. The moment the door closed behind him, Eleanor arrested Ada's eyes with her own. It offered Ada a glimpse of the fierce determination she imagined Eleanor once had before she fell ill.

"Take off your glove."

Ada did not question her and simply peeled it away to reveal a left hand that now had two missing fingers.

"It has already begun. The house is taking you."

"What do you mean?" Ada asked, though she knew the answer.

"Forgive me," Eleanor said, gathering her strength to speak. "I was desperate to save them all. Not just the girls, but the children's souls trapped within the walls. Nothing I did worked, so I petitioned the Guardians—ancient beings who lurk in every corner of our world. Not the Sisters, but those who have no names. No faces. I wished to become a vessel of protection, so that every child who enters Haite Hill would be safe from the Sisters' hunger. The house began to take of me, to use me for that very purpose, but Charles whisked me away before it could claim all of me. You are now the mistress of that house. So now it takes you."

Ada heard her words, but they hung in the air, suspended, their meaning unable to settle in her mind.

"Fear not. If you leave, it will stop, like it did for me. Still took one of my lungs, though," she said with a rattling gasp of a laugh.

Ada was quiet for a moment, listening to the sound of the woman's labored breathing before she asked the question.

"And what if I do not leave?"

"Haite Hill will take of your flesh, but your soul will live on, stronger than any soul lingering there. You will have command over Julianna's spirit, over that wretched Amity, over the Congregation, over the Sisters. Nothing will harm the girls, nor any child who comes after them. You will starve the Sisters, ruining their power for as long as the house remains standing."

Ada heard rustling outside the door, but her world had grown still. There was a happy ending somewhere, one where she and Tom lived out the rest of their lives together with the girls, perhaps with a child of their own, living happily and free. But how could she live knowing what she left behind? Knowing that forgotten children still remained trapped in the walls? And what of those who came after them? Even if she was rid of Charles, who knew how many were still left of the Congregation? The Sisters would still demand to be fed.

She felt Eleanor's hand on her stomach and looked down.

"You have more to protect than just them," she croaked. "A babe grows in your womb."

The door opened to spill out three men.

"Ma'am, you must step away from her," the orderly reminded her. He moved to grab her arm, but Tom stepped in his path to gently do it instead.

Rendered speechless by the revelation, Ada stood as close to him as possible, watching the scene around her unfold without being able to participate.

"Father Conner, I wish to have my final will and testament witnessed before my final rites," Eleanor said to the vestment-clad man who had joined them.

The priest nodded and took his place at her bedside. "Boy, please fetch us an ink pen," he instructed the orderly as Ada handed Tom the will.

"As sole guardian of Margaret and Josephine Haite, I transfer that guardianship to Thomas Garvey upon my death."

Bewilderment crossed Tom's expression, but Ada placed a comforting hand on his arm, letting him know she would explain later. She knew what Eleanor was doing, and her heart swelled with both appreciation and sorrow over it. Tom unfurled the will she'd given him and, when the orderly hurried back with the pen, set to writing out the terms, which Eleanor and the priest initialed.

"Do you wish to be in attendance during the reading of the rites?" Father Conner asked them when the ink was dry.

"Go," Eleanor croaked to Ada with another weak smile. Her last words were out, and she had fallen back into decline. "My soul will be at peace knowing Maggie is cared for, and all will be well."

Ada nodded, fighting back rising emotion as Tom guided her away.

"We do not need an escort back," he told the orderly as they left the room. "The lady would like a moment to grieve privately."

"I'm not supposed to let guests walk back alone—"

Tom darkened. "Do you not understand who this is? This is the wife of Charles Haite, the man who has donated thousands upon thousands of dollars to this hospital. I would hate to hear what your supervisor—"

"Not to worry. I'll leave you to it. Take care." The overly friendly man bobbed his head and ducked down an opposing corridor.

Tom took a deep breath to deflate, the softness returning to his features as he looked at Ada. He held up the will. "Please tell me what is happening."

"You promised you would trust me," Ada reminded him. "And there is one more thing I must do before we return. Post the will to Charles's lawyer as soon as you leave the hospital, then secure a room at the Hollenden under your name. I'll join you there later."

Tom let out an incredulous snort. "And where exactly will you go?"

"I told you, I have something left to do—"

Tom grabbed her arms. "Ada, this is madness. I cannot let you just go out into the city alone. You have to tell me what you plan to do."

Ada met his eyes with determination, trying not to reveal the swirling whirlpool of emotion churning beneath the surface. "If I tell you what I plan to do, you will not let me go."

Tom let out a deep sigh. "You are going to be the death of me, Ms. Ada."

She lifted on her toes to plant a kiss under his mustache. She wished she could feel his lips on hers forever. "I love you, Mr. Garvey."

His cheeks reddened, surprised at her tenderness. It took him a moment to collect himself before he replied earnestly, "And I, you."

"I promise there is nothing to fret over," she assured him. "Please see to the girls. They need your protection above all. I will see you soon."

Tom took her hand and kissed it, murmuring his agreement into her skin.

She unwillingly pried herself away from him, and they continued back down the hallways to the front, as her heart screamed for her to ignore her brain, which knew what she must do. The girls were anxiously awaiting their return and launched themselves at her the moment they entered the children's parlor. Ada dropped to her knees to hug them tight, recalling how they once hated her very existence. How long ago that seemed.

Tom dipped outside to fetch a car, and Ada looked into Maggie's eyes, now familiar with Eleanor's.

"Mama," Maggie said, knowingly.

"Your mama loved you very much," Ada told her, smoothing her bouncy auburn curls from her face. "And I do, too."

"Did you find out what you were meant to?" Josephine asked.

Ada cupped her face with her hand. "Yes. And there's something I must do alone. Can you look after Maggie until I return?"

Josephine, ever wise beyond her years, heard the unspoken words and nodded tearfully before she wrapped her arms around her neck. "Thank you for saving us," she whispered.

Ada kissed her head. "Thank you for saving me."

"Are we returning home now, ma'am?" Mary asked, looking concerned.

"Not quite yet," Ada told her as she stood. "Tend to the girls with

Mr. Garvey and follow his instructions. I will meet you shortly and we will return to Haite Hill."

"Yes, ma'am."

"The car is ready, Ms. Ada," Tom said from the doorway.

"Come, girls," Ada said as cheerfully as she could muster. "I will see you off."

With one hand holding Josephine's and her other arm holding Maggie, she followed Tom to the taxi. A gentle snow swirled in the wind, barely making it to the street before it dissolved like powdered sugar on a happy tongue. Ada managed to keep her emotions locked up tight, even as Tom took the ultimate risk and gathered her into an embrace.

She wished the moment would last an eternity, and she inhaled his scent, determined never to forget it. "I'll see you soon, Mr. Garvey," she said softly next to his ear.

"I'll see you soon, Ms. Ada."

The sun had set when the taxi pulled up to the Haite Company's Cleveland office, but Ada knew Charles was still inside. Everyone close to him knew of the penthouse he often stayed overnight in, and its late-night guests, even though to speak of it was strictly forbidden. She tipped the cab driver and gathered both her wits and her skirts as she headed into the towering building. The city sounds had been soothing, as familiar as the smog and city dust that covered her boots, but she had no time for nostalgia. It was time to make things right.

The letter she'd written to Tom had been penned more hastily than she preferred, but she'd managed to explain it all. She also managed to get to the Hollenden, leave the letter at the front desk, and slip away without any of them noticing. She could only hope the concierge would follow her instructions and deliver it to him first thing in the morning.

Ada entered the Haite building and artfully maneuvered her way through the main floor with flippant pleasantries until she reached the elevator. It took a bit more persuasion to get the attendant to take her to the uppermost floor, but he finally relented. Ada took a deep breath as he opened the elevator door and marched right into Charles's suite to find a scantily dressed young woman perched on the top of his desk. She slid off immediately as Charles jumped to his feet, his skin mottled with rage.

"What is the meaning of this—"

"Did you not receive my letters, dear husband?" Ada asked innocently. "And who might this young lady be?"

Terrified, the young girl grabbed her effects and bolted for the washroom.

Charles's face had begun to resemble a fully ripened tomato as he spat out his words. "Where is that blasted Garvey?"

"He is back at Haite Hill, looking after your daughters," Ada replied. "I came here alone. I require more money for supplies. You've left us a pittance to get through the winter."

"This is simply unacceptable! You should not be here. I've given Garvey plenty to manage you. He and I will have words." Charles grabbed his coat.

"Then perhaps he has robbed you? In fact, I did see him sneaking into the cornfield beyond the house, perhaps he is stowing away his bounty—"

"I will handle it," Charles snapped. "But first, I will have one of my men drive you back to Haite Hill, where you belong."

"Regrettably, I don't think that will work. My husband should be the one to take me, and perhaps you can confront Mr. Garvey about the finances then?" Before he could argue, she continued, "I have told everyone from the front desk to the elevator that you planned to visit, but I was here early to surprise you. They're expecting you to return with me. Unless I tell them the truth—"

"You senseless cow," Charles hissed. "I will make you pay for this."

Ada simply smiled.

"Bennet!" he called out his door, forcing a pleasant voice. "Prepare my car. My lovely wife has given me such a wonderful surprise."

CHAPTER FIFTEEN

Lori, 1981

"Kellie!"

Lori burst into the house, struggling to keep the hysteria out of her voice as she screamed for her youngest daughter. In a mad dash from room to room, she frantically searched for any sign of life, but Kellie was nowhere to be found. She stopped in the kitchen, slowly growing defeated. The lights flickered around her, threatening to go out. "Dammit, Kellie, answer me, *please!*"

Then it hit her like it had on the day of their arrival at Haite Hill—the tower.

Heart thundering in her chest, she raced back through the foyer to the tower staircase. She recalled the moment they first arrived—God, how had it only been two days?—when Kellie looked out the window. *Lori, why is there a lady standing out there?* How could she have been so stupid? Kellie had been seeing the things that haunted Haite Hill this entire time.

Lori pummeled through the tower door and stopped dead in her tracks. It was happening again—she'd been transported through time. She now stood in a child's room, but it was drained of all the cheery playfulness a room like that should be. Near the empty bookcase stood a sagging, splintered desk and a tattered mattress on an old bed frame. The room smelled of death and decay.

"Ms. Ada tried to stop her, ma'am. Please don't be mad."

Lori whipped around to see a frail child standing beside her in ragged clothes. He stared up at her with mournful eyes.

"W-What—"

"She walks in her sleep, like we once did," the boy continued.

"You must go to her," another child said, stepping forward. A girl, as impoverished and hollow-eyed as the boy. Streaks of dirt clung to their skin. "The ones trapped in the lake are not so kind."

Lori didn't stop to consider how or why she was seeing the ghosts of two dead children in the tower. She was running again, fueled by the kind of energy only sheer panic could create. The burgeoning storm clouds above her finally burst, this time releasing tiny ice pellets that stung her cheeks. Hail was not something she anticipated, but she refused to stop until she saw Kellie's little face. After several pounding strides, she reached the edge of the lake, but again, no sign of her.

"Kellie!"

The only thing that screamed back was the Sisters.

Lori didn't know if they had the power to come and physically harm her, but she didn't want to wait and find out. She ripped off her t-shirt, preparing to dive into the lake in her sports bra, when the sight of a dozen white faces below the surface stopped her. Her nightmare of stagnant water resurfaced, but this time, there was no deadly bacteria, just poor, murdered children moaning as they grasped fruitlessly for the surface. She could barely pry her eyes away from their small, rotting corpses, but when she did, a flash of hot pink grabbed her attention.

"Kellie!"

A narrow bridge of quarry rocks cut the lake in half, overgrown with moss. Kellie walked along it like a tightrope, completely unaware of the calamity swirling around her, nor the hail pelting every surface. The ghosts were right—somehow, she was sleepwalking. Lori ran to the bridge, sensing Nikki and Finn nearby. They must have caught up to her. She saw them in her peripheral vision, but could barely hear their voices over the storm and screaming creatures. She managed to push it all away to focus on the task at hand.

She kicked off her shoes and, barefoot, began to cross the bridge, one careful step at a time. The makeshift bridge was only wide enough for one foot, and she thought of every stupid jazzercise video Janet made her watch—*"That's it! Now use your core for balance!"*—as she continued, slow and steady.

The hail turned to icy rain, which still bit at her skin, and she struggled not to slide on the wet, slippery moss. She stopped calling for Kellie, afraid that she'd wake up and panic if she heard her voice. The Sisters seemed to have ceased their screaming, as well, but it was little comfort. Every muscle of Lori's body had tensed.

Just one more step...

"Let her come to me, Lori. It's better this way."

The voice startled her so badly that she nearly lost her balance. Flailing her arms, she found it by sheer luck, steadying herself as an ancient, hunched-over woman waiting at the other end of the bridge came into view. Lori didn't even have to question it. The woman was Amity Goodeman.

"She is *not* yours," Lori growled.

The old woman laughed, a horrible cackling sound reminiscent of the distant screaming. "Neither is she yours."

Kellie suddenly stopped.

Lori scrambled to think fast. "If you do not let me do it my way, your sister will not have my body," she said quickly. "You must allow *me* to make the sacrifice!"

"Who told you this?"

"The Sister who wears Ada's face."

The old lady spat a thick wad of snot into the mud. "Ruth refuses to let go of her childish quest for an earthly body. It is beneath her."

"Yet, there you stand."

The old woman stared at her for a moment longer, then crouched low, folding into herself with a series of cracks and pops. Lori realized she was transforming into some kind of creature...a cat? A bird?

Then she knew.

The screaming vulture spread its wings to take flight, and Lori took the opportunity to dash forward. Her hands found Kellie's arms, and just as she woke up, Lori hoisted her up and into an embrace. She squeezed her tight, crouching to shelter Kellie with her body as the vulture swooped dangerously close overhead before disappearing into whatever lay beyond.

Kellie's eyes opened and immediately widened as she took in her surroundings. "Lori?"

"You were sleepwalking, but I got you," Lori said, trying to straighten her body and keep steady on their slippery perch. "Now listen to me—I have to be super careful not to slip with you into this lake. That means you gotta close your eyes and hold onto me real tight. Nikki is waiting for us at the end."

Thankfully, Kellie didn't argue. "Okay," she whispered. She must have understood, deep down, the danger they were in. She pressed her face into Lori's chest, gripping her so tightly, she thought she'd lose her breath. But the slight pain helped her steady herself, and Lori was able to slowly turn and walk in the other direction. Her toes were sore from gripping the stone, and she knew at any moment, they'd be numb from the cold.

She didn't let herself think about the seemingly impossible feat of balancing on a narrow, moss-covered bridge with a five-year-old, and instead retraced her steps as carefully as before. She would not look down at the poor souls below and their sad little faces, either. That alone would be enough to send her over the edge—literally. She kept her gaze directed ahead and walked.

Step, step, step.

Nikki and Finn came into view, holding umbrellas that struggled to stay still in the wind. Nikki had her hands to her mouth, her own eyes like saucers as she watched Lori tight-rope walk. Finn stretched his arms as far as he could, grabbing them the second they were close enough.

Step, step, step.

And they were there.

Sobbing, Nikki pulled Kellie into her arms, and they huddled together under her umbrella. Finn grabbed a shell-shocked Lori and did the same. Lori felt herself dismantling in the warmth of his arms, and the tension twisting her muscles released along with the breath she'd been holding. It came out like a strangled sob.

"What happened?" Kellie cried.

"You were sleepwalking," Nikki told her, "into that stupid lake!"

"Guess the breakfast date was a bust," Finn whispered his weak attempt at a joke in Lori's ear. By the sound of his voice, she could tell he was just as shaken up as she was.

Her sob turned into a quick laugh as she pulled away to meet his eyes. She was so glad he was there. She'd stopped believing there was any man out there who could make her feel supported, and here he was, hiding in the valleys of Ohio, a stranger who had willingly decided to hold her down during the craziest time of her life. It seemed too good to be true.

But she knew deep down, it was far from over. There was no time for rest when the girls' lives were threatened.

"Finn," she began, "I know you don't know me that well—"

"Bullshit. We're like family, remember?"

"I need you to trust me, okay? I need you to take the girls back to the hotel. Don't come out no matter what you hear."

"Lori, that is so fucking stupid—"

"You and I both know there's a reason I'm here, even if we don't quite understand it. I feel it, Finn. Before you even told me, the house had been trying to tell me what was wrong. I know it sounds crazy, but it's pain—a woman's pain. I feel it. I recognize it. And I need to confront it."

Finn surprised her with a nod. "Let my grandma's spirit help. She lingers here. All the spirits who died here do." He reached down, and Lori realized he was wearing a tool belt. He handed her the hammer she once wielded against him. "And if all else fails, fuck them up with this."

Lori let out another laughing sob and stuck it into her belt loop. Her weapon going into battle, she thought. It would be funny if it wasn't all so fucking terrifying. As if on cue, the Sisters let out an antagonizing shriek.

"Girls, I need you to go with Finn."

"No!" Kellie shook her head. "You come, too."

Lori left Finn's side to wrap her arms around both girls, squeezing them tight. "Please just trust me."

"You better come back," Nikki said through chattering teeth. Both of them shivered in the icy downpour, and Lori remembered the storm was still waging its own war on the world. Adrenaline had offered a kind reprieve.

"Go on, girls, go," she said firmly as she released them from her grip.

"I'll get them safe and warm," Finn promised. "You come back to us, you hear me?"

Lori nodded. "And if you see that Becky chick, keep her far away from them. She is not who she says she is."

Then, before she lost her resolve, she charged into the darkness, toward the woods and the dead cornfield. Toward the sound of screaming. She hurdled through the mud, trying to avoid fallen branches and rocks as the swirling tempest continued to batter her bare skin. She was glad her feet went numb—it would be a miracle if she kept all her toenails.

She wasn't sure what exactly came over her—she'd never been the hero type. Perhaps it was seeing the dead children and nearly losing hers, or the intuitive *knowing* that the women in her bloodline wanted her here, but something had driven steel into her veins. She felt nothing now but the fiery determination to confront whatever had caused all this pain.

In the distance, she saw their contorted white silhouettes, knobby and bent like the outline of birch trees against a forest of dead oaks and maples. But she knew better—they were too colossal to be trees, their gangly limbs moving with the wind in a macabre, maniacal dance. Lori felt her bravery waning, and she slowed her pace ever so slightly, confronted by things that were clearly not of her world.

The Sisters' screams grew louder until they mimicked the volume she'd heard in her dream, drowning out the sound of her heartbeat. The hammer clenched in her fist made it impossible to cover her right ear, and she felt the sharp, agonizing stab of her eardrum popping. She tried not to cry out as she steadied herself, helplessly watching them advance as blood oozed down her neck.

In a flash, her fear turned to anger, and she was suddenly furious at the disgusting, covetous fiends coming toward her. "I have made my decision!" she screamed in haughty defiance. "I will not give you my children, nor will I give you myself! I don't give a *shit* about you or your pain!"

Screeching their displeasure, they abruptly rushed toward her.

Lori froze then, struggling to push past the horror of witnessing the incomprehensible. Forced to crane her head all the way back, her eyes widened as they took in giant, exaggerated casts of pain. Their screams succeeded in popping Lori's other eardrum, adding another wet trickle of blood. The Sisters bled with her, the deep crimson dampening their shrouds so they stuck to their agonized expressions, their long, open jaws trapped like murder victims in plastic wrap. As their spindly arms stretched over their heads with claw-tipped fingernails that searched for flesh, Lori looked down to see ropes painfully digging into their distorted bodies.

She remembered why she was there.

She closed her eyes, picturing who they might have been before. Three women—Ruth, Theodora, and Rebecca. How it must have felt to starve, watching those they love die around them slowly. The fear when they realized what the man they depended on intended to do to them. She thought of Rebecca, forced to bear a child in that horrible cabin, and she recalled her own darkest memory, the one she buried deep in her stomach. Her miscarriage. The sight of something so sweet and promising reduced to blood smearing the bathroom tile. How she cried, feeling so bitterly alone.

Lori screamed.

It was a howl of pure anguish, an echo of every scream uttered by every woman before her. Screams of childbirth, of death, of mourning. The affliction that is womanhood—of every rape, of every torture, of every burning, of every tragedy. She understood now with perfect clarity what the Sisters were and what came out of their wrenched open jaws—the screams of generations of suffering women.

A vision hit her then, as if given.

It came in cruel flashes, like scenes from an old movie. She saw the cabin of misery and death. She saw Becky—Rebecca Crane—left bleeding on her cot, moaning. She watched Ruth Alden, driven mad by grief, steal the stillborn child from his slumbering father's arms. She watched her escape into the woods to offer the child's remains to the cornfields, praying to unseen things. She watched as Ruth returned and Samuel Crane discovered what she had done. Watched as he tied them around a wooden beam with rope so tight it left burns and cut into Rebecca's tender stomach. Heard the crack of Rebecca's jaw when he hit her to keep her from screaming. Heard their screams as he took his time peeling their scalps away from their heads, like he'd witnessed being done to his men when he tried to set up settlements before. She watched him take his time with Ruth, a special punishment for taking his son, and throw what was left of her face into the cauldron. For him to cook and eat.

Lori felt tears stream down her cheeks.

"I'm sorry," she whispered. "I'm sorry he did that to you. He deserved every drop of agony he felt."

The vision shifted, and she watched Samuel Crane being tortured, his limbs seeming to break by themselves as unseen hands twisted him around an old wooden wheel. His death would be slow, but the women were no longer there to suffer with him.

They were the Sisters Three, the ones now standing before her—powerful and free.

CHAPTER SIXTEEN
Ada, 1910

Charles whipped the Peerless around each curve, over pavement still slick from melted snow, and Ada pressed her eyes shut to keep from getting sick from the motion. For their entire journey, he'd screamed and given no sign of stopping. "You will pay for this—do you hear me? You are nothing but a common whore, easily replaced. All women are disposable. It was a mercy for me to allow you to stay in my summer home. You should have remained here quietly, as I instructed you to!"

Ada could hold her tongue no longer. "Sacrificing your daughters is merciful?"

"What did you say?" Charles's voice dripped poison.

"Did you not think I would learn of the Sisters Three?"

"Blasphemy!" he sputtered. "They used to burn women like you."

Ada did not reply. She closed her eyes again, picturing the faces of Tom and the girls. He'd be wondering where she was by now, and she could only hope he'd wait until morning before trying to find her. Her hand found her stomach, where the spark of life patiently throbbed, waiting to grow into a child. Their child. She knew somehow that her body would not reject this one. She felt it in her bones, a maternal *knowing* she'd never experienced before. And she would protect it and the girls with her life.

The town appeared in the distance, dark and empty, its remaining townsfolk retired for the evening, awaiting the next storm. Charles's Peerless roared right through it, upsetting its peaceful slumber as it spewed charcoal fumes into the country air.

Ada looked down at her gloved hands, wondering how much longer it would be before the rest of her fingers disappeared. Where would they go? Would they become the light fixtures? The tub's feet? She shuddered, wishing not to think of such things before they occurred. She'd gotten through much in her rather short life, and this would be no different. Just another thing to endure.

The Peerless continued its uproarious incline toward the house and soon, Ada tasted moisture in the air, letting her know another bout of tumultuous weather was headed their way. Charles whipped around the final bend, and Haite Hill soon loomed overhead. Its windows, illuminated by wavering electricity, looked like glowing eyes staring them down as they approached. Cries in the distance—restless vultures or encroaching Sisters, Ada didn't know—rang out, singing from their unseen realm. Then the loudest crack of thunder Ada had ever heard promptly clashed, jolting even Charles as he ground the Peerless to a halt.

He pulled her from the automobile by her arm as she struggled to keep her balance, and as soon as he wrenched open the front door, he threw her into the foyer. She landed with a painful smack, dazed from the impact as she looked up at the Madonna and Child. They seemed alive in the flickering lights.

Elena hurried in from the kitchen, summoned by the racket.

"Where is he?" Charles roared as he stomped through the first floor of the house. "Where are my daughters?"

Elena saw Ada and rushed to her side.

Ada grabbed her hands and caught her eyes. "Please do not tell him," she whispered.

"You! Maid," Charles barked as he rounded back to the foyer.

Elena assisted Ada as she climbed back to her feet. Then she stood before Charles, casting her eyes to the floor. "I do not know, sir," she replied calmly. "Mr. Garvey cares for the girls in Mrs. Haite's absence. I merely manage the household."

"Are not the occupants of that very household part of that management?" he hissed.

Ada interrupted. "Perhaps they accompanied him to the old corn fields, as he often does?"

Remarkably, Elena played along. "Oh yes, now that you mention it, Mrs. Haite, I did hear the door whilst I attended to the chores."

Charles marched into his study and commenced ripping open the drawers. Ada slipped beside Elena and took her hand, a gesture both of gratitude and protective preparation for whatever would come. Ada hoped the rest of the maids would remain stationed in their quarters, safe from Charles's wrath.

Moments later, he emerged with a pistol. He grabbed Ada's wrist with his free hand and wrestled her from Elena. "You are coming with me!" He began dragging her through the hall to the grand parlor as Elena faltered, clearly unsure of what to do.

"All will be well, Elena," Ada called back in a light voice, hoping she'd have the sense to stay inside, no matter what she heard. "Please see to the maids!"

The night air they met felt static, and Charles's fingers dug into her skin as he pulled her across the veranda and down its stairs. She lost her footing when they reached the mud, but he continued dragging her as if she were nothing more than a rag doll.

"Charles, stop, you're hurting me!" she finally cried.

Another riotous boom ripped through the sky, and the skies released a wet and sloppy snow—not quite rain but not cold enough to produce flakes of white. Ada took advantage of Charles's newly moistened skin to wiggle free of his grasp, but he grabbed her hair, seemingly determined to cause her as much agony as he could muster. She thought of the Sisters then, of their bloodied scalps, and she wondered if they had once been altered by the violent hands of men.

A shriek abounded from the woods.

"Here, you cursed beasts!" Charles yelled. "I have your damned sacrifice! Take her now! I'm tired of the games."

Ada was unable to see anything in front of her, holding desperately onto her hair so he could not peel it from her scalp. But she could *feel* them. She thought of the spark nestled safely in her womb and the story

Julianna told her. Would the Sisters know she was with child? Would they demand to take it?

Charles dragged her across the yard, past the lake, and she saw the apparitions of children with their sad, hollow eyes standing on the surface. Beyond them, the yellow glow in Haite Hill's windows continued to flicker, and Ada swore she saw a young woman in the tower, staring down at her.

The frigid sleet shifted into proper raindrops, soaking through Ada's clothing and ruining the fog that had settled around the corn fields. Although she still could not see the Sisters, she knew they were close, their ancient presence overwhelming all else. They let out another shriek, piercing Ada's ears like the screams of a hundred angry birds.

"Take her now!" Charles cried as the giants crept closer. "I have fulfilled my promises and demand the riches that are owed!" He threw her ahead of him.

Ada couldn't help but cry out at the sight of them. The vision from her nightmares—or maybe her reality—hovered over her, three monstrous creatures like twisted trees, shrouded in blood-drenched white, their hideous faces trapped in a scream. They lowered themselves slowly over her and Charles, the tops of their scalpless skulls raining crimson down upon them.

Ada twisted around and kicked her foot out, aiming for Charles's legs. Surprised, Charles dropped his gun and crumpled, giving her enough time to scramble to her feet. Then she threw her head back and screamed up at the advancing fiends. "He has brought you no children! He has failed, but I am devout! Let me offer my flesh to Ruth, freely!"

The Sisters paused, cocking their heads as they apprehended her with curiosity.

Ada realized blood ran down her own forehead from where Charles had ripped at her hair. Just like theirs. She whipped around to throw an accusatory finger his way as he scrambled for the fallen pistol. She wasn't sure where her words came from, but she screeched them all the same. "*He* is your sacrifice! A ruiner of women! *He* deserves your wrath!"

It happened so fast.

Lightning struck, illuminating in flashes the pale fabric and flesh as Ada fell to the ground, watching the Sisters lift Charles like a spider, splaying out his arms and legs. His face, once burning with anger, became a mask of unabashed horror, watching helplessly as the fiends holding him cracked and contorted parts of his body not meant to be coiled. He stayed conscious throughout the entire excruciating endeavor—scream, crack, scream, crack—until one of his multiple broken bones punctured his lungs, and blood garbled the howling of a man forced to bear the agony he once administered.

Hot blood splashed Ada's face, provoking her to wake from her stupor. She scrambled backward and broke into a run, leaving the Sisters to their pleasure. She could hear and think of nothing until she reached the house, expending every ounce of energy she had felt to fling herself across the veranda and through the door where Elena anxiously waited.

"Shut the door!" Ada gasped as she collapsed on the floor.

"I will fetch bandages—"

"No." Ada grabbed her arm. "You must take the maids and leave this place immediately. It is not safe here."

Elena knelt and took her hand. "I've known of the Sisters, Ms. Ada," she told her softly. "I worked in the hospital Eleanor was sent to, and I came to help you. Both Mary and I."

Ada let out a sob of relief. They were there to help, not hurt her. She'd left the girls in safety. "You should still go."

"No, ma'am. I've seen the ghostly children, and I know the stories. My family once lived in Boston Village, where the Congregation ruined the lives of many. My place is here, helping you to put a stop to all the madness."

Ada's tears poured freely now. "Then you know what I must do?"

"Yes, ma'am. Eleanor told me of the house and the curse that lingers. My deepest regret is that I could not save her from that place."

"She is sleeping peacefully now with the angels," Ada told her gently.

Outside, the Sisters continued their shrill cries, albeit more joyful than before. Ada wondered if Charles was still alive, writhing as they continued to bend and break him, forming him into a human wheel.

"She will come for me soon," Ada whispered to Elena. "You must send away the maids."

"Yes, ma'am. Are the children safe?"

"They are with Tom and Mary in the city," she told her. "I don't expect him to come searching for me until the morning, but he will keep the girls away regardless. I left him a letter explaining my intentions."

Elena nodded. "Let us get you into bed then. If they want to come collect you, they will have to come into the house proper, like the ladies they once were."

Exhaustion and fear had wrecked Ada's body, and she found herself grateful to have Elena to lean on as they went to her room. Her scalp throbbed, and she could tell from the rivulets of blood running down her face that Charles had pulled out some of her hair.

Elena led her to the bed and laid out a towel for her to lie on before fetching water and a cloth. Ada closed her eyes as she cleaned and bandaged her limbs and head, grateful for the caring reprieve before the Sisters came to collect her.

After moments of blissful peace and quiet, she asked, "What are they?"

Elena sighed. "That all depends on who you ask. The Congregation believes they are angels. Some call them Guardians. Some call them demons. The original natives of the land have their traditions. My father's family, who lived here, came from Ireland, but my mother's family comes from Greece. There are stories in our culture of the Three Fates, called the Moirai. I have often thought the Sisters may have once been them, but became distorted over time. They were the personifications of destiny: Clotho, who spun the threads of life from her distaff onto her spindle, Lachesis, who measures the amount of life allotted to each person with her measuring rod, and Atropos, who cuts the thread of life with her abhorrent shears."

"How have they come to be here?"

Elena looked thoughtful. "No one knows why the gods intervene in the affairs of humans. But I do know that moments of great violence and tragedy can awaken things meant to stay sleeping." She patted her arm. "You rest now, Ms. Ada. I will take the maids into town. When I return, I will make sure you stay comfortable for whatever is to come."

Tears sprang back into her eyes. "Thank you, Elena. Truly."

Elena stood and lingered at the fireplace before turning to meet Ada's eyes. "My Irish family, the Brennans, once suffered at the mouths of the Sisters. Their spirits and the spirits of all who linger here are with you." She stopped as if emotion seized her, offered Ada a respectful bob of her head like a bow, and withdrew from the room.

Outside, the storm continued to roar and crash.

With nothing more to do but wait, Ada let herself drift off into a restless sleep. When she opened her eyes again, it was to see none other than Rebecca Crane sitting patiently at her bedside.

"Hello, Ms. Ada," said the ancient being wearing the facade of a young girl.

Ada scrambled to sit up, pressing her back against the headboard. Her racing heart brought the stabbing pain back to her forehead, and she winced.

Rebecca gestured to her wounds with a jerk of her head. "We are grateful for your offering, but you know nothing of what we have endured."

"How must the children feel when you take them?" Ada shot back.

Rebecca laughed. "Do you care for the chickens and cows you consume? How curious your righteousness is."

"I will not give you the children," Ada told her. "I offer your sister my body, as promised. In return, you will give me your word that none of my children shall be harmed."

Rebecca frowned. "The way Charles Haite's wives cling to the Haite daughters makes them all the more delectable to us. But Ruth deserves to wear her own flesh. You are the only mistress of the house thus far who similarly bears the curse of childlessness. We cannot afford to let you go." She stood. "You have an accord, Ada Haite."

Ada swallowed. "What must I do?"

Rebecca approached, reaching out to place a cold hand on Ada's forehead. "First, you must experience our agony."

CHAPTER SEVENTEEN
Lori, 1703

Lori's eyes shot open.

Instantly, her teeth chattered, her breath puffing out in clouds. She turned to see a young woman lying in bed beside her, shivering in her sleep underneath the thin quilt they shared. She recognized Becky's face beneath her bonnet. Tufts of gray hair peeked out from the bonnet of the bundle next to her, and Lori recognized the old woman she knew as Amity—Theodora. It took her a few moments to understand they'd pushed the beds close to the fire for warmth, but it had long since died through the night, weak embers now sparkling faint orange in the cold ash. On the opposite side of the fireplace, a man snored beneath thick blankets and an open Bible. Winter's wrath howled outside, forcing tiny piles of snow through cracks that had not been properly sealed.

Lori located a meager pile of wood against the wall. But before she rose, the girl beside her shifted, revealing a book hidden under her pillow. Upon closer inspection, she saw it was a handmade book made of parchment tied with string. *Ruth Alden's journal.*

Lori waited a beat before she slowly pried it from beneath the sleeping girl. Then she stood, slipping the book into the folds of her dress. Although she tried to move quietly, the cold had forced stiffness into her bones, and they creaked as she moved toward the woodpile.

"What hath come over ye, Goody Ruth?" a voice hissed.

Lori turned to see Becky—Rebecca Crane—sitting upright as she addressed her.

"Master Crane must be the one who tends to the hearth," she continued to chastise.

Lori ignored her and grabbed a log. Somehow, she was no longer Lori, but Ruth Alden. She had been transported back in time.

"Ye will bear the child soon," she said softly, in a voice that was not her own. "He must have warmth."

With a gurgling grunt, the man woke. Samuel Crane's face was gaunt and surrounded by wiry black hair, his dark eyes sunken into their sockets. His skin, a sickly pallor, turned violent red as his fury rose. He looked familiar, like every terrible man Lori had ever met. *"How dare ye!"*

Lori remained calm, continuing to talk as she imagined they used to. "Pray pardon me, Master Crane, but Goodwife Rebecca's birthing pains cometh soon. The babe must have warmth to live."

His eyes widened as they appraised Rebecca. "Is what Goody Alden speaks truth?"

With frightened eyes, Rebecca nodded.

"God hath answered my prayers!" Crane cried out in joy. "Goody Alden, fetch the snow for cooking. Goodeman's Wife, rouse yourself from your stupor, and prepare our meal."

Theodora Goodeman sat up, her lips tinted blue as she mumbled her reply.

"Speak, olde woman!"

"T-there is naught food to prepare, Master Crane."

"Yes, yes." Crane reached for his Bible. "God will provide. Remember thee, for they who suffer will be once more with Him." He flipped through the pages, finding his passage before he began to recite the words with a booming voice, singed with madness, "Beseech thee therefore brethren, by the mercies of God, that ye give up your bodies a living sacrifice, holy, acceptable unto God, which is your reasonable serving of God."

He snapped the book shut to stare at them with wide, yellow eyes.

He thrust out a bony finger. "Will ye offer thy flesh to feed mine son, the truest child of God?"

"I will fetch food for the babe," Lori quickly said as she grabbed their water bucket.

Crane continued, as if he hadn't heard her. "If thou suffer, so we shall reign together with Him. If we deny His will, He will deny us..."

Lori blocked out his voice as she hurried to dress in the warm winter clothing piled near the door. Then she pushed against it, fighting the snowbank built up behind it until she created an opening big enough for her to wedge her body through. Then she slipped out into the cold winter morning, leaving the lunatic to his raving.

Her frayed petticoats and cloak did little to shield her from the biting air, and although she tried to hide her face behind the wool scarf, her cheeks quickly went red from the cold. Though Lori knew she stood in what would one day be the cornfields behind Haite Hill, the world seemed unrecognizable, a snowglobe of quiet, endless white. She remembered the story Becky told her and the girls; there was no food anywhere to be found, and the next snowfall would make it impossible to leave the cabin.

That was when Crane went mad.

Lori located a mound of rocks beneath a cluster of low pines and burrowed herself between them to create shelter. With shaking hands growing numb, she opened Ruth's journal. She squinted to see what had been written, the words barely legible and poorly spelled.

> *The Devil Crane goese madder. I see the three sisters erry morn, angels frum God. They tolde me of his sins to man, the tortures he did to womyn from this land. They want his blood, and only then can we be free.*

A garbled hiss interrupted her reading.

Lori jerked her head up to see three mounds of snow near where she huddled. Shimmering beetle black eyes glared from beneath the inches of snow that had built up while they perched. One lifted its wings, sending a great *whoosh* through the forest as the accumulation on its feathers exploded with movement. The other two followed suit, the noise ruining the peaceful forest.

Lori gently closed the book. "You never wanted women or children. You wanted him. But Ruth Alden failed and tried to give you his dead son instead."

She was met with silence as they stared at her with beady eyes, shrouded in the red, featherless flesh of their heads.

"She created what you became. Their pain created you."

The vultures simply stared.

In fury, Lori ripped the flimsy, handmade book in half, leaving the ripped pages and pieces of the journal to further deteriorate in the snow. Then she filled the bucket with snow and, lifting her heavy, soaked skirts, she marched back to their dwelling.

She was greeted by the sound of a woman moaning, quickly letting her know it had already begun. Rebecca lay before the hearth on the floor as laboring sent her frail body into violent throes of pain. Blood already dampened the quilts beneath her, the child coming soon. Theodora sat beside her, grasping her hand, blatantly unprepared to deliver a baby. Relief flashed over her wrinkled face at Lori's return.

"Goody Alden, heed to my wife!" Crane barked from across the room. He looked frantic, his eyes wide with the kind of hysterical fear found only in a man who doesn't like losing control.

"Ye must take leave as she labors, for a man needn't bear witness to the uncleanliness of women," Lori told him firmly.

"Ye stupid wench," Crane spat. "The snow be too high to venture out."

"There be a path left by Mister Alden and Mister Goodeman, that I hath followed. If I did manage, surely God shall protect His son. Dost thou doubt His love for you?"

Rebecca let out another low wail.

"There be a cave in the woods," Lori pressed. "Ye will find warmth and shelter there."

In an explosive fit of frustration, Crane grabbed his coat and effects and shoved himself into the door. It gave enough for him to squeeze through as she had done, and Lori waited until she no longer heard the crunch of his footsteps. Then she got to work, shoving first the bed, then the kitchen table against the door.

"Goody Alden, what madness doest thou embark upon?" Theodora gasped.

"He will freeze to his death, as is God's will," Lori told her, pushing the other bed to join the rest of the furniture. She could only hope it all would hold.

The old woman gasped. "Thou committest the greatest of sins!"

"Then 'tis my sin to bear." Lori grunted as she picked up another chair. "Now tend to the hearth, and I will ready for the birth of Rebecca's babe."

"I cannot—"

Rebecca cried out as another contraction hit. Lori pushed the last bit of furniture she could find against the door, as she tried to think back to everything she'd ever learned about childbirth. She knew from her studies that women had helped each other birth children since the dawn of time, but though she had biological instinct and a general familiarity with womanly things, she certainly was no OBGYN. Her mind raced as she tried to think of what she'd need, then hurried to help Rebecca up and into a squatting position.

Then she handed Theodora the bucket of snow to put into the iron pot and bring to a boil. The old woman had grown quiet, her face still in the building fire's glow as she added more wood to the hearth. As if she'd resigned to what Lori had told her.

Lori found a cooking knife and let it sit in the iron pot with the soon-to-be-bubbling water. Then she dampened a bit of cloth with melting snow and wiped the sweat beading on Rebecca's forehead. "Is the Lord coming to take me?" the young girl muttered, delirious from pain and hunger.

"Thou will not perish," Theodora clucked. "Suffering is a woman's burden. One we all must endure—"

"Thou will be well," Lori cut her off, hoping the cool cloth would soothe her. "Take heed, thou will soon meet thy child."

"What of the Sisters, Goody Alden?" Theodora asked. "Did they speak to thee in the woods?"

Lori didn't falter. Of course, Ruth had whispered her findings to them before Lori arrived. It was their only hope. "They want *him,*" she replied, changing the narrative. "His sacrifice will ensure our survival." She looked up to meet the old woman's eyes. Remarkably, there was no resistance.

There was a popping sound, and fresh blood gushed from Rebecca as she let out another low moan. Lori peeked between her parted legs to see a crowning head. Though she thought she might feel shock and disgust, she instead felt calm. "Hold her now, Goody," she told Theodora. "The time has come."

There was nothing more that Lori could do than try. Reality had long abandoned her, thrust into a hellish existence she once thought was just a story. She didn't know if her plan would work or if she would be fated to live out the tragic affliction that Ruth Alden and the women of Hope Towne had been forced to endure. She didn't know if the child would survive or if they would survive. She saw the faces of Kellie and Nikki in the back of her mind, and she desperately longed to be back in her world, in her time, with them. If she made it through this, she would never let them go.

Seeing Rebecca, a frail girl not much older than her oldest daughter, lost to the agony of childbirth, pulled her back into the moment. She knelt down to ease the baby from her body. "Nice and steady, honey," she said, forgetting to alter her language. Fortunately, the two women did not notice; the old lady was gently singing in the young one's ear. It seemed to help, and Lori prepared herself for what was to come.

It came faster than she expected; with another resounding scream, the warm, slippery body coated in fluids was expelled into her arms. Lori allowed herself only a moment of sheer, unabashed panic—she had no fucking idea what she was doing—before she remembered to cut the cord that bound mother and child. The baby was still and uncrying, so she nestled him downwards on her arm and daintily swept a clean pinky finger in his mouth. The child sputtered, coughed, and cried.

Lori let out a sob of joy as she fell to her knees, gathering the slimy little creature close to her heart. The baby was alive.

Theodora approached her with outstretched arms covered by a blanket. She handed the baby off, and the older woman artfully swaddled him before handing him to Rebecca. The young, exhausted mother burst into happy tears, holding her child close as it continued to mewl.

"He is a true child of God," Theodora said with a smile.

"I will name him John Matthew, after thy husbands who have gone to Heaven," Rebecca whispered.

"Thou art of angels, young Goody Crane," Theodora said gently, stroking the back of Rebecca's head. "Now, thou must feed him from thy breast."

Lori wiped away tears with her blood-streaked arm. She couldn't believe what had just happened, but she knew their ordeal was far from over. In the distance, she heard the crunch of boots in the snow.

She cleared her throat. "Goodwomen, thou must heed my words. The Sisters hath imparted God's decree—Mister Crane 'tis but the Devil himself who hath planned to strike us all dead. To drag us into hellfire. But God hath shown us His mercy—if we cast out the Devil and shun his sinful ways, we shall liveth and taketh care of His true child, the babe of Goody Crane."

The two women looked at her, and for a moment, Lori felt the impossibility of where she stood, in another century before women who had died long before her birth. Their eyes, brimming with emotion, also revealed a glimmer of *knowing*. That this was more than what it seemed. They did not voice their agreement, but Lori felt it just the same.

Pounding rattled the door.

"Open this door!"

Lori put her finger to her lips, and the women said nothing, the baby nursing quietly at Rebecca's breast. Lori took a deep breath and held it as Samuel Crane continued to batter the door, screaming as his frustration mounted. The furniture she'd put before it rattled, but held firm.

"Thou wicked wench—open this door!"

The women stayed still.

"God will strike ye down!" Samuel shrieked. "And I shall be His instrument! Heed my words, wretched Devil women: I will return!"

Lori listened as the sound of crunching boots stomped away, then faded. Then she stood, washed her bloody hands in the melted snow, added another precious piece of wood to the fire, and joined the two women by the fire. She wasn't sure where Crane had ventured off to, but as the sun set and the cabin grew dark enough that the women and baby slumbered, Lori swore she heard the echoes of a man screaming.

When she opened her eyes again, it was to see Ada.

She knew it was really her this time, her blonde hair in tendrils around a gentle face with kind blue eyes. She sat on the side of the bed opposite where Rebecca, Theodora, and baby John slept soundly beside her.

"Hello, Lori," she said. "I've come to take you home."

Lori looked down at the cozy bundle. A part of her felt strange, almost guilty, leaving them, even after such a short time. "Will they die?"

"All humans die, Lori. But I can tell you they will not suffer at the hands of Samuel Crane. While looking for wood to force open the door, he broke his leg. He was still alive when the vultures began to pick him clean." Ada's eyes sparkled.

"What has changed? What will happen to you?"

"You have corrected the wound, but you have not altered the past. What happened has still happened. The difference is, you have now freed us—all of us trapped at Haite Hill. I wish to go to Heaven with my Tom now. With my girls. And all the children I have taken under my wing. You see, I got to be a mother after all." Ada smiled, a real human smile. "Just like you."

Lori's eyes welled with tears. "I'm sorry I couldn't fix it," she whispered.

"Oh, but you did. And now we are all ready to rest." Ada stood and reached out for Lori to take her hand. "But before we go, I must ask you one more favor. I need you to take a message to Tom."

Lori climbed out of bed and took it.

1981

Lori woke to see the Madonna and Child mural staring down at her from above. The image shuddered so violently that Lori half-expected

Mary's jaw to come loose and devour her whole. But the entire world was trembling, and when a single crack appeared in the ceiling, separating the mother from her baby and ruining the idyllic image, Lori realized where she was—a crumbling Haite Hill.

A chunk of ceiling fell away, leaving an empty hole where Mary's face had been. It landed and exploded inches away from where she lay. The jarring crack of falling plaster pushed Lori to her feet, just as the quickly deteriorating ceiling dropped more pieces like angry hail. The house's grumble became a roar as she fell apart, her bursting windows releasing the high-pitched scream of shattering glass. Wood splintered and plaster crumbled, releasing thick plumes of dust into the air.

Lori sprinted for the door and spilled down the stairs into the morning. She got as far as she could before her legs gave out, forced to sit and breathlessly watch as the once magnificent Gothic manor collapsed. Although she knew she had been delivered back to reality, she couldn't help but hear a woman's cries in the sound of falling stone and breaking wood.

She felt two arms grab her from behind, pulling her back. She didn't even need to turn around to know it was Finn. They both sat watching, awestruck, as Haite Hill fell into ruin.

"I-I think I fixed it," Lori whispered.

"I think you did, too," he said quietly. He reached up to her face. "Your ears..."

She recalled her eardrums bursting, but when she joined his fingers with hers to touch dried blood, she realized they were healed. "It's—it's a long story." Then she remembered. "The girls," she said with a start, rising to her feet.

"Safe at the hotel with Carl and Granddad," Finn assured her. "I told her about Becky... Carl called her sister, and well. Her *actual* niece is still at KSU. You were right. She had us all fooled."

"I have to speak to your granddad," Lori told him.

"Are you good to walk? My truck is parked at the bottom."

Lori nodded, but kept hold of his hand as they headed to the wooded hill. She didn't want to look back. She didn't want to see the three vultures she knew were perched on top of the rubble, watching them as they retreated.

Lori pulled her sore body into the truck, and Finn drove them into town. As soon as they pulled into the parking lot, the girls burst out of the hotel. They nearly knocked her over as they exploded with rapid-fire questions: "What happened?"—"Did you kill those things?"—"Where is the house?"—"Is Becky a ghost?"—"Did you die?"—"Are we going to be okay?"—

Lori squeezed them both tight, so grateful to see them again. "I promise I will explain everything, but first I have to talk to Finn's grandpa."

"He said he was feeling tired," Carl told her from the porch. There was a hint of something in her voice. "He went upstairs to lie down in his room. He didn't look so good to me, Finn. You better go see him."

Concern furrowed Finn's brow as he met Lori's eyes. He headed inside the building, gesturing for the girls to follow. Lori held Kellie tight as they climbed the stairs after him.

"Is his grandpa dying?" Kellie whispered in her ear.

"I don't know, baby," Lori whispered back. "I think so."

As soon as they reached the bedroom and Finn fell into the chair with a dumbfounded look, she realized Kellie was right. It was as if all the long years Tom lived had caught up with him in the few hours since Lori left the hotel. He lay completely still under a single quilt, letting loose a rattling wheeze with every shallow breath. His jaw hung slack, his weathered skin falling from his open mouth. Gone was the cantankerous spirit who puffed on unfiltered Camels.

Lori set Kellie down beside Nikki, who had wordlessly fallen into a nearby couch.

"Hi, Mr. Garvey," Lori said gently as she approached. "It's Lori Byrne from earlier. I met Ada, your wife."

The old man pried open an eye. "Is she free?" he wheezed.

"Yes," Lori gently lowered herself onto the bed and took his hand. Cold to the touch, his skin felt soft and delicate like cheesecloth. "She showed me everything and wanted me to tell you she will see you soon. It's okay to let go. She's waiting for you."

A smile spread across his lips. "Good."

Lori looked up at Finn, who seemed lost. "You should come sit with him."

He nodded, grateful for the direction.

"Come on, girls, let's give them a minute."

"Should we call an ambulance?" Nikki asked, worriedly.

"No, baby. It's his time." She scooped Kellie back into her arms. "He's ready to go home."

EPILOGUE
Lori, 1981

Morning sun spilled over the horizon as Lori stared out at a cloudless sky. The storms were over, and though it was no longer unseasonably warm, the town had the pleasant chill of early spring. But there was promise in the air that lingered on Lori's tongue.

Tom Garvey had slipped away peacefully in the late afternoon, and Finn, though noticeably deflated, seemed to be taking it well. She was more than willing to give him, and those who knew Tom, time to catch their bearings and the space to grieve. She herself was still in a state of shock, even as the girls being the girls grounded her. They both insisted on sleeping in her room, with Kellie in her bed, but neither asked any questions. It was almost as if they didn't want to know.

Lori hadn't slept at all, her eyes watching the shadows creep along the ceiling as the hours slipped by. A strange liminal sensation had settled over her body and refused to let go, as if she were there but not really there at the same time. It made sense—even if only her mind had traveled through the veil separating time and space, her body had still been through quite an ordeal. She had wondered, as the paramedics came to take Tom's body to the morgue, if she should check into a hospital too. But what would she tell them?

She heard rustling behind her, interrupting her musing. She looked up to see Finn had come out to join her. "Hey, you," she said softly.

"Hey, you." He fell into Tom's preferred rocking chair and pulled out an old, crumpled pack of filterless Camels, obviously his granddad's. "Have one with me for the old man?"

Lori slipped into the chair next to him. "Don't tell the girls."

Finn mimicked zipping his lips and handed her the pack.

She fished one out and held it with her teeth to the lit Zippo he held out. She coughed immediately, the harshness reminding her of why the thought preceding the hit was always better than the inhale itself. Especially when they're stale, unfiltered Camels.

Finn chuckled softly. "I don't know how the hell he lived as long as he did smoking these awful things. But that's the least weird thing I don't understand around here."

In moments, the porch was filled with plumes of cigarette smoke. It hung in the air like all the words they should be speaking, but neither found the energy to express. Outside, the world was also quiet, no longer punctuated by random, inexplicable screeches.

It was Finn who finally broke the silence.

"Penny for your thoughts?"

"I just don't know what comes next," Lori said. She tried to hit the cigarette again, then smashed it into the nearby ashtray. "I have nowhere to go."

"Bullshit," Finn said. "You still own that land. It's time for you to rebuild."

Lori looked at him with wide eyes. "Back on that cursed hill? How could I possibly?"

"The house was cursed, not the land, and now it's in pieces," Finn pointed out. "Grandma's gone to Heaven with Granddad, so I'm thinking any lingering ghosts went on to rest in peace, too. And I have it on very good authority that a feisty redhead with super smarts and horrible eating habits sent all the nasty creatures packing, too."

Lori hid a smile. "I still can't believe all that really happened."

Finn took a long drag from his cigarette and added his extinguished butt to hers in the tray. "I'm jealous you got to meet Grandma. I always wanted to ask her how it all went down. You know, like how she was able to have my dad and all that."

"She showed me, you know."

"Did she?"

Lori nodded. "The Sisters took me back in time, to 1703 when Crane murdered them all. I was Ruth, like in her body. I played along and saved Rebecca's child. I locked Samuel out of the cabin and let him freeze to death to save us all."

"Holy shit." Finn stared with wide eyes.

"Yup. Ada was the one who pulled me out of there and brought me home to our time. She showed me how her story ended, too." She hugged her arms as she looked out onto the horizon. "One of the Sisters, the one who was once Ruth, tried to take Ada's body, but the house fought back. Eleanor's curse was stronger, and it took all of her instantly, leaving behind the child in her womb. Her maid, Elena, found the baby fully developed and healthy on the floor. The act of it all weakened Ruth and the other Sisters. It was enough to hold them off for decades. Your granddad got her letter and rushed to Haite Hill to find the baby. The rest is history, I suppose."

Finn shook his head. "Talk about one crazy family history. Guess it's yours, too."

"I'm glad they can be together now," Lori said. "I can't imagine how hard that must have been for Tom. For your whole family."

"I wonder why the curse started to falter. Why the Sisters came back."

Lori smiled sadly. "I think she wanted to be with your granddad. He held out for years, but everyone dies eventually."

Finn leaned forward and took her hand. "I'm so glad you made it all right. I can't thank you enough for all you've done."

Lori felt heat creep into her cheeks as she met his eyes. "I'm pretty sure I didn't have a choice."

"Nah," Finn said. "You have a pure heart. That's pretty rare nowadays."

"So, where will you go now?" She changed the subject. "The carriage house is still standing…"

"I'm going wherever you're going," Finn said immediately.

"Two dates and you wanna move in together?" Lori teased. "I didn't realize I was *that* good."

"Oh damn, look who's got jokes now." Finn looked impressed.

Lori shrugged. "Guess you're rubbing off on me."

"That's it. I'm yours. Tell me where we're going. Driving Carl crazy? Shacking it up in the carriage house? Heading back to New York? I'm already packed up—after Granddad's funeral, I'm totally free. You tell me."

Lori paused to think. "I say we stay here for a bit. I'm planning on having them exhume the land for any lingering remains, and I want to be here when they do. Then I want to build a memorial for your grandparents and those who have died there."

Finn nodded. "That's a brilliant idea. I'd be honored to help you."

"I also want to go to your granddad's service," she continued. "Then I do have to go back to New York for a bit, for the girls. Maybe I can find another job. Figure things out from there."

"Sounds like you could use a jack of all trades."

"Especially one with a truck that doesn't take a shit after so many miles."

Finn's eyes sparkled. "Are you for real, then? We doing this?"

Lori laughed at the incredulity of it all. "This is crazy. We barely know each other—I mean, I don't even know your favorite color."

He grinned. "It's Greene."

Footsteps bounded down the hotel stairs, and the front door burst open.

"Lori, Carl said I can have this candy bar, but Nikki won't let me—"

"No, I said, wait until breakfast, candy fiend."

"Candy for breakfast is never a bad thing," Finn pointed out.

"See?"

"Well," Lori interjected. "True, but I think we need a healthy compromise here. Candy bar and scrambled eggs..."

"Eww!"

Nikki laughed. "Not together, you dork."

There was a crunch of gravel in the parking lot as a car pulled up.

Lori did a double-take, staring at the Dodge minivan for several moments before she realized who it was.

Sean rolled down the window. "Hey, girls!" he called. "How was your weekend?"

ACKNOWLEDGMENTS

As I said when I wrote the acknowledgments for Meadowbrook: writing can be a lonely job, but I'm surrounded by so many amazing people. I credit them completely for any book I manage to complete. I honestly can't believe folks actually like to read what I write, so first and foremost, a huge thank you to the readers who continue to buy my books throughout the years and who support my beloved publishing house.

Speaking of Quill & Crow, to my entire team: Alma, Mel, Kayla, Lisa, the Mat(t)hews, Tiff, Logan, and Stef—thank you so very much for not only keeping that machine moving, but for allowing me time to write. And you know what, thank you to Rho, too! Lisa and Tiff, Kayla and Matt, thank you for your editing eyeballs. To all the Crows—those with us currently and those who have flown on—thank you for all the love and support.

The support of the indie community has also been a big part of this book's completion. I am honored to be part of a growing initiative that is changing the face of publishing. Authors supporting authors is a beautiful thing. I appreciate all the authors who took the time to read and blurb for me.

And last but not least, my beloved Andrew. Thank you for always believing in me and for faithfully reading everything I write. Did you ever think this is what I was dreaming up when you drove me up to Hines Hill ("my house") in the park? Or on all those hikes? I guess this was my love letter to Ohio from us both. And, of course, thank you to my boys for letting Mommy have her writing time. I love you all more than you know.

ABOUT THE AUTHOR

Cassandra L. Thompson has been creating stories since she got her grubby little hands around a pen. When she is not busy managing a feral household (human and canine) with her beloved husband, you can find her wandering around cemeteries, taking pictures of abandoned things, or in the library researching her latest obsession. She has a B.A. in History and an MLIS, but she ignores her degrees to focus on writing and running Quill & Crow Publishing House, both of which require copious amounts of coffee and Crows.

Other Books by Cassandra L. Thompson
Welcome to Meadowbrook
The Ancient Ones Trilogy
My Little Black Book of Horror

TRIGGER INDEX

Abuse of Women
Body Horror
Child Abuse (mentioned/off-screen)
Child Death/Murder (mentioned/off-screen)
Miscarriage (mentioned/off-screen)
Monster Horror
Pregnancy Horror/Trauma
Bigotry/Misogyny
Religious Trauma
Torture (implied/off-screen)
Thalassophobia (drowning/near-drowning)

THANK YOU FOR READING

Thank you for reading *The Agony of Her*. We deeply appreciate our readers, and are grateful for everyone who takes the time to leave us a review. If you're interested, please visit our website to find review links. Your reviews help small presses and indie authors thrive, and we appreciate your support.

More Books from Quill & Crow

The Bone Drenched Woods, L.V. Russell

The Stitch Witches, Krissie K. Williams

All the Parts of the Soul, Catherine Fearns

www.ingramcontent.com/pod-product-compliance
Lightning Source LLC
LaVergne TN
LVHW040050080526
838202LV00045B/3573